Testimony

Not yet thirty, ex-Police Constable Terry Davis, with a gaping throat wound as though a spiked glove or some wild animal – a pit bull terrier? – had done it, isn't expected to live.

Forced to resign for accepting unauthorized hospitality from a known criminal, he had set himself up as a private investigator and paid informant to a Sunday tabloid.

The only witness to this savage attack is a blind man.

When a full-scale murder hunt gets underway, Detective Inspector 'Jacko' Jackson and his attractive, gay Detective Sergeant, Caroline Parker, probing Davis's nefarious dealings – some very close to 'home' – unearth a sinister connection with the unsolved drowning of a teenage girl.

With stealth, patience and finally with justifiable deception, an unexpected solution to a brutal killing is reached and a tragic story of misplaced loyalty revealed.

This first novel by a Nottingham journalist displays degrees of inventiveness, pure expertise and narrative power that ensure him a successful career as a writer of crime fiction.

TESTIMONY

Frank Palmer

Constable · London

First published in Great Britain 1992
by Constable & Company Limited
3 The Lanchesters, 162 Fulham Palace Road
London W6 9ER
Copyright © 1992 by Frank Palmer
The right of Frank Palmer to be identified as the author
of this work has been asserted by him in accordance
with the Copyright, Designs and Patents Act 1988
ISBN 0 09 471050 3
Set in Linotron Palatino by
Falcon Typographic Art Ltd., Edinburgh & London
Printed in Great Britain by
St Edmunds Bury Press Limited
Bury St Edmunds, Suffolk

A CIP catalogue record for this book
is available from the British Library

The lines from *The Last Word* by Auberon
Waugh are published by kind permission
granted by Peters Fraser & Dunlop Ltd;
the lines from 'Busy Doing Nothing'
(Burke/Van/Heusen © Warner Chappell
Music Ltd) with their permission; from 'Great
Pretender' (Buck Ram) by kind permission of
Southern Music Publishing Ltd; from 'Silly
Love Songs' (Paul McCartney) by arrangement
with MPL Communications Ltd; from 'Main
Street' (Edens, Comden and Green – © 1950,
M Witmark and Sons, USA) reproduced by
permission of B Feldman and Co Ltd, London
WC2H 0EA.

Though some settings are real, the East
Midlands Combined Constabulary is fictional
– and so, too, are its characters and cases.

FOR SADIE AND HER FAMILY

Author's Note

The idea for this story was born out of a chance remark by Councillor George Miller, chairman of Nottinghamshire County Council, who became my guide on how people like him beat the handicap of blindness.

In affectionate tribute, I have retained his first name but given the fictitious witness a different surname because his persona is totally imaginary, as is the entire cast of invented characters and the situations they find themselves in.

1

Bleeps sounded, stridently, grating.

He attuned his ears: too close to be from the pedestrian crossings outside the railway station or the police station.

A six-footer darted in front of him making him flinch in surprise. He trailed a distinctive smell, masculine, medicinal maybe.

A car, as battered as the briefcase he held, started on full choke at the third attempt. Another jogger ran by across the narrow street, rhythmically, soundless almost.

Bleeps again. Urgent, demanding.

He counted them: eight.

Can't be from the computerized till in the pub on the corner. Came from behind him; behind the wall.

The metal token dropped. The car-park barrier rose with a whine. The Mini stopped. The driver's door opened.

'Sorry to have been so long.' A familiar, female voice, approaching. 'It's like an ice rink in there.'

She took his arm. He stood still, listening. 'OK, George?' she said, puzzled.

'Is there a car behind this wall?' The frozen air grabbed at his hot breath so that the words came out in a white bubble like a cartoon character. 'Some sort of alarm went off. Perhaps there's been a break-in.'

She let go of his arm, said, 'I'll have a look' and walked back to the Mini to take out a torch.

Her footsteps became fainter. From behind the wall she called, 'Can't see one.' Then, uncertain 'Wait a minute.' Now, horrified, 'Oh, my Lord.'

Her footsteps ran back. 'There's a man in there. Bleeding badly.'

'Quick, Maggie,' said George. 'Get help from the pub.'

She ran across the street. Mumbles became a loud hubbub as she yanked and held the door open. Half a dozen pairs of footsteps, fast, heavy, came towards him, her slower, softer ones behind.

'Where?' A man's voice, cool, authoritative.

'Behind the wall.'

George heard them sprint away. Soon, from over the wall, the same calm voice: 'Get an ambulance. Find some blankets.'

A comforting arm hooked his, guiding him to the pub. 'A whisky,' said George at the bar. 'Make it a double and . . .'

'A grapefruit juice,' said Maggie, a drink order that never varied when she was driving.

They moved away with their glasses to a wall table where he eased himself into a chair with wooden arms. He took three sips and waited for the spirit to do its warming work. 'You all right?' His face, round, rosy, registered concern.

'A bit shaken.' Maggie shivered from shock and cold.

He listened to the sirens of two police cars and an ambulance while his drink gently thawed him. The man with calm authority brought the cold with him back into the pub. He pulled a stool towards their table. 'Fixter,' he said as he sat down. 'Detective Inspector. Good job that Mr . . .'

'Marshall,' said George. 'Councillor.' A pause, letting it sink in. 'How is he?'

'Unconscious.' In the headlights of the ambulance it looked to Fixter as though his throat had been ripped out by a wild animal. 'Heavy haemorrhaging.'

George sniffed. 'You've got some blood on you.'

Fixter pulled a handkerchief from his trouser pocket and wiped both hands. Then he saw the deep dark stains at his knees. 'Oh hell.'

Councillor Marshall seemed to study his face. Inspector Fixter looked away, uneasy, towards Maggie. 'He could have died from hypothermia if you hadn't found him. How did you spot him in that dark corner?'

'He heard him.' She nodded at George who looked beyond Fixter with unseeing eyes. Suddenly the inspector realized why.

His eye-witness was blind.

2

Busy doing nothing.

Brrrr. Brrrr.

Working the whole day through.

Bing Crosby and William Bendix were there. He was the singer whose name he could never remember.

Trying to find . . .

Brrrr. Brrrr.

This is a forest scene, for Christsake. There are no phones in a fucking forest.

Brrrr. Brrrr.

Oh, Jesus. He slid from under the salmon pink duvet. He groped alongside the cold radiator beneath closed curtains with an inch gap which let in a strip of light. He had made this trip many times in semi-darkness. He had not had a bedside phone since he'd taken a 3 a.m. call, said right, yes, straight away, and gone back to sleep until it rang again two hours later with the Little Fat Man spitting in his ear.

Brrrr. Brrrr. He shuffled in paisley pyjama bottoms beyond the foot of the bed. He closed the door before turning on the landing light. In his den he turned on another light. Brrrr. Brrrr.

He picked up the phone but did not answer as he flopped, feeling dizzy, on to a stool at a small square desk.

'Mr Jackson?'

'Yes.' Half grunt, half groan, disorientated.

'Sorry to bother you, Inspector. Control here. Your Chief Super sends apologies.' A likely story, Jackson thought. 'He realizes you're still on leave.'

'What time is it?'

'Zero five twenty, sir. There's a major incident. Victim not

9

expected to live.' Jackson yawned, sleepy. 'Ex-PC Terence Davis.' Wide awake now, stomach churning.

He made notes in the block capitals he used when writing without his specs. 'I'll be there.'

In the bathroom he spooned handfuls of cold water on to his creased face and then studied it in the mirror. Watery, hazel eyes, unfocused and melancholic, gazed back at him. Not again, he sighed to himself.

The headboard light was on when he returned washed and shaved. She lay on her side, smooth-skinned face in profile, glossy chestnut hair scattered on her pillow. 'Trouble?' she mumbled.

'Sounds like it. An old colleague of mine. Dying.' Down to me this, he thought gloomily. If I'd cracked it, he'd be in jail instead of running around the back streets, getting himself bumped off.

She pushed herself upright as he dressed. 'Shall I pack you some cold . . .'

He stopped her with a look of mock horror and she laughed. In her white shortie nightie, frill-less but (to him) thrilling, she followed him barefoot down the stairs to the front door. He pulled on a waxed three-quarter length coat he used for dog-walking, dressed as though he was going out poaching.

They kissed. She broke away, shivering. From cold, he recognized, not passion. They seldom made love in the morning and certainly not before six. 'Be careful.' He opened the door and stepped into the freezing fog.

Work is a habit, he decided as he backed his car, steaming in protest, up the steep driveway alongside a lawn with a solitary silver birch, leafless and white with frost. It had taken less than two weeks to kick it. Cold turkey for cold turkey. He smiled weakly to himself.

What he'd give for another couple of hours in bed, another couple of days off. I'm more knackered now than when I knocked off on leave.

The older you get, the longer you've been away, the harder it is to slip back into good habits, he soon realized as he made an immediate mistake. He took the short cut through the villages. The silver country lanes had not been salted. He tried full beam. The light bounced back from banks of fog. He turned on the wipers. The windscreen filmed over outside. He hunched over the wheel. His breath stuck to the inside.

What a bloody job this is, he thought angrily. And four more years before I can call it a day and do what I want to do. And what he wanted to do was write crime novels based on cases and faces he'd come across with a bit of realism and social comment thrown in. He'd roughed out one already – about the killing of a vice queen. Jackie, a real bookworm, had typed it into shape but only given him five out of ten. 'Solid reporting, quite descriptive,' she'd declared, schoolmarmishly, 'but lacking thoughts and feelings, the intimate picture a novel needs.'

But how the hell can a detective who'd been trained to take an overview, keeping his emotions in check, bare his soul? Particularly if, as he suspected, he hadn't much of a soul to bare.

The thought made him despondent and he dismissed it with another thought that always entered his mind when dilemmas occurred – somebody or something would turn up to point the way. He started to sing out loud to restore his spirits. '*I try to be unhappy but I never do have the time.*'

A narrow bridge bent back on itself and slipped down to join a dual carriageway, moist and black where the salt had melted the ice.

He turned on the radio station which covered the whole of his patch and caught the end of 'Reet Petite'.

Good God. Teenagers of his generation tore up cinema seats to music like this in the rock and roll revolution. A good sound that had stood the test of time, by which all music is judged. If this was topping the charts, there was hope for today's youth.

His rising spirits spiralled down to his thermal socks as the news bulletin catalogued the crimes he had missed while on holiday.

They were still working on the murder of the child left alone in a seaside bedsit while her mum went out for a drink . . . A million pounds snatched from a security van by a shotgun gang who'd used a rail track as a battering ram . . . Further arrests after the New Year's Eve riots in his old home town where shops had been smashed and looted and policemen attacked.

In his uniform days, twenty years earlier, he'd linked arms

11

with the revellers round the Bow as the clock struck midnight. They'd taken turns to wear his helmet. A girl returned it with a kiss. Now the children of those revellers brought in the New Year with a riot. What's happening to the younger generation?

He listened all the way through to the weather forecast which warned of hazardous driving conditions.

Nothing about Terry Davis yet then. The Little Fat Man was playing it close to his chest again.

Enough of this day-dreaming about being a writer; an end to this journey down memory lane. Back to work. Back to the real world. Back to Terry Davis.

Not yet thirty and dying. A corrupt bastard, flash, on the make, but he doesn't deserve this.

Terry Davis joined the police service when he left the army after the Falklands. Had a good war, they said. What is a good war? Not being one of the two hundred and fifty dead, I suppose.

In its wake, Davis couldn't face dull army duties and pointless parades. In the police force he'd never found the buzz he craved.

Police work isn't like that. Even a detective only gets the feeling once or twice a year that he has made a contribution; an arrest that would make the world a safer place; justice for an abused kid, a raped girl, a robbed pensioner. Mostly it's a long, hard, frustrating slog.

So Terry Davis sought excitement in his social life and Golden Jim provided it. They'd met at Gold Spot, Jim's club, then drinks and a game of snooker on his private table at his country house. The seeds were sown.

Golden Jim was about to open a hotel. Every owner of every posh car for miles around got a mail shot.

A desk sergeant spotted the racket and reported it. Davis was getting ownership details out of the national vehicle computer by the multi-storey car-parkful.

Jacko spent two months investigating. The tip was that five thousand names of potential punters had been supplied at a quid a time.

Sure, Davis conceded, he'd made use of the computer. He'd

got info that expensive cars were being targeted by a gang which dealt in stolen radio cassette players.

Sure, he knew Golden Jim. He was hoping to get close enough to him to use him as a source. His bank account showed no big unexplained payments in. Neither had there been any payments out to cover a fortnight in a villa at Marbella which Golden Jim owned.

Enough for a disciplinary hearing to require him to resign for accepting unauthorized hospitality from a known criminal; not enough to get him into court.

Many detectives hate gumshoe jobs, the canteen name for internal inquiries. Jacko never ducked them. If a freebie holiday was all he could get him on, that would do. Turn a blind eye and a corrupt cop gets greedier.

Evidence in open-and-shut cases gets lost. Small-time crooks start asking courts to take into consideration raids that others, not far removed from the Golden Jims of the underworld, have carried out. Insurance firms are hit with police-approved claims for stolen property when the raider fled empty-handed. Not all stolen property recovered finds its way back to its owners. The corrupt cop engineers them all. For his cut.

Jacko knew he could never have been like that. He had that working-class ethic dinned in from childhood. Fair day's work for a fair day's pay. Do the job as best you can, have a drink with your workmates and get home to the wife, kid and dog. Didn't want a bigger house. His place was paradise compared with the terraced street where he was born. Didn't want a bigger car. His dad had nothing but a bike. Didn't want a big-titted woman on the side. Hang on a mo, old man, let's not go that far. He grinned impishly.

He hadn't seen Davis for more than a year. He'd heard that on the strength of an undistinguished six months as an aide in CID he'd set himself up as a private detective and was running around with the in-crowd in a big red racing job.

Now he was dying. He'd have been better off in jail where he belonged.

'Come on.' Jackie's voice spoke to him, as clearly as if she had been sitting in the passenger seat. 'You knew him as a living, breathing human being, warts and all. What are your thoughts and feelings right now?'

13

He searched his soul for several thought-free seconds. Well, he decided slowly, it's a free country, a democracy. If that's the life and death he chose for himself, sod him.

Hard-bitten bastard, he heard her saying, but he believed it, had to believe it. Stay detached. Keep your distance.

The sign welcomed him to Leicester. *This is a nuclear free zone*, it added. He felt no safer.

The dual carriageway funnelled into a shop-lined street where red, white and blue lights in the windows of a sweet mart wished him Happy New Year in English and Urdu. He turned left at a roundabout and drove down a street colonized by banks and commercial buildings. The police station, white and solid, was round a bend from the railway station, red and solid.

The distant drone of a dozen conversations grew louder as he climbed the stone steps and burst into confusing discord as he pushed the doors open.

Thirty or more stood around. Men and women in street coats, a few in uniform, holding plastic cups, in two untidy semi-circles at opposite ends of a trestle table.

Sipping coffee and munching toast, he gazed round what looked like a schoolroom. Rows of plastic moulded chairs stood on an oak block floor. In front of them, a long table alongside a virgin blackboard on an easel.

Sitting at the table was Detective Chief Superintendent Richard Scott, short, tubby, known in the Major Crimes Squad as the Little Fat Man, jowls darkened by day-old stubble. His head was in his hands, down, reading.

Leaning over him, one hand on the desk, stood a fit-looking man, younger than Jacko; thick blond, almost white hair and eyebrows; an outdoor face, brownish red, which had seen its share of sunshine; stocky, muscular body. In the sixties Detective Chief Inspector Steve Keeling, head of West Division CID, would have been a Beach Boy.

Scott looked up, grim-faced. 'OK, folks.' Conversations stopped in mid-sentence. The noise multiplied from the clatter of heavy feet and the scraping of chair legs being pulled into line again.

Jacko sat at the back. Christ, he thought, studying Scott,

14

he looks bushed. It wasn't the loss of one night's sleep. He could cope with that. It was the endless grind of being head of CID in the East Midlands Combined Constabulary. Every case reported on the radio driving here was Scott's ultimate responsibility – and lots more. Jacko knew he could never cope with that workload. He had tunnel vision. One case at a time until the light appeared. He wanted to be the chief of nothing. This was where he belonged. At the back of the class, with the boys and girls.

'Right.' Scott rose wearily. 'Within the last half-hour, your former colleague Terry Davis died in hospital without regaining consciousness.'

Latecomers who weren't in the know drew hugely deep breaths. Some dropped their heads, stunned. Among those heads, Jacko's. For just a second, that self-protective toughness, that island of indifference on the trip here, was gone. He wished Scott had broken it more gently to Davis's old colleagues, and had added some expression of regret.

'First on the scene,' Scott pressed on, 'was DI Fixter. You may as well get it first hand.' Jacko's head was up now, listening, work to do, detached again.

Fixter stood in the front row and turned. He was not far short of forty. His face looked younger, sandy hair swept back. The rest looked older because of a drinker's enlarged neck and paunch.

He and half a dozen colleagues had been drinking off duty in the station's local from eight thirty, he began. Into the pub at half-ten came Mrs Margaret Marshall to report their discovery in the car-park opposite.

In the park was a man in a grey suede coat lying in a still-spreading pool of blood. His throat wound was all too apparent. They tried to staunch the gurgling flow. Detective Udden went with him in the ambulance to hospital. 'Let's hear from him.'

Fixter nodded towards a crew-cut young man. His broad shoulders tapered into a trim, firm waist in a dark suit and out again into chunky hips and thick legs. Only a pale face and exhausted eyes betrayed a night without sleep.

'I didn't recognize him until we got him into casualty and they cleaned him up a bit. I mean, his wound was that bad. Blood everywhere.' He looked down, shuffling on his feet.

'As some of you know, we joined the force about the same time. We kept in touch after he left.' Jacko smiled grimly to himself, steely again, suspicious. 'I saw him last night. Played snooker at the Gold Spot. He was still there when I left around nine to join the boys at the pub.'

His head was up now, eyes over the heads in the back row, avoiding their faces. 'At the infirmary he went straight into surgery. They did their best but . . .' Head down again, mumbling. 'I'm afraid . . .'

Fixter gripped his shoulder. 'Sit down, John.' Udden, hollow-eyed, did as he was told.

'It came as a great shock to us all, especially those who served with him,' said Fixter. There were murmurs of sympathy tinged with a touch of belated anger directed, Jacko guessed, at Scott for his insensitive introduction. He sensed the battle lines, born of professional pride and envy, being drawn between squad and divisional detectives.

'Only loose change, no notes, were found in his pocket at the infirmary. That's right, John?' Udden nodded dumbly. 'John's sure he had a few tenners in his pocket when he bought a drink at the club. His credit cards were intact in an inside pocket. Just to complete this segment, it's right, isn't it John, that he told you he had someone to meet but didn't say who or where?'

Another mournful nod.

Fixter's eyes embraced his entire audience. 'We sent a couple of men round to the club. Davis left just before nine thirty. So there's an hour's gap we need to fill.'

A preliminary search of the scene, he went on, had located no weapon. Davis's red Mazda was not in the car-park where he was found or in the garage of his home, a suburban bungalow.

As he spoke, Fixter backed away to the table. He stopped and picked up the statements the Marshalls had given him. As he stepped forward, holding them, his listeners saw the bloodstains that darkened his brown trousers a much deeper brown at the knees and below.

George Marshall had dozed for most of the ninety-minute trip from St Pancras after a day in Westminster on council business, accompanied, as always, by his wife Maggie, he said.

16

The train arrived on time. Twenty-five steps from the platform and a dozen strides into the echoing booking hall. 'He actually counts them.'

Right, down a curved covered walk-way into the street and right again towards the car-park. 'Knows every step of the way.'

At that corner a slovenly woman hurried by. They walked down a narrow street where a post office vehicle idled to keep warm.

From the barrier, Maggie surveyed the icy car-park, too treacherous for George to walk over. She stood him by the wall.

He heard a car, diesel-engined, hissing out of the car-park. Another car purred in pursuit. A smaller car spluttered out.

Mumbled conversation and muffled music burst into life as the pub door swung open. A couple stepped clumsily on to the pavement. The sounds faded as the door snapped shut on its springs. Stale fumes drifted from the humming extractor fan.

'All this he remembers and describes in great detail,' said Fixter, admiringly.

Between the two series of bleeps, he felt the six-footer passing by, smelling, he thought, of something like dressing embrocation and he heard another jogger on the opposite side of the street with longer, lighter steps.

Mrs Marshall had only the haziest recollection of a woman in a long brown coat and wearing a head scarf rounding the corner at the railway station. She was certain a youngish man was walking ahead of them towards the car-park.

George described the woman as slovenly because of the way she walked with scraping heels and smelt from stale scent and tobacco smoke. Naturally, he had no knowledge of a man walking ahead. He was adamant three cars came out of the barrier – one diesel-engined, for certain, one that purred so was likely to be big and expensive, and a Ford whose cold engine sound he recognized because they had an Escort before their Mini.

'He's a remarkable witness.' Fixter spoke with engaging enthusiasm. 'He's got what the visually handicapped call obstruction awareness.' Jacko was warming to Fixter.

'He's sure the person who passed him as he stood by the wall

17

was male because of the weight of his footsteps, around six foot because the sound of his breathing came from above him and he's five feet six.'

Fixter turned back to the table. He held up a plastic bag. Inside was a square black box, the size of a cigarette pack. 'This is what alerted him. His bleep, clipped to his inside pocket. It's a radio pager with a visual display panel which flashes up messages.'

There were two on it. Both had been photographed in case the battery went on the blink and wiped them out. The last said, *Waiting at Grand. Jason.*

The message bureau had passed it at ten twenty-four. It took an average twenty seconds before the bleep indicated to the wearer that a message was running on the display panel. Another minute or so and the bleep and the message were repeated. To stop the sound, an orange button had to be pressed at the side. Davis, dying, had been unable to silence the piercing noise.

'George may not be much of an eye-witness.' Fixter smiled quietly. 'But he's one hell of an ear-witness. So . . .'

He turned towards the blackboard on which Chief Inspector Keeling had been writing with squeaking white chalk. 'We need to trace . . .' With pointing finger, he ran down a list: *Who he was meeting. The slovenly woman. The youngish man walking ahead of the Marshalls. The three car drivers. The six-footer. The jogger. The couple leaving the pub. Jason.*

'Let's hope they're half as good as him.' He walked towards his chair amid mutters of appreciation for what had been a fine briefing.

Scott rose, a mischievous grin on his face. He liked to brighten briefings with a joke and Jacko knew one was coming. 'And let's hope this doesn't become a case of the blind leading the blind.'

The laughter was half-hearted, embarrassed and uncomfortable and Keeling actually winced. Only Jacko guffawed heartily.

He had heard the phrase many times. Always reminded him of his grandma. Most Sundays, he went round with his sister and their parents to her tiny cottage for tea. No woman was allowed to help her prepare it. She knew the exact second when the buns would be toasted to perfection. She was undisputed head of the household. His grandfather, a reformed drinker, was dominated by her. Jacko had the chore of drying the pots afterwards. Gran did the washing up. Whenever he put a cup on the wrong hook or a knife in the fork compartment, she would sigh, 'It's a case of the blind leading the blind.' He was only six or seven when the illness that took her sight also took her life.

'This will be a joint division and squad operation,' Scott decreed, ill at ease. He doled out the jobs. Fixter would wash and change and head the scenes team. Another squad would bring in muggers, convicted or suspected of operating in the city's streets.

Publicity, he said, would be down to Chief Inspector Keeling, operational leader of the inquiry, but was a problem. Davis was single, living alone. His parents were away, skiing, but neighbours didn't know where. His name could not be released until they had been traced but he wanted immediate appeals for any passers-by, particularly the motorists and pedestrians George Marshall had mentioned.

'An even bigger problem might be establishing the exact cause of death. Steve, explain, please.'

Keeling stood. 'It was a gaping throat wound, absolutely appalling, but we don't know what caused it. Mike' – he nodded at Fixter – 'reckons it looked as though some wild animal had done it. There is a missing dangerous dog, a bull terrier, believed stolen, but there are no reports of similar attacks.

'They cut away some tissue, swabbed the rest and inserted tubes and stitching at the hospital and that means some evidence has been lost. At first sight, they were more like puncture and pull marks than rips so we can't rule out something like a spiked glove.'

Everyone pulled pained faces as he sat while Scott stood again.

'So it's not a straightforward mugging and the answer may be in his background.' He looked to the back row. 'Jacko. That's down to you.'

The next briefing would be at six. Everyone started to stand and talk. Oh, good, Jacko thought. Only a twelve-hour day on a day off. He headed through the crowd for the door.

'Jacko.' Scott called him back to the table where he now sat alone. 'Parker will be your partner.'

A second's silence, awkward, unsure.

'OK?'

'Fine,' said Jacko without conviction.

'Concentrate on his last twenty-four hours.'

Jacko knew that and he knew that Scott knew. He looked down at him awaiting the real reason for his summons. There were lines on his forehead and around his dark brown eyes. 'My merry little quip didn't go down too well, did it?'

A strange mixture, thought Jacko. Full of public bravado normally, tough at times. Yet, in private, caring and compassionate and absolutely honest.

'Bollocks to the blind bastards.' He answered loud enough for Keeling, standing nearby, to hear, laying his unquestioning loyalty on the line. 'My gran would have loved it and she was totally blind.'

3

Tab Private Investigations was a deep disappointment. No squeaky swivel chair. No green filing cabinet. No office bottle in a locked drawer. No Chandler on the bookshelf.

Not the mean streets this; a commuter suburb, once a self-contained village, now tied in ribbon development to the city.

Jacko was uneasy. He would have welcomed a pen set on the desk. He was an old-tech, Quink ink, 2B pencil man. Ballpoints had been banned at his grammar school.

Two tape recorders, one silver-cased, the other in black plastic, and a Canon Sure-Shot stood on shelves where books and binders were neatly stacked. Beneath a window with fawn vertical blinds was a walnut veneer desk packed with gadgetry – a word processor with screen and print-out, a mushroom-coloured phone with buttons and an answering machine.

He decided on the division of duties. He'd handle the old-fashioned paperwork. Caroline Parker would decipher the new tech.

She was a modern girl, different. Short black hair. Deep brown alert eyes. Compact body, sizeable, shapely bosom and backside. And a smile (for Jacko at least) that told much about her. Solitary, secretive, sometimes sad.

For three years there'd been rumours, no more than hints really, at HQ that she was lesbian.

'A pity,' Jacko had told his wife, gossiping over supper one night.

'Why?' snapped Jackie. 'She needs your support, not your pity.'

He tried telling himself it didn't matter, was none of his business. After all, that fast bowler in his army cricket team

21

was homosexual. Having a French boyfriend hadn't stopped him taking a lot of wickets. But I never saw them kissing, did I? And, if I had, I would have winced like Keeling at Scott's joke. Because it was, well, not normal, not natural. He regarded himself as an ordinary man with ordinary views. So it did matter, though he never tried to explain why to his wife.

He and Caroline got to down to work. The bungalow was as cold as the road outside. They toured it anti-clockwise, getting a feeling for Davis, looking for something, anything, out of place. A bedroom where fitted wardrobes hid a dozen changes of smart clothes. Bathroom and toilet with a tiled shelf filled with male cosmetics. A soulless lounge, clinical and barren. An expensively fitted kitchen that had sampled little home cooking.

Definitely a bachelor pad, they decided. No potted plants or pot-pourri in baskets. No sweets in the fridge. No woman's touch. Like Jacko's place between marriages.

A couple in their fifties, Davis's parents probably, smiled down from the chrome and black plastic wall unit in the lounge. Around them, lines of books, crime, mostly non-fiction. On top of a radiator shelf stood a trophy, mock granite with cross cues in mock gold: *Gold Spot Club Championship – Runner Up*. It held an unframed snapshot to the wall which showed Davis receiving it from a fat, beaming Golden Jimmy Goulden.

In a drawer, packets of photos, some of army days, and holiday snaps in an exotic eastern setting, stripped to white trunks, rippling muscle under a sun-kissed skin. Alongside him, Detective John Udden. Close, those two, thought Jacko, too close.

'It's a place that a woman sometimes visits,' Caroline suddenly announced. In the palm of her small hand were two hair grips and a pair of ear-rings, silver-starred and studded, which she had taken from the dresser top. Among the male toiletry in the bathroom she'd found a black make-up pencil. Beside the only ashtray in the home of a non-smoker was a Silk Cut lighter.

Twenty cards hung on a thread between silver wall lights above a gas fire with fake logs. Most were from couples. Mum and Dad. John and Lisa. Someone called Chrissy had sent a solo card, a cartoon Santa, with love and kisses. Golden Jim had not extended his greetings. Neither had anyone called Jason.

The letter box rattled. A folded *Daily Express*, the policeman's paper, dropped on the mat. No, said the well-wrapped delivery boy, when Jacko called him back to the door, the occupant of No. 62 was never up this early and, no, he didn't take the *Mercury* at night. 'Didn't leave me a Christmas box either,' he added bitterly. Jacko understood. No seasonal tip meant sodden *Heralds* and *Mirrors* being delivered for a week or two into the New Year on his round as a boy. He gave him a pound coin.

The gas boiler clicked and fired. The bungalow began to defrost. Lights flickered on and off in windows around like a fog-bound fishing fleet.

Jacko saw the silhouette of a postwoman through the fluted glass and opened the front door to her. Yes, she said, as she handed over two items, she knew him. A slim, handsome chap with no regular visitors she'd ever seen.

There was a postcard from his mother. On the front what looked like a circus top on a concrete block sitting in the middle of snow and cloud-capped mountains. On the back a 'Murren, Switzerland' frank above a neat feminine hand: *Flight and hotel fine. Icy but expecting new fall. Dad did the black run à la James Bond.* God, thought Jacko, with a shaft of real sorrow, how awful it's going to be for them.

A letter, headed James Goulden Leisure Holdings plc, said: *For services rendered.* An enclosed cheque matched the sum on the invoice: £5000.

'Christ,' sighed Jacko, finally taking off his waxed coat, 'if I'd had this in my hand fifteen months ago he'd be alive today. In jail but alive.'

Caroline appeared not to hear him. 'Listen to this,' she called from the office. He joined her and heard one of four messages on the answering machine. Caroline played it back twice. 'Phone in a transcript and tell them where his folks are,' said Jacko. It was one of several calls they added to a bill Davis would never pay.

There was only one other interruption that morning. It came just before they left two uniformed constables on guard and drove to a pub for hot soup, sarnies and real ale for Caroline, Coke for him. The bell rang loud and long. Jacko opened it to a man he knew well, a reporter from the commercial television station which covered the East Midlands. An eager beaver, ambitious but trustworthy.

'Thank Christ it's you.' Only partially concealed relief filled his fair young face.

'Can't help you, Tony. I'm just a tail-end Charlie. See Scott or Keeling.'

'Both have gone to ground. All I've got is a suspicious death. Your PR's slow.'

Mmmm, thought Jacko. The police are fond of over-using the media and giving the minimum in return. He said nothing.

'Can you confirm it's Terry Davis, the ex-cop?'

Jacko shook his head, partly defensively, partly in admiration. No point in seeking his source. He'd guard it as jealously as he would his own.

'Guide me, for Christsake. I'm running short of time.'

They cobbled it up together on the doorstep. Mystery death. Self-employed businessman in late twenties. Believed head injuries (to be on the safe side, thought Jacko). Died on operating table. Murder-scale inquiry launched. Discovery made by couple collecting their car after a train trip from London. Efforts being made to trace victim's family on holiday abroad.

'Still not much,' said Tony, in a dingy green anorak over his smart on-screen suit. 'I'll still need a pic when they officially name him.'

'You won't get one here.'

'Oh, come on, Jacko. I'm snookered without one. Give us a steer.'

Jacko thought, then smiled. 'Try the Gold Spot Club.'

'Thanks, pal. I owe you.'

Jacko said so-long and shut the door.

Caroline looked up and tutted. 'One of these days, you'll drop yourself in it.'

Jacko regarded goodwill as a bank. Put some in. Draw some out. Now he was in credit. He considered that he knew all there was to know about press relations and other relationships, too. What could she know? he asked himself. He resented her reprimand but said nothing.

Till late afternoon when it became prematurely dark they

seemed to Jacko to blend together with the understanding of a well-rehearsed piano duo. Yet something was missing from their performance. Technically good, true, but no emotion; no feeling. He liked to flirt with female partners; not with bed in mind, but sexual chemistry made him show off and that brought out the best in him. But there was no point in fancying a lesbian, was there?

With less than twenty-two hours to live, the day had dawned for Terry Davis at eight when he turned off his alarm clock, they discovered. He popped his grey sleeping trunks under the pillow.

He took the top of the milk with cornflakes in a bowl which he left unwashed with a tea mug in a stainless steel sink in the trendily modern kitchen. He looked through the *Express* and put it, unfolded, on the black leather couch.

Ninety minutes later he left the bungalow in his Mazda to keep a diaried appointment to collect a set of coloured photos from Mid-Shires Portraits in the city centre.

He drove on to a law firm to sign a statement detailing his observations on a worker suing his employer over an incapacitating back injury. The photos showed the employee playing soccer.

At noon, they established, he was on an industrial estate doing a security survey for a small new firm. He pub-lunched the manager, hard-selling burglar alarms he'd just been contracted to market. No deal.

Mid-afternoon. Fifteen hours to live. He is in the office of his accountant discussing his first year in business as Tab Private Investigations.

He had grossed £25,000. Ten thousand came from Golden Jim Goulden plc in two instalments. The first half was paid into his bank thirteen months earlier as he was setting up. Hush-money, Jacko guessed, for keeping quiet about the car number racket that should have put Golden Jim behind bars, too.

The second five thousand came in July so today's cheque, Jacko deduced, had been intended to keep him on the payroll on a six-monthly basis.

His second major source of income was as a tipster, a paid

informant, to a Sunday paper that specialized in sin, soap opera, sport and the Royal Family. They made three payments.

In the summer, he received a £5000 cheque for *excl tip and asst re Mum's Deadly Dilemma*. Caroline dug into a grey cabinet to decode that cryptic note.

The bottom drawer was filled with an untidy pile of envelopes packed with burglar alarm brochures. Beneath them were old Jiffy bags containing loose-leaf pages from a refillable notebook, carefully dated and held together by elastic bands. A bit of the methodical policeman in Davis had remained, Jacko noted. In the three drawers above, his files were tagged from A to Z. She found the answer under F in a bulky file labelled *Frost family*. They spent a long time studying it sitting together on the couch.

In May a youth called Lance Frost had stood trial at the city's Crown Court for the murder of a neighbour's daughter, aged fourteen, in a local park. He'd been spotted cycling away before her body was found at the edge of a lake. Frost had been questioned by Detective Inspector Fixter. In the presence of his stepfather, he signed a partial confession.

When Lance came to give evidence on oath, he said, 'It wasn't me who killed her. It was my stepfather.' His mother followed him into the box and swore that her husband had not been at home at the vital time. The jury freed Lance. It caused a sensation at the time, massive headlines, but now was more or less forgotten except, Jacko guessed, by the dead girl's family.

Davis had been hired by the solicitors who acted for the defence. He charged them £140 plus expenses for two days' work. A copy of his report to them recorded that the stepfather's own mother had also blown his alibi. It noted that he had declined to undergo an hypnosis test which Davis had suggested to verify his claim of innocence.

Davis had multiplied his legal fee by selling on the story to the Sunday tabloid which carried it across two pages under the headline: WHO IS THE KILLER UNDER MY ROOF? ASKS COURT DRAMA MUM.

He'd acted as the family's agent in financial negotiations with the newspaper which settled for a payment of £5000 *on publication of exclusive interview and photographs of Frost family*. Davis's signature witnessed the deal.

26

The police reopened their inquiries after Lance's acquittal. He and his mother stuck to their court stories. By then seven months had elapsed since the girl's body had been found. There was no hope of gathering forensic evidence against the stepfather. He was never charged.

Someone, however, had anticipated that he could have stood trial. There were two copies of an unsigned draft agreement guaranteeing Mrs Frost a further £5000 *on conviction of her husband for exclusive rights to her account.*

No charge meant no conviction and no further pay-out. The story dribbled out of the news.

'Someone in that family', Caroline ventured, after a second read-through, 'seems to have got away with murder.'

Jacko nodded, concentrating. He'd never be immune to murder; always worked obsessively hard on them. Some, like Davis's, he treated as a job to be done, on autopilot, almost. Others, child murder especially, became a personal crusade. He read the file three times, soaking up the detail.

Experience was telling him it would crop up again in the current inquiry.

There had been a second payment from the same newspaper for £2000 just five weeks before this day of death. The accompanying invoice itemized, *Excl assistance re Soccer Star's Shame.*

Jacko found the link under G in the thickest folder in the cabinet, marked, *Jim Goulden plc.* In it was another cutting with a headline to match the invoice.

It reported the confessions of an international footballer about his gambling debts, claimed he had undergone therapy to kick the addiction and promised to turn over a new leaf. 'It's a mug's game,' he had declared. The story ended with a quote, rather stiff, from a spokesman for Golden Jim's Country Casino. 'We never discuss our clients. All our dealings are confidential.'

Mmmm, thought Jacko, Davis used publicity as a weapon in collecting Golden Jim's debts and got paid on the side for it, the unscrupulous bastard.

The third payment from the paper had arrived by post just twenty-four hours earlier and had not even been banked. *Asst re Dog-Fight Gang – £200.*

Jacko found the cross-reference in a thin file at the front of the top drawer, labelled, *Animal Alliance.*

In November Davis had done a week's work for them, charging £400. He had bumped up his fee by selling on info he had gathered to the paper. On the first Sunday of the New Year, just two days before he died, they carried a double-page exposé: DOG-FIGHT HORROR – WE NAME THE GUILTY MEN.

All three stories had been billed as 'Another Great Exclusive'. All three had been written by a reporter called Jason French.

The rest of his earnings, less than ten thousand, had come from services he advertised in a display advert in Yellow Pages: *Personal – Legal – Commercial – All types of inquiries undertaken. Confidentiality guaranteed.* Jacko laughed, more of a snort, really.

Without his retainers from Golden Jim and his snouting for Fleet Street, Davis would have been on skid row. His foray into burglar alarms was new. No commission from it had yet found its way into his accounts.

He'd been a big spender. Easy come, easy go. His mortgage and car hire purchase ate up a third of his income. His gadgetry cost three thousand. The tan on his snapshots had been acquired in a crowded, dusty, jerry-built seaside village in Indonesia and cost almost two thousand. At least, Golden Jim had not paid for that holiday, Jacko noted.

He had £2000 in a high interest account, was overdrawn in his current account and his accountant can't have been very impressed, he guessed.

Teatime. Around thirteen hours to live and a neighbour saw him arrive home in his Mazda. He brought that evening's *Mercury* in with him. He didn't add to the washing up by eating anything. Four messages awaited him on his answering machine and Caroline transcribed them.

The first was a voice from the past for Jacko. He recalled it from an angry interview fourteen months earlier. 'Oh, Terry. Jim. Your cheque's in the post. But let's not rush into anything again without my say-so. Hallrightie?' Golden Jim had attempted to gentrify his rural accent in a way that some people think is necessitated by new money. Aitches, instead of being dropped, come out like hay-tishoos. Pompous fat prat, he thought.

The second was another male voice, local again, younger, hesitant, like a nervous young clerk relaying a message. 'Yes, Mr Davis. She says what we agreed on Saturday is OK so the arrangement stands.' He hesitated, as if expecting some reply, then added a lame, 'Thank you.'

The third was a woman's voice. Light, chirpy, coquettish. 'Hi. It's Chrissy. It's OK for tonight as it turns out. Give me a ring at work if you can't make it. By-eee.'

The fourth was a man's voice, unpolished by new money, echoing and slightly slurred, either in drink or disguise. 'We've got your number, Davis, you sneaky little shit. And your number is up. Got that, you bastard?'

He'd been seen to leave home in his car just after seven in the evening. Jacko and Caroline followed his trail. Davis arrived at the Gold Spot Club ten minutes' walk from the railway station before half-past. He asked for Golden Jim but was told he was at his casino six miles out of town. He had two gins and slimline tonic but hadn't eaten. 'Either he was watching his slimline figure or he had a supper date,' Caroline speculated.

He played three frames with the off-duty Udden. Both were speedy, proficient players. He hung around for thirty minutes after Udden left, locking up his cue and chatting. 'See you, sweet,' he called to the barmaid when he left. She was the last person so far traced to see him alive. Within an hour, he was dying with his throat torn away.

They drove back in the fog which had not lifted all day. Jacko was well pleased. Not only had they amassed a solid report, they had glimpsed into Davis's soul. A paymaster, a lover, an enemy. My, my. He'd been right about him; right to shunt the bent bastard out of the force. Lying on a slab at the Royal Infirmary hadn't altered that. Jacko was vindicated and he felt good.

In their absence, the briefing room had been transformed into an incident room with a score of desks. Sitting on them were computers with screens and phones with wires running across the oak floor.

They took adjoining desks, logging the exhibits they had brought back. They asked for the answering machine tape to be dispatched to the science lab for voice-printing.

They retained Davis's diary and contacts book, thumbing through them, trying to answer two outstanding questions. Where was Jason French? Who was Chrissy?

Jacko phoned the Grand. Yes, said the receptionist, Mr Jason French was booked in but had been out all day. Davis had three numbers listed for him. There was no reply from his Birmingham home. His London news desk didn't know his movements.

'So let's bleep him,' said Caroline, picking up their phone. She dialled the third number under French, J., the message bureau. She gave another set of figures to the operator and dictated, 'Please phone Inspector Jackson. Urgent.' She added the station's and their extension numbers.

Within ten minutes, the extension rang. Caroline picked it up. She handed it on to Jacko with a clever dick smirk which annoyed him.

'Jason French.'

Jacko thanked him for calling, said he couldn't talk over the phone and arranged to meet him at the Grand at eight. 'Great stuff, this new tech,' he said, replacing the phone.

Caroline ignored him. In the contacts book, she'd found lots of people with the initial C., three with the first name of Chris but only one Chrissy. No surname, two numbers. One had the local prefix for Loughborough, a town ten miles north. The other was the number of the central police station.

She dialled 9 for an outside line and dialled back into the station's main switchboard. 'Could I speak to Chrissy, please?'

'One minute,' said the operator.

'Juvenile section,' said another female voice.

'Could I speak to Chrissy, please?'

''Fraid not. She signed on at two but went home ill soon afterwards. Can I help?'

'Sergeant Parker here. Can I check her home number?' It corresponded with the contacts book.

'Don't disturb her,' the voice pleaded. 'She's probably sleeping. She looked quite ill. If it's urgent why not have a word with her husband?'

'Where will I find him?' Easy-going, very casual.

'CID. Inspector Mike Fixter. You know him, don't you? Shall I transfer you?'

'No,' said Caroline, sounding casual still, feeling every muscle tighten. 'It'll keep. Thanks.'

Jacko closed his eyes and sighed from the pit of his stomach when she whispered it all to him. He looked anxiously at the clock on the wall. Ten minutes to go to the six o'clock conference. 'We can't produce this out of the hat in front of Fixter, can we?' Caroline shook her head.

There was only one thing to do, he decided. Pass the buck to the Little Fat Man. He walked tentatively towards Scott at the far end of the room. He waited until he had finished a heated conversation with the collator. 'A private word, guv, please.'

'Can't it wait?' The Little Fat Man was tired and in a temper.

'Now please, sir.'

He led the way out, Scott following, disturbed. Jacko was a close friend who only called him Sir in front of top brass.

In the privacy of the corridor, he learned that the constable wife of a senior officer was probably having an affair with Davis. And Davis's blood had been splattered, for all to see, over his brown trousers.

'Oh, Christ,' Scott groaned.

4

She'd been lying in a darkened fuggy bedroom in a white slip over cotton bra and pants and slipped on a candy-striped housecoat when Caroline rang the door bell. All she was told was, 'The Chief Super wants to see you.' WPC Chrissy Fixter didn't plead illness, didn't argue. She seemed to know what was coming. Doomed, thought Caroline, guiltily; her marriage and career destroyed and it was clever dick me who shopped her.

Chrissy had been sick in the toilet as soon as she realized the reason for the activity that engulfed the station. Her sergeant had sent her home. Period pains again, know-all male colleagues had said. Some men, mused Caroline, think that women can suffer from no other sort of pain.

She threw on the handiest clothes. Green blouse, a mustard two-piece suit and, on top, a fawn trench coat she left unbelted. She put on black shoes with mid-heels and tan-coloured tights, which sagged at the ankles. It was if she was saying, What do I care now how I look?

She wore no make-up so her lips were pale and her skin dry. She ran her fingers through her long jet-black hair and didn't bother with a comb or grips or rings for her pierced ears.

Nursing her black shoulder bag, she chain-smoked on the ten-mile drive and Caroline's car became as foggy inside as it was outside. Not a word was spoken. It was uncanny the way she asked no questions. Because she knew the answers, Caroline supposed.

She turned over her mind to try to find a safe subject, a little opening for saying, 'If you ever need a shoulder to cry on . . .' Not with anything in mind, certainly not seduction (this girl's a proven heterosexual, for all the good it's done her), but as a colleague who hates to see suffering. Odd the way the world admires male bonding but sees something kinky in women being close. Not a subject for small talk, though, was it? Not when you're being whisked off for questioning over adultery and death. Finding no safe subject, Caroline kept quiet.

Chrissy ran up the station steps, lifting her knees like a colt. Her leather shoes clip-clopped on the terrazzo tiles.

Tartish, Jacko thought, but hellishly sexy. He was vulnerable to vulnerable women, liked to chat them up, and he was beginning to suspect Scott had assigned Caroline Parker to him as some sort of malicious joke.

Chrissy Fixter sat down in a straight chair opposite the Little Fat Man who had commandeered the Divisional Deputy's office and glass-topped desk. 'Sorry to have to bring you in.'

She fiddled in her coat pockets. From one she brought out a crushed packet of Silk Cut and from the other a disintegrating book of matches. She ripped one off and lit up. Scott slid a glass ashtray towards her.

'Does Mike know?' She spoke at last, low, with a bit of a whine.

'You've taken the words out of my mouth.' Scott spoke quickly. 'Does your husband know about you and Terry Davis?'

A long pause. She tapped the cigarette into the tray as though morsing distress signals. 'Not from me.' She shook her head. 'No. I'm sure he doesn't'

Gradually, the story came out, Caroline noting it down. She was a probationer when Davis joined the force. 'We met at parties. Only socially.'

She was already sleeping with Mike Fixter. Three years ago they married. She for the first time; he for the second. She was twenty-six. He was thirty-nine. No children.

They'd invested in a place, mock tudor, at Loughborough, a busy market town with a university sprawled alongside a road approaching the M1.

'Lots of Terry's mates were upset when he had to leave the force. Some of us threw him a farewell party. Mike couldn't go, could he?'

'Why not?' Scott asked.

'Well, Terry left under a bit of a cloud, didn't he?'

'Do you know why?'

'The grapevine said he'd misused the vehicle computer

33

for personal gain.' She arched her plucked eyebrows. 'He drove me home after the party. Nothing happened. He just asked if he could keep in touch, said he'd miss the camaraderie.'

He'd phoned a couple of times and eventually they met for a drink when Mike was on nights. They finished up at his local. 'And, well . . .'

The careless shrug told it all. No slow seduction with flowers and dinners. Straight into the sack. They'd been doing it ever since when Mike's shifts allowed.

Jacko, a silent observer throughout the interview, took a non-judgemental view of matters sexually. He just mildly wondered how people found the time and energy. 'When was the last time?' Scott asked.

'Ten days ago. At his place. We met on New Year's Day but only for a drink. We half arranged to see each other last night.'

For the first time she faced up to Scott's gaze. 'It wasn't just sex. I did like his company. He, well . . . He made me laugh.'

She spoke as if she didn't expect anyone to understand. She was wrong. Too many detectives, Jacko knew, spent too much time working and drinking and got home too late to give their wives too many laughs.

'When Mike told me he was going out, I phoned Terry and left a message on his machine.'

'What were the arrangements?' Scott lent back on a solid leather chair, keeping a palm on the glass top.

'When I had the car, I drove to his place. When I used the train, we'd meet in the station forecourt.' Scott pulled a perplexed face. 'At the railway station, not the police station,' she added in explanation.

He nodded understanding. 'And last night?'

She shook her head. 'He phoned me at work about five. Said he couldn't make it. Had something on. He didn't say what. It was a very short conversation.'

The next question was obvious. Scott didn't ask it. It would have meant the rest of their interview proceeding under caution. Jacko knew he didn't want that yet. She was being co-operative, courageous almost, faced with the prospects of a lost marriage and career as well as a lost lover. He didn't want to stem the flow. He backtracked.

'On your dates, did you ever discuss business?'

'Not police business, if that's what you mean.' A snapped-out answer, nothing left to lose.

'Not exactly, but since you mention it, did he ever ask you for favours – tapping into our computer for vehicle numbers, for example?'

'No. Never.' A set face, angry.

He nodded again, seeming to accept her word. Then, relaxed, 'So how was his business going? Did he discuss that with you?'

She screwed her eyes, either in thought or to keep out cigarette smoke. 'He never acted short of money.'

She knew he worked as some sort of security adviser to Golden Jim but she had never met him. 'Come to think of it, he was a bit worried that his contract with him might not be renewed.' She didn't know what the contract was worth or what, if anything, had gone wrong between Davis and Golden Jim.

Yes, she said, she did know a journalist called Jason French, had a drink with him in the Grand one night six weeks ago. 'Terry did some legwork for him. Said the pay was very good. He handed him an envelope. I don't know what was in it. Didn't ask.'

Scott changed the question line, swiftly, suddenly, a skilled interviewer's ploy. 'Apart from you, were there any other women in his life?'

She looked away and shook her head. 'Not that I know of.'

'Would you have minded if there had been?' Jacko recognized a hard question with an easy answer if she wanted to grasp it. 'I wouldn't have minded provided I didn't know.' 'How could I complain with a husband at home?' Something like that.

Instead: 'Yes. I think I would.' She tapped out more morse with her cigarette. 'Were there?'

'Not as far as we know. Did anyone know you were seeing Terry?'

'We were very careful. We only used his place and drank at his local.'

'But you were with him in the Grand when he met a journalist. You can't be more open about it than that.'

'We just dropped in on the way to pick up his car by the Town Hall.'

'Did anyone know, Constable Fixter?' The questions were hardening up.

'Not that I know of. It's possible, I suppose, there might have been some station gossip. Only my best pal knew, for sure.'

'So if your best pal knows, Terry's best pal might know. Who was that?'

A shrug, uncertain. 'Johnny Udden, I suppose. I don't know of any other really close friends.' Him again, thought Jacko.

'If Terry did tell Udden, did Udden tell your husband? After all, they worked . . .'

'No.' A facial squeeze shot vertical lines up her forehead. 'All hell would have erupted. He'd have probably kicked me out. No. I'm sure of it.'

Towards the jugular now, slowly, a stalking animal. 'You were telling me about yesterday. Did you bring in your car?'

A headshake. 'I was on office duty. Two till ten. I used the train.'

'And he phoned at five to cancel your date. So what happened at ten?'

'I logged off and caught the twenty-past.'

'Which way did you go to the railway station?'

'London Road.'

'Via Campbell Street might be quicker.'

'And darker. Besides it would have meant passing the pub and I didn't want to bump into Mike and his mates.'

'Turn out your pockets and bags, please,' said Scott, brusquely.

'Why?' Vertical lines shot from black eyebrows to the roots of her black hair.

'Please, Chrissy,' said Caroline with a tense smile.

She deposited three damp torn paper tissues from her pockets on to the desk. Lipsticks, sprays, a metal edged purse, a ring of keys, a pocket book clattered down as she emptied her bag. A silk square landed softly on top of them. Golden girls, arms

36

akimbo, danced on a brown background. Caroline picked it up. *Made in Bali,* said the label.

'A present from Terry?' she asked, feeling it in her fingers. Chrissy nodded.

'Wear it last night?'

Another nod.

'As a head scarf?'

An offended look, her dress sense questioned. 'Here.' She touched her throat. 'You don't see head scarves these days.'

Mrs Marshall did, thought Jacko. Last night. Worn by a woman rounding the corner from the direction of the car-park in which your lover died.

Scott hunched himself forward. 'I'd like you to give us a full and frank statement. In fairness to you it will be taken under caution. We'd also like to inspect your car and your house.'

'But surely . . .'

He raised a silencing hand. 'You know the rules. Let's do it by the book.' He stood. 'I'll send you in some fresh cigarettes.'

She looked up alarmed as he moved sideways from behind the desk. 'Can I see Mike?'

He turned at the door, Jacko following. 'Sorry, no. He's very busy.'

Jacko had been expecting floods of tears. Not a dew drop. Only when she was alone with Caroline did they come, running down her nose, wetting the white cylinder of yet another cigarette, reddening her blue eyes. And when it was down in writing Caroline patted her shoulder ever so gently.

Inspector Mike Fixter had spent all morning with forensic scientists at the scene, just 300 yards from the warmth of his office.

He was called away in the afternoon when a traffic warden reported the missing Mazda car illegally parked in a side street near the tucked-away Town Hall which regally overlooks a square with trees and a fountain. Nothing of note had been found inside.

37

The 6 p.m. briefing had been short. Chief Inspector Keeling reported that the pathologist had removed the skin from around Davis's throat, treated it with preservatives and pinned it to a board for further tests. Forensics had found no dog hairs on his clothing.

His parents had been contacted in Switzerland and were flying home. Scott approved the immediate release of his name. 'If any journo presses for a motive, tell them we have an open mind,' he told Keeling. Everyone around the table knew that was policespeak for 'We haven't a clue.'

The background team, it seemed to Fixter, had not made much progress. He'd heard that Old Jackson was the Little Fat Man's favourite son. He looked old enough for the roles to be reversed. Mid-forties, an ill-pressed grey suit, greying sideburns, bespectacled, his face more lined than Keeling's who'd had no sleep.

Jackson, he moaned later, dwelt for a long time on Golden Jim Goulden and the Frost family. Everyone knew that he hadn't nailed Golden Jim over the computer leaks. Everyone, Fixter especially, knew that young Frost was a sex killer who had fiddled his freedom, not a homicidal mugger.

Fixter told his sergeant that he suspected Jackson of padding it out to hide the fact that, while everyone else had been freezing their nuts off in the streets, he'd sat indoors, a cushy number, and failed to find a secret lover.

'All the same, these Big-Time Operators from HQ,' he grumbled and his sergeant laughed. There was never any love between the Major Crimes Squad and Divisional CID.

Scott, he complained, had been an indifferent chairman at the briefing, exhausted, perhaps. Preoccupied, certainly. There'd been no tactical discussions and he hardly encouraged any debate. Fixter had to volunteer to beef up the team tracing and pulling in local muggers. Plenty to pick from, he sighed; some hard to find when word of the round-up got out.

The phone rang in the Divisional CID office where he was working on the muggers' file. Udden picked it up, said OK twice and put it down. 'The Chief Super wants Mr Fixter and Jackson wants me in half an hour.'

'Who's he?' Detective Bullman, a veteran with the face of

38

a ferret and hunting instincts to match, looked up from a collection of mug shots.

'The Little Fat Man's bum boy,' said Udden. 'He did Terry Davis.'

Sitting alongside Scott when Fixter walked into the Deputy's office was Keeling, in mournful mood, as though someone had told him his pet dog was dead. In a corner away from the desk sat Jackson, who looked down when he entered.

Scott nodded Fixter to sit opposite him. He recapped from the statement Fixter had painstakingly typed.

He'd logged off at eight thirty and got to the Royal Mail within five minutes? Two sergeants and two constables were already there? Udden joined the party just after nine?

All of it was confirmed by nods.

'How many pints did you have?'

'I was on my fourth when it happened, sir.' Fixter spoke placidly, then pointedly added, 'The plan was for John Udden to drive me home after a curry.'

'How tall are you?'

Fixter squeezed his chin into his thick neck, a look of disbelief. 'Six foot one.'

Scott made a show of making a note. Then he wanted to know what Fixter knew about Davis.

'I never got to know him that well. I saw him around now and then but never worked directly with him. They say he was a useful lad when it got nasty at the football down at Filbert Street but I never saw him in action.'

Scott stopped making notes. 'At the pub did you go to the lavatory?'

Fixter looked at him in astonishment. 'I don't follow, sir.'

'You'd had four pints. Did you use the loo?'

Fixter seemed to seek guidance with a look towards Keeling whose eyes remained down. 'Yes.'

'Can you remember when?'

Fixter gave his head a mystified shake. 'Just before Mrs Marshall raised the alarm.'

Scott caught Keeling's eye and nodded. The funereal look deepened. 'There's no easy way of saying this, Mike, so I won't

39

try. Your wife has given us a statement in which she admits she was having an affair with Davis.'

Fixter looked from one to the other, a weak smile on his face. A bad-taste joke, perhaps?

'Were you aware of this liaison?'

'I don't believe you.' It hadn't sunk in.

'I'm afraid it's true. Did you know, Mike?'

'Balls.' Angry now. 'There's nothing to know. You've been listening to canteen gossip.'

'We have her statement.' Scott spoke quietly, patting a form on his desk.

It was sinking in now. He rocked, like a mental patient, back and forth in his chair. 'It's not true.' He shook his head, vigorously.

'You see our situation.' Scott cleared his throat but still croaked his words. 'You were absent from your company at a crucial time. There's Councillor Marshall's statement about a six-footer darting in front of him. You said yourself he's a great witness. There's blood on your clothes . . .'

'But no motive.' Fixter had stopped swaying. Rigid in his chair. Upright. 'Do you hear?' Face twisted. Sweating. Raising his voice. 'Because I didn't know. You must believe that.' Shouting now. 'I didn't know. I did not, repeat not, know.'

Jacko's mind was far away. To the day he'd learned about his first wife and her sergeant lover. At least he'd heard it from her and not from some Chief Superintendent who'd then made him a suspect in a murder inquiry.

Depression had replaced his earlier euphoria. He wished he'd never heard of Terry Davis, wished he'd pleaded sickness and stayed in bed. This job was too close to home; much, much too close.

Udden walked cockily into the incident room and sat down uninvited in the absent Caroline's chair, lounging immediately. 'Want me?'

'Only for a bit of background,' said Jacko, pleasant enough.

He'd met Davis, Udden said, when he transferred from Rutland, a rural sub-division so law-abiding that it was said in the canteen police cadets had to fight each other for a bit of public order training. They became pals because of their mutual passion for surfing and kept in touch after Davis was drummed out.

'Was that wise?' An elder statesman's face, a reprimanding tone.

'Whatyamean? You proved nothing against him because there was nothing to prove.'

'Oh, really.' A taunting tone. 'And what about his freebie holiday with Golden Jim?'

'Show me a Chief Constable who foots the bill when he jets out with his wife to study policing in California.' Udden jutted out his chin, freshly shaven and splashed with cologne.

'And what about your surfing holiday in Kuta?'

'Paid my own way.' The question had jolted him straight. 'My bank statement will show you that. And how.' He lowered his voice and chin, a peace-offering. 'It was fixed up and paid for before his trouble.'

And, since his trouble, they'd had the odd summer's day surfing and winter's night playing snooker. 'I thought he might come in useful some time.'

Odd, thought Jacko cynically, how policemen always dredge up that excuse for indiscreet relationships.

Jacko jutted his chin forward. 'And were you useful to him?'

'Whatyamean?' Growled this time, nettled.

'Did he ask for favours – vehicle numbers, criminal record details, addresses to assist him in his work?'

'Do me a favour.' A scornful smile. 'He was earning more than you. He didn't need help from me.'

'What about his social life?' Jacko worked his way round to his real quest. 'Any girlfriends?'

'I only met him at sporty stag dos.'

'Last night was stag. Did you invite him along to see Inspector Fixter and the boys?'

'I've already made a statement about that. He told me he had a business engagement. What, when and where he didn't say.' Chin up again. 'Neither of us discussed our jobs.'

'Your inspector's wife, Chrissy. Do you know her?'

'Only from the occasional party.' Guarded, watchful.

'Did Davis know Chrissy?'

41

Jacko realized he had telegraphed it and Udden had seen it coming. He dropped his chin into his neck, on the defensive. 'No. Why?'

In seeking evidence of motive before evidence of opportunity, Jacko had showed his hand. A mistake. He was angry with himself. Maybe he was depressed over the Fixters. Maybe he disliked Udden because of his association with Davis, a proven crook. Or maybe everyone was getting tetchy. Whichever, he'd mishandled it and he knew it.

When they moved on to what happened in the Royal Mail, Udden was prepared to swear on a box of bibles that Fixter had not left his side. He was doing, Jacko recognized, what most policemen do. Closing ranks. If the shit hit the fan for his inspector, no one was going to be able to say he blew the whistle.

With increasing acrimony they went over and over it. No, Udden was sure Fixter didn't know about Chrissy and Davis. Davis had told him about her but he hadn't told Fixter. Yes, he was sure that Fixter never left his view in the pub.

Jacko reported it all back to Scott. 'I cocked it up but I know he's not telling the truth.'

Scott nodded. 'Even Fixter admits he took time out for a pee.'

'Udden's got vested interests. His mate's the victim and his boss is a suspect.' Jacko waited for Scott's reaction. None came. 'Take him off the case, Richard.'

Tiredness and frustration came to the boil within Scott and the lid came off, steaming. 'Don't you come in here telling me what to do. You screwed it up. You sort him out.'

'Right,' said Jacko and walked to the door, slamming it behind him.

I've already put in fourteen hours on a day off and I'm still not finished, he thought angrily, as he collected his waxed jacket. Then he bollocks me. I should have told him to fuck off.

Walking down the steps into the fog he was reminded of a story from his spirit-reviving well of happy tales.

This inspector, see, comes out of the Chief Constable's office, ashen-faced. 'He gave me the biggest bollocking of my life,' he tells his superintendent.

'I never stand for that,' says the super. 'I always tell him to fuck off.'

Next day, same inspector, another terrible bollocking. He stops the Chief in full flow. 'Excuse me, sir, but why don't you fuck off.'

In the corridor, tears in his eyes, he meets his super. 'Thanks a lot. I took your advice, told him to fuck off and he suspended me.'

'Oh Lord,' said the super, 'you didn't actually let him hear you, did you?'

He was smiling again by the time the Grand Hotel loomed into view.

5

The face at the door of the hotel bedroom was pretty enough for television. 'Combe iron.' The voice condemned him to a lifetime in the print world. A Brummie has as much chance of reading 'News at Ten' as a Ukrainian. In broadcasting terms they're what's known as duff utterers.

Jason French would survive, Jacko decided, surveying, not without envy, features that were dark and handsome.

The room was a mess with newspapers scattered on a bed that was coming apart. On top of the pile was that night's *Mercury*. Two main stories featured on the front page. SECRETARY THREATENED TO KILL ME, CLAIMS GP. It was a follow-up to the previous night's story Jacko had scanned at Davis's bungalow: SEX TRIAL GP TERRIFIED ME, CLAIMS SECRETARY.

The main story was headed: CAR-PARK DEATH RIDDLE. BIG POLICE PROBE. Their reporter had just as good sources as Tony from Television. He hadn't run the name but had quotes from regulars at the Royal Mail and the post sorting office opposite, plus a photo looking down at Fixter's team on their hands and knees.

It would have been difficult, Jacko had to concede, for the *Mercury* to have missed the story. The Royal Mail is the nearest pub to the paper's offices, a long straight building with lime squares dotted among slabs of fudge, across the road from the police station.

When relationships between press and police were strained – and this happened about every other week, in his experience – the police would refer to their near-neighbours as Fairies from the Fudge Factory. Journalists would claim the whiteness of the police station gave it an Aryan feel and referred to it as Gestapo Headquarters. All good fun. Neither in the others' pockets. As it should be in a democracy.

'How can I help?' French monotoned.

'It's about that.' Jacko nodded to the front page.

'You on that?' French was re-reading the sex-case doctor story.

'Only background.' Jacko's eyes were on the car-park riddle.

'I'm trying to sign up the receptionist but she won't talk.' His accent gave the impression that he was bemoaning his luck but he was wearing a broad smile.

'Wrong story.' Jacko smiled, too.

French glanced at the death riddle article and shook his head. 'Means nothing to me.'

'We've only just released his name. A pal of yours, I'm afraid. Terry Davis.'

'Jesus.' The smile vanished. 'That's a shaker.' He sat on the bed, troubled, and read the paper. 'What happened?'

'Murder.' No response as he read on. 'Did you see him last night?' A headshake without looking up.

Jacko had not known what to expect. He had easy-going, trusting relationships with several journalists, Tony from Television especially, but they were local. National men would screw their own grandmas for a story, he'd heard. He'd already decided to proceed with caution. 'Did you have an appointment to see him last night?'

'Yes.' French finally looked up. Davis, he said, had phoned him at home on Sunday evening. 'Said he had a cracker for me. About a murder. He refused to go into details without an agreed price. There was no rush. I was coming across on this trial.' He nodded at the paper. 'So we fixed to meet in the bar downstairs.'

'What time?'

'Ten. His idea, but it suited me. You can't approach witnesses until they've completed their evidence so all my work is done after the court rises.'

'What happened?'

'He didn't show. So I bleeped him to hurry him up.'

'What time?'

'I'd been waiting for fifteen minutes or so.'

French spoke with the confidence of someone used to dealing with much bigger fish than a DI. He flopped back on the bed, pummelling up a pillow behind his dark, curly hair.

Jacko sat on a chair with a pink velvet cushion. He pulled out his notebook and put it on an antique writing table. 'A contact of yours, you say?'

'Now and then.' French swung his legs off the bed. 'Does this have to be formal or can we eat while we talk? I'm famished.' So, too, was Jacko.

Over his too-loose Benetton grey shirt, French – fit-looking, early thirties – pulled on a too-loose jacket which matched his too-loose silvery grey trousers. They took the lift down and walked beneath crystal chandeliers.

The basement restaurant had ceiling fans, hand-printed friezes, tropical plants in tubs, water that ran into bowls shaped like giant oyster shells, a grand piano in the corner. Jacko felt like Noel Coward walking into Raffles. Only his wax coat spoilt the colonial illusion. A bow-tied waiter took it from him, holding it at arm's length, like an unexploded bomb.

They decided against starters. Jacko skipped all items involving turkey and settled for halibut. French ordered the most expensive steak but sportingly opted for dry white wine.

Jacko was surprised how smoothly it was going. He'd half expected him to plead ethics and refuse to discuss his sources. Now he was having to guard against being pumped for information. He let French do most of the talking between mouthfuls which the journalist enjoyed so much he occasionally hummed in happiness as he ate.

In May the previous year, he said, his news desk got a call from Davis offering information. Every paper gets scores of such offers every day on the phone or in personal visits to the office, he explained patiently. All have to be checked.

The call was transferred up to French because Leicester was part of his Midlands patch. 'He was cagey on the phone. They always are. They want cash in hand before they open their mouths. You have to talk them into putting their goods in the shop window before you can price them.'

They met here at the Grand. 'He had big bucks in mind. Twenty grand. I told him for that price we'd need Dirty Den from "East Enders" involved.' Jacko smiled, enjoying himself and the meal.

After the financial facts of Fleet Street life had been spelt out Davis scaled down his demand and outlined his story.

He said a teenager called Lance Frost was going to stand up in court and say his stepdad had committed a murder he had been wrongly accused of.

'I told him the dailies would saturate the story before we came out. It would only work for a Sunday if, first, the boy was acquitted and, second, the family talked exclusively. He said he could deliver if the price was right, had authority to act as the family's agent and was willing to sign a deal there and then. "Hang on, I sez, and wait for the verdict." If Lance was guilty there was no story.'

French stayed away from the trial because he didn't want to alert his rivals to his interest. Once Mrs Frost had given evidence he signed the contract Davis had drawn up. Payment would be 'on publication'.

'An important phrase, that,' said French, topping up Jacko's glass and totally refilling his own. 'If Lance had been found guilty there would have been no publication and no payment.'

The jury cleared Lance. Davis spirited him and his family away in his car. French met them at a hotel with a photographer. 'Dead easy, though the stepfather bottled out. We got the story. They got paid.'

'Five thousand,' said Jacko, a statement, not a question. A who-cares shrug. 'Did you follow it up?'

A brief headshake. 'It was just a one-off.'

'You see' – Jacko broached this carefully – 'we found a contract anticipating the stepfather would be charged. Again Mrs Frost's story was for sale. The price and the name of the newspaper hadn't been filled in.'

'He never mentioned that.' A moment's reflection, trying, Jacko suspected, to decide if Davis had been planning a double-cross. Then, dismissively, 'Once the police closed their file, the story was dead.' Another pause. 'Were you on it?'

Jacko shook his head. No, thank Christ, by the sounds of it, he thought.

French rested his chin on a hand, taking a breather from his T-bone steak. 'It was a cock-up. The kid did it all right. He's not all there.' He tapped his temple.

'Hear from Davis again?'

'When a guy like that has had a bit of success pound signs flash in his eyes. He was often on. Tips about a kidnapping and a snatch from a casino. Daily paper stuff.'

'Golden Jim's Casino, by any chance?'

An in-the-know smile, sneaky. 'He was his next success.'

Davis had phoned about a couple of months ago with news that an international footballer owed big gambling debts. 'Hang on, I sez.' French had an attractive way of telling a tale that made Jacko overlook his Minnie-the-Moaner delivery. 'That's dicey without documentary proof. "Got it," he sez. We met here.' He nodded at the ceiling and the cocktail bar above. 'Sure enough, copies of all demanding letters from Golden Jim. All I had to do was knock on the footballer's door and wave them.'

'And he admitted everything?'

'Ah, well, now. We had to pay him.' He spoke as though it was the most natural thing in the world. 'He contacted his agent and we settled a price for his confessions.'

'And Davis got two grand for the tip?'

A nod. He stopped munching suddenly. 'You don't suspect our superstar, do you?'

'Hardly. He's got thirty thousand-plus who saw him till quarter past nine last night and ten team-mates who were with him bollock-naked in the bath till quarter-to. I think we can rule him out.' They laughed, at ease with each other.

French picked Stilton cheese, as every other visitor to Leicester does. Jacko, who had it every other day, chose banana split.

A week later, French continued, celery snapping between big white teeth, Davis was on the phone again.

'He claimed to have the low-down on a gang of dog-fighters. I met him here but all he had were a couple of names and addresses and some gen an old biddy from an animal rights organization had given him. So we didn't pay him a lot. Took me three weeks to crack it. He reckoned he'd done a spell with CID in his police days. Detective, my arse. He hadn't a clue how to go about it.'

First, said French, he'd called at the addresses posing as a salesman wanting to buy a fighting dog. He'd been passed on

48

to other breeders. All the time, he was wired up and picking up hints on training and leads on other owners.

Finally he was referred to a farmer everyone called Big Vyn. 'I met him a couple of times with his cronies. By now I thought I had their lingo off pat.

'He invited me round to his place to settle on a deal for a dog. A houseful of his mates were there. Out the blue, he said, "What's a reporter want with a fighting dog? What's your game?" I nearly shit myself. Had visions of being thrown to his dogs and being torn limb from limb. Know how my cover was blown?' Jacko shook his head, enthralled.

'I reckon some tame cop checked out my car number on your computer at Big Vyn's request. Leaks like a sieve, that computer of yours.'

Jacko nodded, non-committal. Can't have been Davis that time, he thought.

'Instead of finishing up as dog meat they offered to stage a dog-fight for me for five grand. All spectators and owners to be masked. No mention of the venue. I just wanted to escape in one piece so I told them I was sure the editor would buy it.

'He turned it down flat. "How can we, a dog lovers' paper, sponsor a dog-fight?" He told me to run with what I'd got. I'd stacks of tapes so there couldn't be any legal comebacks. The trickiest part was confronting all the people we were going to name. It's a rule, see, that if you've used subterfuge to obtain info you have to reveal yourself and allow them the right of reply. The only reply I got was a punch on the nose.' French rubbed it.

'Violent men, are they?'

'Scum.' He shook his head at the bloody memory. Then, seeking the pat on the head that all writers crave: 'See the piece?'

'Yes. Good stuff.'

He visibly puffed out his chest. 'It was nice to do some proper journalism instead of Dirty Den crap.'

'You said you made a lot of secret tapes of gang members. Could I have a listen?' Jacko headed off a question he knew was bound to come. 'There are one or two messages on his answering machine with no names. We need to identify them.'

'Threatening messages?' French was missing nothing.

Jacko offered a deal. 'You let me have the tapes. I'll give you an exclusive once we have interviewed them. OK?'

The answer was a surprise. 'Not sure. You see,' he said, almost apologetically, 'there's another rule. We don't release unpublished stuff to the police without a court order. It's the same with TV.'

'Why?'

'If we've run it, all well and good. The public have seen it and if the police want a copy, fair enough. But if we haven't published it – and we didn't run much from the tapes – there's a problem. People might stop talking to us in case everything they said is handed on to the police. All I can do is ask and, if the editor approves, I'll drop them in.'

Christ, thought Jacko, annoyed, they pay out cash bribes all over the place and come over all coy when they could hold the key to a murder.

He had only one question left and he approached it with extra caution. 'Did you meet him socially?'

'Wasn't my type. He thought he was God's gift. He loved all the cloak and dagger stuff but he couldn't hack it. Faced with the dog-fighters he hadn't a clue how to begin.'

Jacko seized the opening. 'How do you mean, God's gift? To women?'

French avoided his eyes for the first time, looking away either in thought or enlightenment. 'Only ever saw him with one.' His eyes moved up to the ceiling. 'In the bar when he dropped off the casino documents.'

'Did he introduce her?'

'No.' Eyes down again. 'She was a good-looker. Dark, long hair, slim. Can't recall her name. We only had a quick drink together.' Jacko let it drop.

Soon French motioned the waitress who had served them in friendly, never familiar fashion. 'Put it on my room.'

Jacko remembered Standing Orders which cautioned against accepting hospitality and felt symptoms of a panic attack. 'No. No. Let's split it.'

French lent forward on the table. 'Listen. If we can afford to settle the gambling debts of some thick footballer we can stand you a plate of fucking fish and chips.'

Jacko put a fiver on the plate for the waitress, his conscience salved, and the bomb-disposal waiter returned his coat. They parted with a handshake beneath the chandeliers.

Behind the stone-framed window set in red brick, beneath ornate gables and steep slate roof, Jason French lay on his unmade bed, thinking.

Two possibles were bubbling up. Brave Private Eye Who Helped our Great Dog-Fight Exposé Received Death Threats before he was Murdered. Not bad. No sex in it. But not bad. He'd play along and try to get those tapes.

It was second best, anyway, to My Secret Love for Murdered Private Eye by Tragic WPC. She was a WPC all right. Davis had said so when he phoned him after their meeting here. He'd more or less said he was screwing her. She was married. He'd seen the ring.

Tomorrow he'd commission inquiries from a local freelance, a silver-haired old-timer, cunning as a fox, to try to come up with her name and address. Then he'd put it to her.

Her superiors were bound to know. Look how Jackson went into fine detail about everything else but skipped round her. It would cost her her job so five grand would come in useful. That was about what it was worth for an exclusive talk and a sexy picture.

It wasn't Beirut, but this is the East Midlands, not the Middle East, and you gotta earn your crust. He'd stick down the Silver Fox for a couple of ton if he came up with the address.

He wished he'd remembered to tell Jackson a favourite story. About a cameraman who got stuck in a snowdrift. A motorist stopped to help but had no tow line. The photographer trudged to the nearest garage to borrow one. That week the last line on his exes was: *Money for old rope: £10.*

Just about summed up Fleet Street these days. Money for old rope.

Jacko went off straight away, more or less, back to back with Jackie, who stirred and mumbled but did not wake.

She always left an inch open in the heavy lined curtains to let in a chink of light from the street lamp. She'd discovered in

51

frightening fashion on their honeymoon that he had a terror of total darkness.

A war baby's hang-up, he later told her. His grandmother's blindness, she suspected.

She'd been roused from deep sleep by shouting and banging and found no husband at her side. 'Jacko,' she screamed. 'Here,' came a muffled voice from inside a wardrobe. She leapt out of bed, turned on the light, opened the door. He stepped out, blinking and sweating, naked and sheepish. 'Sorry.'

He had awoken in their rented, isolated cottage half-way up a pitch black Irish mountain. In blind panic, he was trying to find the switch to a light, any light, and walked into the wardrobe instead. They kept the hall light on and the door slightly ajar for the rest of their honeymoon and at home ever since she always left that gap in the curtains.

At five, he sprang upright, like a keep-fit fanatic doing sit-ups, yanking the salmon pink duvet from her. 'Jesus.' It came out as a hiss.

Not again, she thought, clutching for her covering. She opened her eyes and found pale light from the street lamp penetrating through the fog into the room. 'What's the matter?'

'His notebook.' He addressed the foot of the bed. 'There was no current notebook. Not on him, in his office or his car.'

She sat up and put an arm over his shoulder, pulling him down to the pillow. 'Let's get some bloody sleep.'

He turned on his side. 'Whoever heard of a detective without a notebook?'

'Sssh,' she whispered. She put her arm over his hip, hand on his flat stomach, snuggling close.

'Sorry,' he muttered.

'Sssh,' she sighed.

Soon sleep returned.

6

Golden Jim Goulden didn't rise in welcome from behind his under-used desk. Once he was settled in his solid brown leather chair it had all the makings of a block and tackle job to get up again.

He weighed more than twenty stone and Jacko had heard it was said of him in local snooker circles that he made Minnesota Fats look thin. He was wearing an immaculate brown suit, a feat of tailoring on his frame, lots of gold rings on chubby fingers and a sad face.

He came from an itinerant family which settled in the city after the war. Could barely read or write. 'But, my Christ, can he add up,' said a business associate Jacko had questioned in the Davis corruption inquiry.

For a huge man he walked with surprisingly light, short steps – the result of an iron girder falling across his feet, breaking bones in both.

In the scrap trade it was said he could look round a derelict factory and work out his tender on the back of an envelope. Made a fortune at the expense of a few convictions for receiving stolen goods and one unproven case of offering bribes to a surveyor.

He lived in an old stone country house in landscaped grounds with a row of stables, but no horse was to bend its back under his weight. He bought a string of racehorses and installed his own trainer. He became a professional gambler. He would make a 500-mile round trip to an obscure track, place a single bet in thousands, then head home with his winnings without a celebratory drink. No pin-pricking for him. He knew exactly what would win.

One day his trainer told Golden Jim, 'We won't be trying this time out.' He didn't put on his stake. The trainer did, at long odds, and the horse went like a bat from hell. Next week he had a new trainer whose predecessor was in hospital with broken ribs and nose. No complaint was filed.

He converted a barn into what he called a hospitality suite where he entertained his friends and contacts. Blackened horseshoes hung on whitewashed walls in the loft. A bar and fruit machines were installed.

He moved in a set which vied with each other to flaunt the fast money they were making. They'd binge on behalf of charity at benefit dinner dances, auctioning off anything they'd won on the tombola. Or they'd throw nobbins into the ring at gentlemen-only fight nights where young boxers, no-hopers, beat each other brainless as paying guests in DJs drank doubles and smoked Havanas.

And always there'd be a photographer present to take pictures of them for county-set magazines with their guests who invariably included a show business nonentity and sometimes an Assistant Chief Constable who, Jacko thought angrily, should bloody well have known better.

On the ground floor of the barn was a snooker table, salvaged from a hall above Burtons, the tailor's shop in the High Street.

Every sizeable town in Britain had such halls. All were closed in the fifties when black and white television started keeping men home at nights. Then came coloured television and, with it, a twenty-minute programme called 'Pot Black', and snooker was back from the dead.

Golden Jim, who'd never lost his love of the game or his expertise at it, set up a chain of snooker clubs, in disused warehouses and workshops, of which this place, Gold Spot, was typical.

Twenty tables, shaded lights above each, stretched out in two lines like gravestones laid flat and mossed over. A grey carpet ran the length of the long wide room to deaden the footsteps of prowling players and hide the oil stains from machinery that once stood there, working.

Only half a dozen tables had been in use when Jacko and Caroline walked through to keep their afternoon appointment. Golden Jim couldn't see them in the morning, his secretary said, and Jacko knew he was a late riser and a long luncher. And such a messy one, it was joked, that before he left his usual table at the Grand the waiter had to hoover his suit.

They had walked up three steps into a raised lounge with tables and chairs and a long bar at which Terry Davis had his last gin and slimline.

Davis had learned his snooker in the hard school of the NAAFI, well enough to qualify for a one-black, seven point handicap against the resident teaching pro.

He'd become a regular when he joined Golden Jim's inner circle. His membership was 'comp' – a status conferred on only a few like the odd journalist or council employee who might be useful one day.

Soon came Golden Jim's invites 'back to my place' for games on his private table and parties where guests arrived in big cars with phones and wore designer clothes and often more gold than their women. And the talk was of what discount was available where for cash-in-hand. And what property and shares they'd shifted as land prices spiralled.

Beyond the lounge bar, behind a green door marked 'Private,' was this office from which Golden Jim ran his leisure companies which included part-ownership of three betting shops and his casino in a converted manor house near his home. He was a man of that money-grubbing time in Britain and Jacko loathed him.

'Sad business,' said Golden Jim, very sadly.

'Yes.' Jacko drew a chair closer to the desk, nodding Caroline to a low couch as he sat.

It was almost fifteen months since they had last faced each other across this desk. The subject hadn't changed: Terry Davis. 'Naturally we're looking into his business associations seeking a motive,' Jacko began, low-key.

'Naturally.' A playful smile, cat with a mouse.

'He was in your employ. Correct?'

'Only on a contract basis after you got rid of him.' He threw out his arms expansively. 'But we won't go into that now. In these circumstances.'

'Ohhhh.' Jacko held on to the sound like a singer holding a note. Then, hurriedly, 'But we will.'

He pulled out several photocopies from the inside pocket of his grey suit. 'Within a day of setting up business, after we booted him out, he got this from you.' He held up a duplicated invoice in two fingers, then folded it back to read it. 'For services rendered. What services? He'd only been in business for a day or two.'

Golden Jim picked imagined fluff of his hand-stitched lapels. 'We don't want any unpleasantness at a time like this.'

'Was it back pay? For providing you with the guest list for your hotel's grand opening in the Cotswolds?'

He folded his hands together and rested them on the desk, which was topped with green leather. 'We've been through all this before.'

'And we're going through it again.' Jacko eased himself forward, threatening. Caroline groaned inwardly. Distant yesterday, bullish today, she thought. She wasn't sure whether she liked working with this inspector. 'At the station, under caution, with your solicitor present if you wish,' Jacko went on. 'Now, what was it for?'

'It was a retainer.'

'In advance?' Jacko cocked his head. 'That's not your normal style of business, surely?'

A pause, taking control of himself. 'I was unhappy about the way things had turned out for him. He was hounded out your force and you know it.' His stomach wobbled beneath his waistcoat as he stirred, subsided and reset. 'Still, we all make mistakes.'

'The only mistake I made was not proving it. He was collecting more car numbers than I did as a boy. And, lo and behold, all the owners got invited to your hotel.'

Golden Jim shook his head, sadly, not in anger. 'We got those names from credit card companies, high-class motor dealers and the like. All perfectly legitimate.'

'Perhaps you could show us the documentation?'

'Certainly.'

Jacko was momentarily stopped in full flow. Last time I saw him, he recalled, he was screaming for his lawyer and exercising his right to silence. Now he's offering documentary proof. He's plugged the gap. He wondered how many motor dealers had had their gambling debts written off in return for back-dated correspondence. 'Odd you didn't mention that at the time.' Weak, but all he could manage.

'You were interviewing me under caution. I wasn't obliged to say anything and my solicitor advised me not to.' He switched on a smile as sincere as a TV games host and beamed it on Caroline. 'Your inspector has misread it, I'm afraid.'

Caroline, in a deep blue two-piece under a white mac, had been following the exchange like a Centre Court tennis ball. Now she kept her head still. 'If that's so, how come Davis isn't still pounding the beat instead of getting himself killed?'

'How do you mean?'

'His trip to your place in Spain.'

The smile flicked off. He twiddled his fingers. Finally: 'He won that in our club championship. My company sponsored the prize. All perfectly above board.'

You've got to give it to this man, Jacko brooded. All the ends tied up. Well, nearly all. 'Why didn't he use that in his defence at the disciplinary hearing?'

A heavy shrug, unhappy. 'Perhaps he'd given up the ghost. You couldn't get him one way so you got him another.'

'Or could it be . . .' A pause, postulating. '. . . that he didn't put up that defence because he knew we'd knock it down? He didn't win. He was runner-up.'

'The winner couldn't go.'

'So we'll check with him and have a look at the competition rules. OK?'

A scowl, enraged, a cornered bull. 'The poor boy's dead. He's not here to defend himself. And you want to drag all this up again. It's becoming a personal vendetta.'

'We're looking for a motive for murder. There were only two people who know the truth . . .'

'The truth? The truth?' Wobbling again, jelly on a plate. 'You come in here claiming to know my style. You know nothing. You're not interested in the truth.'

'Two people knew the truth about the reason he got this' – Jacko wafted the cheque – 'on the day after he set up business.' A softer voice, patient. 'And one of them is dead, poor boy.'

Golden Jim, open-mouthed, looked from Jacko to Caroline. 'It's an obsession with him.' He lowered and shook his head. 'He's obsessed.'

*   *   *

Just a few seconds' silence now. Long enough for a flash flood of thoughts, experiences, memories to sweep through him.

Obsessed? Of course I am. About bent policemen anyway. Since those army days.

He'd been well pissed, no disputing that, but he'd gone through his noisy stage and was fast asleep on the bus taking him back to his base in Paris.

'Drunken bastard.' He awoke in agony, his head being pulled by his hair away from the window where it rested and forced to look down at the aisle where a heap of vomit was piled. 'Piss off, prat,' he slurred. 'Nothing to do with me.'

He was pulled down the aisle, past a typist he fancied, down the bus steps. 'What have we got here?' said the MP corporal hauling him into the back of the paddy wagon.

'D and D,' said the red cap who pushed from behind.

'Disorderly? Bollocks. I was sound asleep.'

'I'll teach you to call me a prat,' said the red cap. He didn't see it coming, just felt the pain forcing the wind from his body, along with about five litres of beer. All over the corporal's razor-creased trousers it went as he collapsed under blows that jarred his head and jolted his body till oblivion rescued him.

Four days in the guardroom, ten days confined to camp, reveille parades in full pack, cookhouse fatigues every night. He phoned her. 'Sorry I can't see you for a week or so.' God, he loved her, was crazy about her, sent her poems even and he'd never done that before or since.

'And I'm sorry,' she said in that sexy broken English of hers, 'but I can't see you again. You are, well, like a small child.'

Few cops, he felt, in the entire British police force could know from such personal experience just what wrongful arrest and imprisonment could do to a man and his life. Every case he brought he sought to make copper bottom. Every arrest he tried to execute humanely. Every testimony he gave avoided embellishment.

The truth? Of course I know the truth. About Davis and Golden Jim at least. This overweight, overfed, overpaid bastard is right, he told himself. I am obsessed.

58

And in that short silence, those few seconds, he felt an inner, impotent, innocent rage. The sort he'd felt when he went to jail over a pile of spew that wasn't his.

'So . . .' Caroline broke the silence. 'Why did you pay him five thousand when he was just starting out?'

'Told you.' Golden Jim stared at her face, mobile, dark alert eyes, like a solitary sparrow. 'It was an advance. "For services rendered" is just a commercial phrase. Terry had rendered me no services at that stage.' He nodded at Jacko. 'No matter what he thinks.'

'Why pay him then?' Caroline's tone was conciliatory.

'I hired him as a security consultant. I felt I ought to help him get on his feet. He was penniless.'

'What were his duties?'

'He gave the once-over to our security systems and . . .'

'Nonsense.' Jacko was back from his reverie. 'He wasn't in the burglar alarm business then. His records show that. Now, answer the question.'

Golden Jim, composed again, continued to address Caroline. 'And, as I was about to say, he vetted applicants for posts where a lot of hard cash would be passing through their hands.'

'Ten thou a year for that? Two hundred a week?' A mocking tone. 'How else did he earn that sort of money?'

He fidgeted, just slightly, in his chair and studied his hands.

'How else, Mr Goulden?' said Caroline, firmly, catching her inspector's mood.

'He collected certain bad debts for me.'

'How did he operate?'

'Discreetly. Those were his orders. We only asked him to make follow-up calls when a polite reminder went unanswered.'

'Threatening phone calls? Midnight knocks? That sort of thing?' Jacko was baiting him again.

He lent back, Golden Jim forward. 'How dare you? How bloody dare you? Nothing of the sort.'

'Good at his job, was he?'

'Some debts are irrecoverable and have to be written off but mainly it's just a matter of time. A matter of honour, you know.'

59

An ambiguous answer which Jacko let go, changing the subject suddenly, chasing two loose ends. 'When you saw him, either socially or on business, did he ever have an escort – a lady?'

'He knew all the staff and chatted the girls, but no one steady that I know of. I never pry.' A broad beam.

'Do you own a dog?'

'You tell me. You spent weeks prying into my private affairs.'

'No. You tell me.'

'Horses, yes. Cats, a few. Dogs, no. Don't go shooting.' Still beaming. 'Or killing anything. Or anybody.' A light laugh.

'Why did you fall out with him?'

The beam snapped off. 'I don't follow.'

Caroline flipped through her notebook. 'We've interviewed a witness who said, and I quote, "He was a bit worried that his contract with him", meaning you, "might not be renewed."'

Jacko was delving in his notes, too, head down. 'On top of that you left a message on his answering machine: "Your cheque's in the post but let's not rush into anything again without my say-so."' Head up. 'It's a simple question. Answer it.'

He jerked straight. 'What are you suggesting? That I had a motive to kill him? Would I pay him, then kill him?'

'Well.' An evil smile. 'He's not in a position to cash it now, is he?'

'Outrageous.' A real wobbly this time.

'We can do this at the station if you like. If not, answer the question.'

Golden Jim sighed so deeply that part of his stomach disappeared into his chest, expanding it mightily. 'We had a disagreement over the way he handled one debtor.'

'Which one?'

'Private and confidential.'

Jacko sorted through his photocopies. 'This one?' He waved a copy of Jason French's 'Soccer Star's Shame'.

Golden Jim glanced at it and nodded glumly.

Jacko shook his head sternly. 'That's so private and confidential that three million people have read about it. Stop wasting our time. What was the disagreement about?'

'This little shit –' he poked a fat finger at the star's photo – 'has been a guest of mine. Been to my home many times. One night he drops three thou at the casino. We don't see him for weeks. We write the usual polite letter, then a formal one. No phone call. Nothing.'

A shrug, puzzled, betrayed. 'I asked Terry to pay a personal call. Nothing heavy, just to see if he would make an offer, come to some arrangement. He's on four figures a week, lives in a big house, runs two cars but he just didn't want to know. These superstars think the world owes them a living. Well, not out of me.' He slapped his chest, hard, angry.

'Terry reported all this back but asked me to leave it with him to try another tack. Next thing I know, this smart-arse reporter's on the phone. Naturally, I tackled Terry. He admitted leaking it. Said he thought the threat of publicity would make him pay up but it misfired.' He flopped back heavily in his chair.

'Did it?' asked Caroline.

'Did it hell. He sold his story and he still hasn't settled with me.'

'Did Davis receive anything from the paper for his tip-off?' asked Jacko, mischievously.

He frowned, considering a thought that had not occurred before. 'Better not have done. We don't want publicity like that. I run a respectable place with high-class clientele. I told him to clear things with me in future. I made him sweat for his retainer. To let him know who's boss.'

'When did this take place?'

He nodded at the cutting. 'The day after that appeared.'

'Did you see him over Christmas or the New Year?'

The mourner's look reappeared. 'I was blanking him. Didn't have him around. Now I feel, well . . .'

'When was the last time you saw him?'

'Monday.'

'Where?'

'Here.'

'Did you give him any fresh jobs to do – debtors to call on, job applicants to vet?'

'No. He requested the meeting. Full of apologies. I told him I wanted time to think. Afterwards I realized he'd probably sweated enough. Next day I released his cheque.'

'When you gave him assignments, how were your instructions communicated? Did you give him memos or what?'

'I called him in and briefed him. He took it down.'

'In what sort of notebook?'

He thought. 'One of those bulging black things.'

A Filofax, thought Jacko, to go with his trendy car, his phone, his designer clothes and his overdraft.

'Did you see him or speak to him on Tuesday, the day he was killed?'

A sad head shake. 'Tried to. Left that message.' He nodded at Jacko's notebook. 'He was here that evening but I wasn't.'

'No,' said Caroline, with a bird-like smile. 'There was a big charity do at your casino, wasn't there? A hundred or more guests plus the cameraman from Mid-Shires Portraits, taking shots for some glossy. We've collected his proofs. There's a nice one of you with a big clock in the background. The photographer says you virtually posed it yourself. The clock shows five past ten. Interesting that. And convenient.'

Just as interesting was watching Golden Jim's face, round as a big clock, as it ticked from a look of satisfaction, tocked to a look of suspicion. Then, clang. 'Surely you don't think I was providing myself with an alibi?'

Jacko waved a hand. 'What we do think is that we need a list of all your high-class clients who have had visits from Davis about their debts, all job applicants he vetted and your bouncers.'

'Out the question.' He slapped the desk.

Jacko gave him his hurt look. 'Then we'll take out warrants and visit here on your next tournament night and your casino on your next charity night.'

A smile, unperturbed. 'You'll find some very influential people there, including a few who outrank you.'

'Look.' Jacko forced a sickly smile, then let it slide away. 'You are not dealing here with little old me looking for a leaking computer which would have carried six months, probably suspended, if I'd cracked it. You are dealing with murder, which carries life. And with a Detective Chief Superintendent who came to us from Scotland Yard where he turned over two government ministers in his time. He doesn't give a shit for your high-powered friends. Now, which way do you want it?'

Golden Jim met his gaze, unflinching. 'One of these days, friend, you're going to find yourself in deep, deep trouble. Mark my words.' Caroline did and she saw the menace and the hatred in his face.

7

A score of dogs bounded out of the mist to greet them; differing sights, differing sounds ranging from a docile Great Dane to a yapping Yorkie and cross-breeds in between.

They were on a concrete path alongside a front garden covered with less grass than a Filbert Street goal-mouth at the end of the season. Holes for bones had been started, never to be filled in. The bark on the only tree was peeling away. The fern had changed from evergreen to ever-yellow. From too many legs cocked up against it, Jacko suspected.

Mary Dalby tried to shoo the dogs away.

'Where do they all come from?' asked Caroline, an enchanted, almost motherly, look on her face.

'People just bring them in.' Animal Alliance, Mrs Dalby went on, was founded because she disapproved of the RSPCA's destruction and spaying policies.

She lived in three white-washed terraced cottages knocked into one. Two acres of land ran away from red-tiled outbuildings at the back. Poles fenced off paddocks in which seaside donkeys lived in genteel retirement.

The porch was covered with old stained newspapers. The floor of the kitchen was littered with bowls and puddles. In the sparsely filled lounge, a colony of cats squatted. In more ways than one, Jacko judged, from the smell of the room.

Most leapt, spitting, on to the high back of the settee and on top of a scratched sideboard out of the path of the gleeful pack of dogs which invaded their territory.

'Sit down,' said Mrs Dalby. The problem for Jacko was where. The original fabric of the settee had been lost under strands of every colour of fur in the animal kingdom and caked mud from the goal-mouth garden. And his brand new deep brown trench

64

coat was making its début today: Jackie's Christmas present. 'Your Bogart mac,' she'd called it. In it he felt warm, smart, smug almost.

Caroline smoothed her white raincoat over her trim backside and perched on a worn arm of the settee. Mrs Dalby cuffed two cats off a cushion to find room for her broad-beamed cords. A huge ginger cat kneaded the cushion beside her before curling up into a comfortable ball. A black cat which had lost half an ear and half its tail jumped on to a fold-up canvas chair and signalled with a spit its intention to lose the other halves in defence of its new domain. All that was left was a chair which seemed to have been cut out of a narrow barrel with a round cushion half-way down. He pulled his new coat tight to him and wedged himself in it.

'Perhaps you could start by telling us a bit about your organization,' began Caroline, too casually in the view of her inspector who wanted it over quickly and out.

Mrs Dalby had formed Animal Alliance after her husband's death. Life became so empty she decided to give a loving home to strays. 'That poor little mite was the first ten years ago. Weren't you my little darling?'

Their eyes followed hers to a threadbare mat in front of the gas fire. On its side lay a whippet, bald patches on its mangy coat; so still that Jacko suspected it had died unnoticed and, from the smell of it, was in the early stages of decomposition.

'Dumped because she wasn't fast enough.'

'How could anyone treat any dog like that?' said Caroline, shaking her head.

'What's its name?' Jacko asked idly.

'Lady.'

'Lady?' he repeated, involuntarily, incredulous. An ear twitched. A rheumy eye opened. Unsteady as a drunk the dog rose to its feet. Then, a panther on its prey, it sprang off the mat into a sitting position on Jacko's lap.

'We're not just a shelter,' she went on. 'We take positive action, too.'

'In what way?' asked Caroline. Oh, for God's sake, thought Jacko, speed it up

For instance, Mrs Dalby was saying, a year ago informants had given her the name of a catnapper, a man who snatched pet

65

cats off the street and sold them to a university for experiments. She'd gone in for some Miss Marples style snooping, keeping watch in her old van through several cold nights, hoping to find out who made the collection.

'The idea was to build up a dossier.' They love their dossiers, these crackpot activists, Jacko thought, trying to concentrate. 'I followed a couple of vehicles from his place but lost them.' The dossier went unbuilt.

The smell of home-cooked horsemeat and decaying teeth filled his face, gagging him, turning over his stomach like a manure heap. He slid his right cheek alongside Lady's left. Their breath warmed each other's ear, sending a tremor of revulsion through him and a passionate shudder through her.

'So when we got inside information about the dog-fighting ring we decided we needed professional help.'

'What information?'

Before imparting it she gave a long lecture and Caroline found herself recognizing in her an eccentric, a zealot, but one she approved of, while her inspector pigeon-holed them both as long-winded bores.

'Dog-fighting has been outlawed since they banned bear-baiting but it still goes on. A nasty lot, the owners. Scrap merchants, car dealers, a few gypos and miners, social security spongers.

'They buy bull terriers, mostly Staffordshire or Old English, but more are getting pit bull terriers imported from America. And they give them names like Killer, Butcher and Satan.

'They train them in backyards on treadmills to toughen their legs and weighted pulleys to strengthen their shoulders. It's rumoured – though we haven't proved it – that they steal cats off streets and throw them into their backyards so pups learn to kill and acquire blood lust.'

Jacko, cheek to cheek with Lady, blinked to blank out a murderous thought about the dog on his lap and her mistress.

'The fights are arranged under strict secrecy, naturally, and take place in scrapyards, gypsy camps, disused pit tops, farm outbuildings and the like. A ring is formed by boards. They call it a pit. A line is drawn across the centre. The dogs and their handlers take a corner like boxers. Then they let them go. They separate them for breathers now and then. When a dog has had enough, it turns its back and stays in its corner. Doesn't come up to the mark. Know the phrase?' Caroline nodded.

'But often they're so brave they don't know when to give up. They fight till they drop. Spectators even take videos. The RSPCA has got hold of some. Blood everywhere. You can see flesh hanging from their jaws, dripping blood like a slaughterhouse.'

'Sick,' Caroline pronounced and she looked it.

Mrs Dalby tickled a tan mongrel which had nuzzled against her knees. 'They bet in hundreds and a champion dog can fetch thousands. You're not going to believe this but the police and the RSPCA raided one fight, arrested some of the men and rescued their dogs. One, an American pit bull terrier, had killed its opponent, ripped its throat out, they say, but was badly wounded itself. It's the Champion of Champions, apparently. That's what they call it. A beautiful black beast but completely wild, extremely dangerous. They kept it, isolated, at an animal shelter until it had almost recovered. And know what? A gang broke into the kennels and stole it. That's how valuable they are. It's big money.'

The dog Chief Inspector Keeling had mentioned at the first briefing, Jacko deduced.

'We've got a dossier on their activities.' Mrs Dalby talked non-stop. 'But never any positive proof. Then we had a bit of luck. A friend of ours was in a pub near here when she overheard two men discussing dog-fighting and arranging a scuffle, a training bout for young dogs. She followed them to their cars and got their numbers. We decided that, well, after our disappointment with that vivisection operation, we ought to engage some expert help.'

She got Terry Davis's name out of Yellow Pages where Tab Private Investigations was in the list of private detectives. He drove out in his red racer the day she phoned him. Two days later he phoned to say he had traced the names and addresses of the two men.

'Very efficient,' said Mrs Dalby.

Hardly, thought Jacko. One call to the vehicle computer would have done it. His lover, Chrissy Fixter, leaked it. Or his playmate John Udden. His speculation lasted only a moment. Suddenly, and with abject horror, he realized he was the subject

67

of a leak himself. A damp patch was seeping through the thick lining of his brand new coat on to his lap. Dear God, he mentally growled. People whose emotions have been overstretched have been known to wet themselves but it had never occurred to him that a dog, mad with desire, would lose control. Hurry up, Parker, he urged.

'Two days later, Mr Davis reported that he had found a pub on a council estate in the suburbs where the gang hung out.'

Brrrrrump. A sound like a sheet being ripped. Jacko frowned.

'He suggested we hand over our dossier to a big Sunday paper for them to expose the gang.'

'Yes,' said Caroline, doing all the questioning; far, far too slowly for Jacko. 'We've read that story and see you were quoted in it. Did you speak to Mr French, the reporter?'

'Only briefly on the phone. He gave us a nice mention.'

'Wasn't that a bit risky? They are violent men.' Only a suggestion, uncertain.

'They don't frighten me.' Mrs Dalby threw back her shoulders. 'It brought in a few donations from the public.' Her shoulders relaxed. 'We were pleased with the story.'

'Did you see Mr Davis again?'

A sad shake. 'He submitted his bill by post. We settled by return.'

'Have you got it?'

Mrs Dalby rose and walked to the sideboard where she lifted a sleeping cat off the top of a black box file.

Brrrrrump. Brrrrrump. Jacko knew what it was now; hardly great detective work. The smell of part-digested horsemeat was telling him. He threw Caroline a look of hapless horror which she didn't seem to catch.

Mrs Dalby sat down with the invoice but, preoccupied, she didn't pass it over straight away. 'You don't think, do you, that he was murdered because of the help he gave us?'

'Hard to say,' said Caroline without apparent thought. 'Probably not, but we have to look at every possibility. He was working in a job that made him lots of enemies.'

Satisfied, she handed over the invoice. Caroline looked at it and asked 'Was there any financial arrangement with the paper?'

'Oh, no.' Surprise. 'They did it for nothing.'

'Did the paper pay Animal Alliance anything?'

'Oh, no.'

The crook, thought Jacko. He stings her for £400, then pockets £200 from the paper. That's her profit from a dozen jumble sales. And all for the price of one phone call to Chrissy Fixter or Udden.

'Have you had any direct contact with the gang?'

'No, but we hope you and the RSPCA will do something about them.'

Some hope, Jacko brooded. The publicity will have driven them further underground.

'So you've no tips, no leads on this missing dog Champion?' Caroline persisted.

'It will be around here somewhere. Bound to be. Getting ready for its next fight. To kill or be killed. Awful, isn't it?' A sorrowful expression.

'If you hear anything, tell us. Don't go it alone. It's dangerous.'

Mrs Dalby nodded. 'Immediately.'

'Good.'

Good, Jacko repeated to himself. Done and dusted at last. Caroline made no move to get up. Instead, she too started tickling the mongrel at Mrs Dalby's feet and talking about her own dog – 'One glance in a pet shop window and I melted' – its price, its pedigree or, rather, lack of, its walkies, its eating habits, its toilet habits. On and on she babbled while Jacko sank back.

Brrrrrump. Brrrrrump. Brrrrrump.

Jacko came to with a start, wriggled his wedged hips free from the chair that imprisoned him and stood faster than a diver breaking surface. 'Well. Yes. Thanks very much.' Lady back-flipped on to the mat, sighing, dejected, rejected.

Caroline lingered over her goodbyes and followed him down the concrete path towards their car. 'You were a bit brisk.'

'Me?' Voice raised, anger barely under control. He climbed behind the wheel, furiously slamming the door shut.

Caroline got in the passenger seat. 'What's the matter?' she asked, tentatively.

Jacko started up and worked rapidly through the gears before she had fastened her belt. 'Say what you mean.'

'What do I mean?'

'Brusque, you mean. Rude. What about her farting, peeing whippet? It emptied both tanks on me. Look at the state of this new coat. It smells like a bloody pigsty.'

'Give it to her jumble sale then,' said Caroline carelessly.

'This . . .' – Jacko tensed and let go of the wheel with one hand to touch a sleeve – 'happens to be a present from my beloved. You might not have anyone . . .' He stopped then, shocked (or was it shamed? He was never to be sure) by what he'd started to say and tried to salvage himself. 'Just because you're not married . . .' He stumbled again, petering out.

'What do you mean, sir?' Prim and proper.

'Nothing.' He tried to hide his embarrassment with gruffness.

'You're not comfortable with me, are you?'

'What are you talking about?' He played for time to collect a racing jumble of guilty thoughts.

'You've been so distant. You never tell me what tactics you want. We seldom seem to talk.'

'Sorry.' He sighed, relieved. 'It's just that they pulled me off leave and I can't help thinking if I'd cracked the Davis job fifteen months ago, well . . .' He shrugged. 'I'm just a bit brassed off, that's all.'

Silence. Talked myself out of it. As he was beginning to congratulate himself, he felt her turn in her seat towards him. 'It's more than that, isn't it?'

He looked straight ahead through the windscreen, sweaty hands tightening on the wheel. He could think of nothing to say.

'It's because I'm gay, isn't it?'

'No!'

'Yes, it is, sir. Be honest.'

'No!' He knew he was protesting too much but couldn't stop.

'If you're unhappy and want to ditch me, I'll understand. I know I'm not everyone's favourite female.'

He gripped the wheel tighter still and closed his eyes momentarily. He felt unclean, shitty.

She sat back and twisted her hands together on her lap.

'Look,' he said, softly, glad of the excuse to keep looking

ahead. 'I really don't give a damn about people's colour or anything. I mean, in an inner city riot when the bricks rain down, it doesn't matter whether the officer next to you is que . . . gay or not, as long as he watches your back.' He paused. It was coming straight off the top of his head, rather than from deep in his heart, but he knew it was sounding right. 'Honest.' Another pause. He gambled on a quip. 'You're dogged. I'll give you that.'

He laughed loudly, too loudly, glancing sideways, anxious to gauge her reaction. She was playing with her fingers but she wore a broad smile. Soon he was telling her all about his mongrel dog. All the time he was running their conversation through his troubled mind. Finally, he decided she'd been straight with him and that was all that really mattered and he was at peace with himself and his partner.

8

The freezing fog that had clung to the city with deadening hold finally loosened its grip, scattered on winds from the Arctic which brought deep snow and sent the temperature on the electronic clock on top of the *Mercury* fudge factory plunging as low as minus nine.

Jacko shivered as he trudged in green wellington boots into a police station that had lost its white glow against its new backdrop of virgin snow.

The response to the appeals had been immediate. The drivers of a diesel-powered Vauxhall, a purring BMW and a coughing Escort all came forward. So did the couple whom George Marshall had heard leaving the Royal Mail pub. None had seen anything significant. All they had done was to confirm what a reliable witness the police had in George.

But, Jacko grumbled to Caroline over a drink, Keeling wasn't using him properly, to the full. The chief inspector was in day-to-day charge of the inquiry now. The Little Fat Man was spending long spells on the coast where the hunt for the bed-sit child's killer was bogged down.

'He's used George's ears but not his nose,' he complained. 'Christ, my grandma could tell the split second a toasted bun was ready.'

'Why not tell him?' asked Caroline.

'I have told him. He won't listen.'

Nor would he act on Jacko's feeling about the Frost family. 'Where's the connection?' he'd asked.

'Davis worked for Lance's defence.'

'He was a sex killer and this is not a sex killing. Davis worked for Golden Jim, Animal Alliance and Fleet Street, too. Rule them out first.'

Jacko suspected he knew why he was so sniffy. Keeling had taken over the inquiry from Mike Fixter after Lance's acquittal and had got nowhere. Jacko's interest was being viewed as an intrusion into a divisional matter, a private grief. He chafed with frustration.

Every night Caroline caught the 10.20 p.m. to Loughborough. It was a week before she found the passenger Chrissy Fixter had claimed travelled opposite her on the ten-minute journey. A tobacco executive from Nottingham who only went to London once a week, he remembered her because she smoked a brand of cigarettes which wasn't his firm's. He'd noticed nothing odd about her, bloodstains or anything.

During this time a witness came forward to add eyes to George Marshall's nose and ear evidence.

Leroy James was sixteen and black. He had shot up in height three inches in a year and outgrown his strength. 'You've got the skills,' his soccer coach had told him. 'What you need is stamina.'

Every Tuesday he played football on a floodlit all-weather pitch at a community centre in Highfields, a blighted district across an iron and tarmac bridge from the *Mercury* buildings.

When practice finished Leroy jogged home to build up the stamina he needed if he was ever going to catch the eye of Leicester City and play at Filbert Street, his one ambition. Since Christmas he had had a track suit to run in, royal blue, like his favourite team, a present from his parents.

'Weren't you passing that car-park about that time?' asked his father after reading the police appeal for witnesses in the *Mercury*.

When his son told him what he had seen, his father said, 'We must go to the police.'

Mr James quite liked the police, he told Jacko. Some of the younger ones, he said, could be offhand, rude sometimes, but many of the older ones he knew by first name and they shared a hot flask of coffee on a cold day at the taxi rank from which his cab operated.

Jacko took Leroy's statement. 'I had a Coke after football and set off for home between ten fifteen and ten twenty. I turned left after the bridge. At that corner I saw a man. He was about my size, six foot. He wore a black donkey jacket and one of those

73

coloured tea-cosy hats like Rastas wear but he was white. He was walking fast but not running. He had his head down so I didn't see his face. I crossed the street and jogged south on the pavement. Just before the pub, I saw a man, white, small, quite tubby, standing on the opposite pavement against the wall near the car-park entrance.'

With his Bogart mac at the cleaners, Jacko put on his old waxed coat and walked with them across the sanded road where Leroy pointed out where he had seen who.

'When you passed that man in the donkey jacket did you get a whiff of anything – aftershave, sporting embrocation, alcohol?'

Leroy gave a long, thoughtful headshake. 'He was too far away.'

'Were you wearing anything like that yourself?' Another headshake. 'Jogging up to the station, did you see a smallish woman wearing a head scarf?' Nothing jogged in his memory.

Jacko looked at his father. After twenty or more English winters his hair was the colour of snow but his face and personality had remained in the sun. 'This may seem ungrateful but we'll need to examine his trainers and track suit.' Jacko felt ungrateful. 'For elimination purposes.'

Mr James gave him his sunniest smile. 'We surely understand, sir.' A voice as grainy as sharp sand.

They left Leroy with Caroline listing the names of his team-mates he'd had his Coke with after training. Mr James drove Jacko through the filthy slush to his home, a terraced two-up, two-down off London Road, in his taxi and dropped him back again with suit, shoes and an assortment of tins and pots from the family's first-aid box. He refused the fare he was offered.

By then his son had given Caroline a dozen names. Both she and Jacko walked down the station steps with them and waved them goodnight.

It was more than a week before Jason French made contact. 'Sorry for the delay,' he said, humming with joy at his first mouthful of Rogan Gosh in a restaurant in the Asia Minor quarter.

He pushed an envelope containing his tapes across the table-cloth. 'Had one hell of a game over them. The management were fine but the union kicked up. Said providing the police with unpublished material might jeopardize journos' lives in places like Belfast. I had to sneak them out and do a tape to tape.' He took a long drink of lager.

'I owe you one,' said Jacko.

'By the way.' French stopped eating and humming to eye Jacko. 'That bird I saw Davis with at the Grand. I've been digging around and her name is Chrissy Baxter or something like that.' Then, very casual, 'You don't happen to know where she lives?'

Jacko looked down at his buttered Chicken Bhona. 'Never heard of her.' He felt the butter melting in his mouth. I owe him one, all right, but not that one.

They chatted amiably for the rest of the meal when Jacko excused himself to go to the toilet. When he returned, French stood. 'I'll do this,' he said, digging in a pocket, flamboyant with his employer's money.

'I did it when I went for a pee.' Jacko watched his face cloud with disappointment. He fished the receipt from his pen pocket and stuck it in his. 'Put it on your exes. It's no good to me.' The least I owe him, he thought.

It took several days for the experts to report back that none of the voices on French's tapes matched the voice who left the death threat on Davis's answering machine.

Jacko phoned him to ask for the names of everyone who had cropped up during his investigation, taped or not.

Caroline added names provided by the RSPCA Intelligence Branch and a long list had to be worked down. They started on those with convictions for violence. Each was visited at home on a differing pretext. None of them noticed a tiny mike shaped like a Girl Guide badge in Caroline's lapel.

In an alcove in the incident room, separated from divisional detectives, Jacko's small team from HQ worked slowly and thoroughly down other lists. Grinding, monotonous work; the fact, not the fiction, of a detective's life.

One by one, bouncers in Golden Jim's employ and clients in his debt were being cleared and crossed off. Painstakingly they were going through the grey filing cabinet they had manhandled from Davis's office. Find anyone who kept an appointment, not in his diary, with him on the Saturday before he died, Jacko ordered. Or a firm he had dealings with, which had a nervous male clerk with a local accent who might explain the second call on the answering machine. They were going through all his old notes. Find out what murder he wanted to discuss with Jason French on the night he died, Jacko told them. Slow work, hard work, spirit-sapping.

A journey from home which should have taken half an hour was lasting more than an hour as snowploughs battled to keep one lane open on the dual carriageway. Leicester Sound had revived 'Release Me' to herald the homecoming of Engelbert Humperdinck. Local boy makes good, babbled the DJ.

This is what a real detective's life is like, Jacko told himself. A frustrating slog. Romance, adventure, thrills, spills? My frozen arse. He was tired and depressed.

Four weeks into the investigation, Keeling called a meeting of sergeants and above. A council of war, he called it, and the reason for it was that he had to go away. 'A week in the Alps,' he explained, only a trifle embarrassed. 'Booked ages ago. Unavoidable.'

Fancy, thought Jacko bitterly, sloping off to the slopes at a time like this.

In his absence, he went on, he wanted to keep the momentum going. What momentum? Jacko asked himself.

He went back to where it all started – with the statements from George and Maggie Marshall. 'We've eliminated all the motorists he mentioned and the couple coming out the pub.' He turned to Jacko. 'What about this James boy? Could he have killed him, jogged past George and doubled back?'

Caroline, the only woman present, answered for him. 'A whole football team saw him go at ten fifteen. There's no trace of anything on his suit or trainers.'

Keeling looked down at the statements. 'We can rule the James kid out. Agreed?' Everyone nodded.

He looked round the table. 'Which means the six-footer George heard is the man in the donkey jacket the James kid saw?' More nods.

'So we still need him and the woman in the head scarf and the nondescript young man Maggie reported seeing.' They agreed on a new press release.

There was some inconclusive discussion over whether Maggie's young man and George's six-footer could be the same. 'In which case,' said Keeling, summing up, 'the six-footer can't be the killer. He wouldn't have had time for more than a quick look inside the car-park. Not long enough to rip out anyone's throat. George would have heard.' He paused, thinking. 'We'll treat them as separate persons and issue three descriptions.' There was no dissent.

He shuffled a different statement to the top of the pile in front of him at the head of a T-shaped conference table. 'Forensics and the Home Office pathologist are sure it wasn't an animal. No fur or paw marks on the clothing or the surface or foreign fluids in the wound. They're convinced it's a man-made claw of some kind, a metal spiked glove. A pair of gloves, perhaps, because there were indications of wounds each side of his throat. So we're still without a murder weapon.'

'And his notebook.' Half a target and Jacko sniped.

'You're obsessed with that notebook.' Keeling hit back sharply, no smile. 'Those Filofaxes have wallets for credit cards. His mugger may have taken it, expecting to find them in it. How's that end going?'

He turned abruptly to a DI who had replaced the suspended Fixter in charge of the divisional team. 'We've rounded up and eliminated most of them. Some have done runners. We've a team in London tracking them down.'

'May not be a mugger.' It was the collator who spoke, musing, more or less. He was a squad sergeant, a tall, dark, melancholy figure, who'd anchored many major inquiries, the desk man, a pivotal position. 'They hit their victims over the head. They don't rip their throats out. It doesn't tie up with any other recorded street crime.'

'You should see some of the horror videos we've recovered,' said the DI, petulant. 'That's where they get their new ideas from.'

'Even so,' said Jacko evenly, 'let's not lose sight of other possibilities.'

'Like what?' asked the DI.

'The Frost family, for instance.'

'Not them again.' Keeling sighed, impatient.

'Davis wanted to see Jason French about a murder. We've been right back through his police career. He was never on a murder. His only involvement in murder is the Frost case as a

77

private eye. It has to be that. Did Lance, for instance, wear a donkey jacket?'

Keeling looked towards a divisional sergeant who'd been with Fixter on the case. He shook his head. 'There's your answer.' A pause, gathering himself. 'No one is losing sight of other possibilities. That's what detective work is about. An overview. All you seem to be interested in is an intimate picture of just one family.'

'And Davis's book,' Jacko chipped in, grinning.

'You're not a bloody novelist, you know.' Smiles from the divisional men, and a few short sniggers.

Not yet, Jacko thought, but when I've finished, when I've quit this bloody job and no longer have to work under patronizing prats like you, I'm going to write books about one or two cases and you, you bastard, will not be getting a very good write-up. He was angry, about to flare up.

Caroline broke in, sensing it. 'We've got explanations for both calls on his radio-pager and we've traced two of the four callers on his answering machine. We've had no joy yet on the death threat. We can't rule out a dog-fighter.'

'What was the weapon?' The DI was wriggling, delighted, unable to contain himself. 'Champion, your wonder dog?'

Longer laughter from the divisional men, smiles from the squad officers, Caroline's icy. 'I accept it was something like spiked gloves. It could be symbolic, though. Made to look like the work of a dog. You know, a message. This is what anyone gets who breaks our code of silence.' Round the table there were several nods acknowledging good thinking.

'How about Jim Goulden?' asked Keeling.

'The perfect alibi and no signs any of his henchmen did it for him,' said Jacko.

'Could be an out-of-town contract,' said the DI, a busybody. 'Our London team will put out feelers on that.'

Keeling wrapped it up, turning first to the DI. 'Pull in the rest of those muggers and be quick about it. Kick a few constables' backsides if you have to. I want a result.' Then to Jacko. 'Maximum effort on that death threat.' And, pointedly, 'Concentrate on that.'

Jacko nodded and stretched, about to get up. The divisional detectives sat still. Fixter's sergeant spoke for them.

'Can we eliminate Mike, chief, in view of the James kid's statement?'

Jacko knew Fixter's enforced absence was upsetting them. And he knew they blamed his team. They had been cold-shouldered in the Royal Mail where they poured scorn on 'the BTOs from HQ'. The collator had retaliated by leading a breakaway drinking school to the Barley Mow, the law court's local, on the same street as the Grand.

'He can't be George's six-footer who James saw. The dress is wrong. It proves he didn't leave the pub. OK, Davis's blood was found on his trousers but everyone saw him kneeling at his side, trying to save his life. It's a bit rough on him.' Pause. 'At a time like this.' Everyone knew he was talking about Fixter's marriage break-up.

Keeling seemed undecided. He looked appealingly at Jacko. He's bottling it, he thought. Sod him. He wasn't going to help him out. He looked away.

Caroline jumped in. 'We suspect WPC Fixter could be Davis's source on the car numbers of the dog-fight gang.' Speak for yourself, thought Jacko. He suspected Udden.

'That's nothing to do with Mike,' snapped the sergeant.

'And . . .' She left it there, jumping back.

'And what?' asked the DI, spoiling.

'And . . .' Jacko intervened, languid. 'The Fixters could have a PR problem.'

'What you talking about?'

'Jason French is sniffing round. He knows WPC Fixter was seeing Davis.' Furious faces opposite him. The sound of inhaled breath.

'How?' asked Keeling, alarmed.

'He had a drink with them both in the Grand.'

'And how do you know that?'

'French told me. I played doggo.'

'Did all this come out over your tête-à-tête in the Grand?' The DI again; deep sarcasm. 'Which went on his bill.'

The shits have been checking on me. Jacko felt his pulse pounding. 'What's that supposed to mean?' Calm as he could but a tight voice.

'Just that some of us might find it odd that you got rid of Davis over unauthorized hospitality when . . .' A shrug, point made.

79

He fought hard to control his fury. 'Matter of fact, it came out over a curry which I paid for.' A frightening thought. I can't prove that. I'm in trouble here, if this comes to push and shove.

'OK, gentlemen.' Keeling broke it up. An incompetent chairman to the last, fumed Caroline inwardly. 'I'll raise your point with Mr Scott.'

Everyone got up. 'A word, please.' Keeling looked at Jacko who sat again. The room cleared in two separate groups, heading for their separate drinking schools, Caroline looking anxiously over her shoulder.

Keeling lent forward on the top table. 'I don't know what happens at HQ but on this patch the officer-in-charge handles the media and then only through the Press Office.'

'I had to deal with French personally to get hold of those tapes.'

'That doesn't mean you have to socialize with him.' He hunched his brawny shoulders. 'I don't want so much as a no-comment to appear from you. Or it's back to HQ.' Shoulders back, confident. 'We can manage without you.'

Enough, Jacko told himself. I've had enough. You can't go on ducking this. 'Actually, I don't think you should be managing this inquiry at all.'

Shoulders forward, combative. 'What do you mean?'

'Look at it from the public's point of view. We've got a love triangle. A bent ex-cop dead. An inspector as a suspect. And who's on the job? Their old mates. It's a classic case of the police investigating themselves.'

'You're not suggesting . . .' Anger on his face, simmering.

'I think Division is doing an honest job and that's the truth, but sometimes it's public perception of the truth that counts. What would the public make of it? That's the test.'

'I shall be reporting your views to Mr Scott when I discuss Fixter with him. Fair enough?'

'Fine,' said Jacko, standing.

Negative, voice print experts reported on every tape they'd made of dog-fighters on the list which Jason French and the RSPCA had helped to compile.

Back, Jacko decided, to the basics he'd been taught as a rookie CID officer twenty years ago. His mood was morose, wishing he'd kept his mouth shut, certain his days on the inquiry were numbered.

He asked Control for details on every incident, no matter how trivial, investigated by the police on the day Davis died. Just to see if anyone on their lists was out and about and up to anything odd. Routine, really, but Keeling had not been there before him and he was not surprised. He had no flair, no feeling. 'Vision', his old mentor used to call it.

He compared all the names on the incident reports with his lists. Only one tallied: Murray. The first name was wrong: Joseph not Gerald. But the address was on the right estate.

'This Joseph Murray you nicked. What happened?' he asked the arresting patrolman over the phone.

'Drink-driving. Hit another car in the middle of the afternoon.'

'Anyone with him?'

'His brother, also pissed. Name of . . . Just a minute.' He heard the pages of a notebook being flicked. '. . . Gerald.' The mention of the name sent a thrill through him. 'A bit bolshie but we let him go. We took Joe in and booked him. Twice over the limit. We kept him till he sobered up, then bailed him. His brother picked him up from the station.'

'What time?'

'Around ten – just before we were knocking off.'

Gerry Murray lived on one of those suburban estates thrown up in the fifties, now up for sale to the tenants. Those who bought them announced their bargain purchases by hanging new front doors, reddish brown mahogany mostly, with brass knockers.

His estate had few mahogany doors. His own, council maroon, had a knee-high splinter at about the height a locked-out drunk would kick it in.

He was thirty, thirteen stone, an unshaven scruff – baggy black cords, thick tartan shirt hanging outside them.

Caroline sat close to him on a dirty settee while he gave a statement about the crash. He described himself as a land-scape gardener. Jacko looked through a cracked pane into a high-fenced back garden which was in a worse state than the Animal Alliance's. Inside, the house wasn't much cleaner.

A scratching noise came from the back door. Murray got up and opened it. A dog followed him back. 'Won't harm a fly,' he assured them.

All three were looking at a brute of an animal that had the Churchillian build of a bull dog, broad back, muscular shoulders, short, strong legs, a longish muzzle, tapering, with a powerful jaw and eyes that glinted black on a white face.

'What is it?' Jacko was sitting in an armless chair, in his recently cleaned Bogart mac.

'An Old English bull terrier.'

'What's its name.'

'Mugger.'

He did not make the mistake of repeating it. Mugger walked towards him with a slight roll, a spring in its step, and sniffed his mongrel bitch's scent on his grey trousers. Jacko looked down, holding his breath. Jagged pink lines ran through short fur over its big, bony skull.

'Wonderful with kids,' said Murray, proudly. 'Got any?'

'One.' Hardly audible.

Mugger turned away and sank on to a threadbare mat in front of the grey ashes of a dead fire, stretching out his front paws, resting his head on them, watchful, menacing.

Jacko breathed again. 'What are those scars on its head?'

'Ran into a fence of barbed wire.'

When the time came to leave he got up slowly, no sudden movements, and Mugger followed him all the way to the door, dark eyes never leaving him.

Positive, said the voice print expert.

Three days later they were back at the dented front door with the biggest two men in the squad and a dog-handler.

'Suspicion of murder?' Murray bayed. 'Me? I wouldn't hurt a fly.'

He was interviewed at the station in a soundproof room with a desk on which stood a twin tape recorder. Caroline did nearly all the talking. She'd more or less assumed charge of this end of the inquiry – 'the Dog Watch', Jacko called it – and he was happy to leave it to her. He fancied the Frosts and made no secret – to her, anyway – of his longing to have a crack at them.

She took a small hand-held cassette player from her shoulder bag. 'Now listen to this.' In silence they heard the message on Davis's answering machine. She changed cassettes. Murray heard himself talking about the crash and his dog. She read over the expert's report.

'Now.' She lent forward in her swivel chair. 'Why did you make that call?'

He screwed his eyes shut and groaned. He didn't come out fighting, up to the mark. He caved in and talked.

He and his brother Joe owned a dog each, he said. Fought them sometimes but never to the death. 'The money is in breeding, in stud fees. They fight to get a reputation. For the form book, like.'

In December a stranger called asking about pups for sale. 'Said he was a salesman whose dad used to own fighting dogs in the Black Country.'

He put him in touch with a farmer called Vyn Baldwin who had a Staffordshire bitch with a new litter. 'Next thing I knew was that Baldwin was all over the paper. Mr Big of Dog-Fighting, they called him. His photo was in with three of his mates. That Sunday night he came round with them, threatening to break my legs. I thought my number was up. Believe me, you don't mess with that crowd.'

Finally they accepted that Murray's only motive had been to

put business Baldwin's way. 'He told me he sussed the reporter because he was asking silly questions. Next time he came, he got a mate to follow him to a pub where he met up with a man in a red sports car. He clocked both index plates. He could only get the name of the newspaper group from one. Must be a company car. But he got hold of Davis's name and address from the other.'

'How?'

'Dunno. Honest. I don't know.'

Can't have been Chrissy Fixter or John Udden shopping Davis, Jacko decided. Someone else is tapping into that vehicle computer; a new nark inside the force.

'On that Tuesday lunchtime I went drinking with Joe in our local. Got talking about how I'd nearly been stitched up. We couldn't get at the reporter so we decided to put the frighteners on his mate. I got his number from the book and put in a call from the pay-box at the boozer.'

He nodded towards Caroline's tape machine. 'I must have said what's on there but I don't remember it all. I didn't mean it. True as I stand here.' He sat on his chair, cowed, with the eyes of a whipped dog.

'We piled into Joe's car at closing time. We were going to take a run round to Davis's place. Just to put a brick through his window or kick in a door. On the way Joe crashed into the back of another car.'

He went home, slept it off, phoned the station and was told to collect his brother. 'Took a cab straight back to the pub for a couple before closing time. I never saw Davis. Never seen him. I don't know what he looks like.'

The two detectives returned with two pairs of trousers found among a pile in his bathroom. Both had what looked like blood smears on the shins.

They went back to the estate, the pub this time. When Joe staggered in, he was arrested again.

Jacko let the brothers go the following lunchtime. Forensics said the blood on the trousers belonged to a dog. The pub landlord and two customers remembered the Murrays returning soon after ten and staying till closing time. They were alibi-ed. 'Could still be useful though,' he told Caroline and he shared an idea.

84

'Risky,' she declared, watching his back. 'Could cost you your job, this job certainly, if it goes wrong.'

Jason French sounded surprised to get the call. 'Never heard of the Fixters! I've got their address, called four times. Some decorator reckons they've gone visiting relatives in Australia.' His tone was good-humoured, win some, lose some. 'Spirited her away, have you?'

'Not my end of the inquiry.'

'But is it true?'

'I'll do you a deal.'

Exclusive by Jason French, it said the following Sunday over a story which began: *Brave private eye Terry Davis may have been brutally slain because of his undercover work exposing evil dog-fighting. Police have already questioned two men and taken away clothing for examination.* The article recapped details of Davis's death, credited him with much more work than he'd done and was immodestly fulsome in praise of the paper's own courage in *putting this shame under the spotlight.* It ended with a quote from an unnamed police spokesman: *'We are treating this as an urgent line of inquiry.'*

By the time it was published the Home Office had granted a permit to monitor Murray's phone and the council had loaned a boarded-up flat in a block opposite.

'The drinks are on me,' said the first caller that Sunday.

'But it wasn't down to me, Big Vyn.' Murray was spluttering, agitated. 'Only wish it had been.'

'That's right, mate. You keep stum.'

The next caller suggested he should make the reporter his next target and Murray, beginning to revel in his standing, said maybe he would and laughed.

Big Vyn's mood changed within a couple of days. 'What did you tell the filth?'

'Nothing. Why?' Stammering again. 'What's the problem?'

'Jim's been on. His friendly fuzz is in a sweat. Claims there's an inquiry going on about car numbers again.'

Listening to the tape, Jacko's eye gleamed behind his spectacles and his stomach tightened.

'I know nothing about that. Honest.'

'He's a great snout. If you've grassed him you're done.'

'I don't know what you're talking . . .'

'He saved our hides. Remember that do near Beacon Hill? Why do you think we called it off?'

'I didn't even know Golden Jim got inside gen.' Murray's voice had risen an octave. 'I'm getting sick of this. I try to get a sale for you and what happens? I get blamed for the stuff in the paper. I'm accused of killing someone I've never seen. Now you have me reckoned as a fink.'

Next day Baldwin's muddy Land Rover sizzled to a stop in the rain. A wiry man in a cap got out. Murray let him in.

Jacko, on surveillance shift, began to fret when the maroon door stayed shut for half an hour. He decided, if Murray wasn't tough enough to take care of Baldwin, Mugger was. He kept his nerve but was relieved when Baldwin emerged, all smiles.

Almost immediately Murray phoned his brother. 'There's a big one in the pipeline. The North London boys are coming up.'

'When?'

'When the heat's off a bit. Anyway, Jim says Champion isn't fit yet.'

At last, thought Jacko, closing his eyes, a thankful prayer, as Caroline turned off the tape. I'm going to get him and his new nark. A wonderful thought, weeks of work worth while. For a while he even forgot about the Frosts.

'Did you know Goulden was into this?' asked Caroline.

He squeezed his chin so his head flicked, neutral, neither a nod nor a shake. 'He's the type.'

'He won't keep it at home, will he?'

'Hardly,' Jacko conceded. 'It would devour his cats, then start on his horses. Probably farms it out to a trainer.'

All they could do, they agreed, was to keep on the phone tap, find out the date and place and raid it. They'd sit on it, let it stew.

Their phone rang. Caroline answered. 'Chief Inspector Keeling's back.' Jacko reached for the receiver but she put it down. 'Wants you in his office.'

Keeling's face was deeply tanned and frowning just as deeply. Trouble, Jacko told himself. 'Seen this?' He pointed to French's paper, on his desk, opened at his last exclusive.

'Yes.'

'Who's responsible for this statement?' A finger jabbed at the police quote at the end.

'Me.' Jacko had not been invited to sit.

'I made it plain you weren't to talk to the press without my say-so.'

'You weren't here to ask.'

'Did you clear it with the Press Office?'

'You told me to concentrate on the dog-fighters and that's what I've been doing.' A side-step, quickly blocked.

'I also told you I didn't want to see even a no-comment from you.'

Jacko looked down, about to lie. 'I thought that instruction only applied to the Fixter angle.'

'Nonsense and you know it. That friend of yours is still chasing Mike Fixter.'

'I am sorry, but that . . .' a nod towards the paper – ' . . . has given us a break.' He briefed him on the taped conversations.

'So what?'

So what? So what? Keep calm. 'So it puts Golden Jim firmly in the frame. There he was, paying Davis two hundred a week while he was helping to expose his own gang.'

'All it indicates is that he may be in possession of a stolen dog. First the Frost family. Now a bloody dog. What are you playing at?'

Playing? Playing? Keep it shut. 'I'm taking an overview, like you said.'

Fury beneath the tan now. 'I'm having you taken off this case.' He palmed the paper. 'This is deliberate defiance of my orders. I'm getting on to HQ. I've already told them of your reservations about my handling of this job and mine about you. Now I'm going to tell them it's you or me. That will be all, Mr Jackson.'

That night he took his team to the Barley Mow. 'I can't remember when I've been to such a nice wake,' said the collator, his melancholy deep.

'I want off, too,' said Caroline in solidarity.

'That's bad thinking,' said Jacko, urgently, the beginnings of a pep talk. 'It would do your promotion prospects no good at all.'

'What prospects?' A sad smile.

He looked at her, a friend's look, fond, concerned. True,

he thought. She possesses a higher intellect than me, would make a far better chief inspector than Keeling. But she'll never reach high rank. Chief Constables might tolerate, just about, an exclusive by Jason French: WPC STOLE MY HUBBY, SAYS HEARTBREAK WIFE. But, never ever: WPC STOLE MY LESBIAN LOVER.

Some people whose taxes pay the Chief Constables their wages distrust and dislike homosexuals. They feel children, all children, endangered by them. Chief Constables, he knew, have to think of their precious PR.

But does it matter? he was asking himself. It shouldn't matter, you know.

'Drink up,' he said. 'I'll go back and collect my Bogart mac.' They smiled at each other, his warm, hers still sad.

10

For days now Detectives Udden and Bullman had been loudly complaining in the canteen about the seventy-hour weeks they were working on the operation to round up street criminals. To Jacko, on a nearby table, it had sounded as if they were enjoying themselves, especially the overtime.

It was if they alone were discovering that muggers don't live in mortgaged fixed abodes but drift between squats, a night's doss here, a week's there, depending on the drugs and the women their last crime will finance.

Udden, judging by his talk, exercised his body more than his mind. Bullman was the reverse, an office politician whose pent-up fury surfaced in drink when he railed against 'those BTOs from HQ, those prats'.

They talked of their waiting game in Highfields, watching addresses until the suspect turned up to be lifted, literally, Jacko guessed, into their van.

Highfields is a walk away from the city centre with its glittering shops and discos; yet, in Jacko's mind, a world away. It is connected to the commercial heart by an iron bridge with half-moon girders that gave him the impression of a drawbridge, waiting to be pulled up, to divide the Haves and Have-Nots. Highfields is on the wrong side of the railway track.

It was Bullman's beat and, with his partner, he worked the streets where girls, teenagers looking forty, waited for their next trick, where winos huddled in doorways for warmth that cider couldn't provide, where kids as young as ten called the police pigs, but not Pinky and Perky. A hard beat, Jacko acknowledged, a tough patch, a hunting ground for the canteen cowboy. Every big city he knew had its Highfields and every big force had its canteen cowboys.

'Look out for Jogger Jones,' a teenager had told them in return for a blind eye on one cannabis cigarette they had found in his pocket. 'He hangs around somewhere off London Road.'

A cold night tonight, damp, raw, no hint of spring and a black beanpole of a youth is running, gracefully, on the dark, wet pavement.

Udden pulled on thin leather driving gloves he kept in a ball inside his leather jacket. He was out of the passenger door before the van had braked to a halt. A few strides and he blocked the jogger's path. They stood face to face, silent, until the jogger stopped running on the spot. 'You Jones?'·

'Not me.' He wasn't even out of breath.

Bullman's sprint around the front of the van had left him panting heavily. 'We want a word with you.'

'Why?' Uncertain, suspicious.

'In here.' Udden put an arm round his shoulder. The jogger leadened his legs.

'I'm on my way to training.' Alarm now in his young black face.

Udden bear-hugged him, pulling him away from the brightly lit window of a shop. 'We're offering you a lift.'

'I don't want one.' A puzzled, pleading look. Bullman opened the back door to the van. 'In.'

'No.' He was pushed and pulled.

'We're the police.' Bullman's voice began to bubble.

'But . . .' He was pushed by Udden, pulled by Bullman – 'I've done nothing . . .' – into the van. He sat on a bench with his knees under his chin.

The two detectives lowered their heads and climbed in, forcing him to shuffle further inside on his track-suited bottom to make room for them.

'Now.' Udden squatted opposite, leaning forward, face to face again. 'What have you been up to? Purse-snatching?'

'Bollocks, you bastards.' Outrage, not bravado.

His head rocked from an open-handed blow. He raised a hand towards his numbed ear. Udden grabbed the wrist, forcing it back, pinning it against the van's inside. The youth felt the wind exploding out of his chest from a stomach punch.

A hand fumbled inside the elastic that held his track bottom

90

taut. 'Where's your knife?' He couldn't speak. 'Or is it a spiked glove?'

'Bastards.' A gasp, like a last living breath.

He swung his free shoulder towards Bullman. A scream of agony echoed as his wrist was grabbed and his arm went into reverse thrust.

The hand came out of his trouser band. Then three painful jabs beneath his rib cage. His chin fell forward on Udden's knee. The knee jerked up. The crown of his head cracked against the van's side.

He was dazed; yet frighteningly aware of all that was happening. That hand again, feeling round a nipple. 'Well, well.' Fingers fumbled inside the breast pocket of the shirt under his sweater and track top. 'What have we here?'

The fingers came away from his pocket and the hand from inside his clothing. Another hand tugged his hair, pulling his face downward. He opened his eyes. He was looking at a small silver sachet, screwed at one end, held between gloved finger and thumb. He looked up at Udden's smirking face, then down again, Bullman still grasping his hair. Udden removed his gloves and unscrewed the top of the sachet.

'Well. Well, Mr Jones.'

'James.'

'James, sir.' Bullman tugged harder. The skin on his scalp seemed about to strip away. He saw what looked like white flour in the corner of the silver paper.

Theatrically, Udden stuck the middle finger of his right hand and dipped it into the substance. He held the finger under his nose, sniffing deeply, beaming. 'My. My.'

He rescrewed the foil and handed it to Bullman. 'We're going to have to speak to this little nignog about this.'

Bullman slipped the foil into his coat pocket. 'Among other things.'

He climbed out the back and walked round to the driver's door. The youth held his elbows tight to his stomach and rested his face on his knees for the short, silent journey.

A hand grabbed each arm when the door opened again. Pain darted into his right shoulder. Fingers tightened on his arm muscles as he was bustled up steps.

He slumped down in a chair in a bright, windowless room,

stretching out his legs, crossing one white trainer over the other at his ankles.

'Be our guest, jigaboo.' Udden stood over him.

Bullman pulled a similar chair backwards across the floor towards the youth. He sat astride it, lowering his chin on to the back rest. 'Make yourself at home.'

Udden aimed a kick under his knees. Anticipating it, the youth sprang to his feet, nimble as a cat. Udden pushed him down again. 'Now you're going to tell us about the car-park job across the road.'

The youth sat erect, feet on the floor. 'Already have.'

'Bullshit.' Udden grinned down, malevolent.

'I gave a statement to Inspector Jackson.'

The grin vanished, a complete wipe-out. 'When?'

'My old man brought me here.'

'What's your name again?'

'Leroy James.' He stretched out his long legs again, spotting the change of mood as the two men swapped worried looks.

'Wait here for a minute.' Bullman left the interview room. Udden sat down, staring at the door.

'Has a James featured?' Bullman asked the collator, back from his break at the Barley Mow.

'Several times.' The sergeant typed on a keyboard and an index flashed up in white letters on a black computer screen. 'First name Leroy?'

A dumb nod.

'Loads on him.' He keyed in a new code. He lent back to let him read the results. Bullman couldn't concentrate. 'He gave us that sighting of the six-footer in the donkey jacket.'

'Is he in the clear?'

Another code. The screen changed. A list of names and addresses, his team-mates, flowed into view. 'Pick from a dozen.' Bullman seemed in a trance.

'Why?'

He shook his head. 'Just a bit of hassle . . .' He corrected himself 'Duplication, that's all.'

He was wearing a bright smile when he walked back into the interview room. 'Sorry about this, kid. We've mixed you up with someone else. Come on, we'll drop you wherever.'

'No thanks.' James stood. 'I'll walk.'

Udden threw a hand over his shoulder. 'It's no problem.'

James tried to wriggle free but the pain stopped him. 'No thanks.'

Udden looked at Bullman; a distress signal, a panic sign. 'We'll walk you down the stairs then.'

At a side entrance, Bullman held out his right hand, half-heartedly. 'No hard feelings, eh? We thought you were armed.'

James ignored it and looked down at his trainers. Udden put his hand on his right shoulder. 'No harm done, eh? Let's forget about everything.' James winced as he shook his shoulder free. Without another word, without turning, he broke into an ungainly trot, right shoulder lopsided, a graceful bird with a broken wing.

Bullman and Udden walked to the canteen, sat at a table out of earshot, heads close together, rehearsing and perfecting their story.

The desk sergeant refolded his *Mercury* when the counter bell rang in the inquiry office, got up and walked out of his glass-fronted office.

At the long counter stood a West Indian, mid-forties, prematurely white hair. Alongside him was a tall, thin youth, padded anorak hanging loose over his shoulders on top of a blue track suit.

'We'd like to see Inspector Jackson, please,' said the older man, politely. 'He wrote to us a couple of months ago.' He took a letter from his pocket and slid it across the counter. It thanked them for *their prompt and valuable assistance*. Jackson had written *Kind regards* in almost illegible handwriting above his scrawled signature.

'Why do you want to see him again, Mr James?'

'To make a formal complaint against two of your officers.'

He retreated into his office. Through the glass panel they saw him on the phone. He put it down and returned to the counter. 'He'll be down in a minute.' He looked at the youth, three shades paler than his father's deep blackness, except for bruising on his cheek. 'Take a seat.' He nodded them towards a wall bench beneath a row of police posters, one with a photo of Davis, appealing for witnesses to his movements on the night he died.

Jacko, his brown mac already on, walked into the inquiry office. He sat alongside them.

As they talked, they were watched over by the sergeant, a grey-haired veteran, an old-fashioned cop, the desk man who had spotted Davis's computer racket.

Jacko led them upstairs, into the Deputy Commander's office, sitting them down, before making a series of phone calls from the desk. He took a long statement from Leroy, who vividly recalled every detail, every quote, a terrific witness, clear and calm. Caroline took the father's statement in an adjoining room. The police surgeon arrived by the time they had finished.

Leroy stripped naked in the unabashed way of sportsmen. Jacko took notes at the doctor's dictation. 'Tenderness to the abdomen, torn muscle in right shoulder as well as the cuts and abrasions you see. A bad beating, I'd say.'

Jacko walked into the next-door office where Caroline waited. 'Take Leroy and a couple of the boys. Get him to identify the scene and do some door-knocking for witnesses.'

He turned to the collator who had typed his own report. 'Bring them in.'

He returned to the Deputy's office. 'Can you give us ten more minutes?' The doctor nodded.

Jacko questioned them separately. 'He cut up rough,' Bullman protested, vehement, only just in control of his temper. 'We suspected he had a weapon. We used minimum force to restrain him.'

'Why should an innocent kid cut up rough?'

'You know what they're like. They regard all cops as white trash.'

'He alleges you planted some dope on him.'

An explosive look, primed. 'Bullshit. We've not seen a grain of dope all day. His old man's probably consulted one of those black law centres. It's a try-on.'

Udden sat with the back of his neck cradled in his hands, passing the time with callisthenics. He nodded to his notebook on the desk. 'I made notes immediately afterwards. He was threatening us.'

Jacko opened it. The last entry described how a polite request for assistance turned into a free-for-all and used the rehearsed phrase: 'Minimum force only was used to restrain him.' There was no mention of drugs. Nor had any been found in a search of their desks and lockers.

Jacko read out the medical report to him, laying down the bait. Udden released his neck and lent forward, elbows on the desk, resting his chin in his hands. 'That proves it. Look at these hands.'

He removed them from under his chin and held them in front of Jacko's eyes. 'Not a mark on them. Now would he have got all that without some bruising showing up here?' He clenched and opened his strong hands repeatedly. 'Proves what we're saying. He's got himself knocked up in a street fight, daren't tell his dad.' He smiled. 'Go on. Take a good look. Be my guest.'

'Thanks.' Jacko got up and called in the police surgeon. 'DC Udden here has very kindly given us permission to examine his hands.'

The doctor put his black briefcase on the desk and opened it. 'All I want you to do,' said Jacko, 'is to remove the debris beneath the nail, middle finger, right hand.'

The doctor cleared the underside of the nail with a small steel blade. Carefully he deposited the scraping on to a plain piece of paper on the desk. White powder glinted among congealed black grime. It looked like flour.

Udden's jaw sagged. Sweat broke out on his forehead.

Jacko turned to the collator. 'Lock him up.'

Mrs James looked up from reading the news of her old home town in a fortnight-old *Gleaner*. Not for her, Jacko noted, the militant black press which will have her son on the front page when the story gets out.

'He's in bed,' she said. 'More shocked than hurt.' Jacko nodded. He was shown to a settee in front of a gas fire, on either side of which Leroy's parents sat, facing each other.

'It's very, very unfair.' Mrs James, plump and slow-moving, folded the paper across her wide lap. 'You bring them up to respect the law. Now this.' A loser's shrug, cheated.

'If it's any comfort, we're throwing the book at them. There'll be no private deals to let them off lightly.' Jacko's voice trailed.

'You read these stories about police brutality and don't believe them until it happens to your own.'

Her husband sighed, dismayed, defeated. 'We feel betrayed.'

'I know.' Very quietly, head down, looking at his wet shoes. 'So do we.' Head up, face encouraging. 'But you've brought up a smashing boy. Hope I do as well with my own.' Patronizing, he knew, but heartfelt. 'Don't let him go off the rails because of this.'

'What would you tell him, then? What would you say if it happened to your own?'

Head down again, in thought. 'You've done exactly what I would have done – bring it out into the open.' Pause. 'I'd tell him the pain he's feeling now won't be suffered in vain.'

'Fine words.' A harsh snort. 'But he's going to ask himself how many other black kids have been treated like that and forced to confess to something they didn't do.'

'It worries us, too. All anyone can do is try to play it straight themselves and see that others around them do.' They chatted for a while, aimless talk, then he rose unsteadily from tiredness. He promised to drop by.

On the half-hour trip home he didn't fiddle with his car radio for news or music. He drove in thought, dark thought, tyres swishing on the wet dual carriageway.

I fudged it. But how can you say, well, Mrs James, the truth is that racism is endemic in the British police force. Listen to them in the canteen. Topping each other's stories of the aggro they've caused, the trouble they've provoked, for a bit of fun, to break the boredom. And have you ever walked across to their table and said, 'If I catch you at it, you're nicked'? No, you haven't.

Listen to them talk about the few black recruits we've got – not just behind their back, sometimes to their face. 'Get back to the jungle . . . Go eat your bananas.' And have you ever walked across and said, 'Cut it out'? No, you have not, you coward.

And if a black recruit feels driven to complain, what do the chiefs do? Investigate the complainant rather than his complaint. A malcontent, they'll call him, not fitting in. A black officer will put up with it for so long, then his pride won't let him take any more and he quits.

And the chiefs go on TV lamenting the fact that they can't seem to recruit the Leroys. And have you ever proposed a motion in the Police Federation telling them what a blind bunch of bastards we are? No, you haven't.

Kids, black and white, grow up without having ever got to know to a bobby on the beat. Never laugh and joke with them, give them a bit of cheek.

All they see of them now is when they scream up in squad cars, demanding to know who they are, where they've been, where they're going. Sometimes with reason, of course. Middle-class liberals like Jackie's friends bang on about civil rights; all well and good, unless your grannie has had her purse snatched or your son is stealing to feed an addiction or you live next door to a three-day blues party.

The truth, Mrs James, is that there are too few parents like you and your husband. Too many coppers like Udden and Bullman; too many middle-ranking wankers like Keeling who demand results, order arses to be kicked and then piss off to the *piste*. And who'll be in charge tomorrow? Makes you sick, doesn't it, Mrs James?

'It's my fault.' Chief Superintendent Scott looked up from studying the medical and forensic evidence, the denials and a damning statement from two students who saw the pushing and pulling and the police van rocking. 'It's down to me.'

'Why?' Jacko was on a bench seat in the CID Chief's office at HQ near Newark to which he'd been summoned.

'They were so desperate for it not to be Mike Fixter. They got frustrated, cut corners. Maybe I pushed too hard.' A heavy cold had thickened his public school accent and deadened his normally alert brown eyes.

'Balls.' Jacko was the only man in the squad who dared to speak to Scott so bluntly. They were close at work and off duty, laughing at each other's stories over drinks in the Fairways, the HQ local. 'How can you blame yourself? No one can excuse what they did.'

Scott picked up a pen and initialled his approval for charges of assault occasioning actual bodily harm and conspiracy to pervert the course of justice. Jacko knew the case would eventually get a big show in the *Mercury* and maybe in the nationals. He hoped Scott would not give him that tired old apologia: 'All wars corrupt and so does the war on crime.' He wanted to go on respecting him.

Scott looked back at him. 'What I mean is they should never have been on the job in the first place. They were personally involved. I should have listened to you. And that is down to me.'

He hooked an elastic band round his fingers, pianist's fingers, with none of the podginess his love of French food had added to his stomach. 'The Deputy's had Keeling on complaining about you.' A pause, tantalizing. 'We've taken him off the case. All divisional detectives, too. It will be a squad only show from now on.'

I can't say, 'Told you so' now, can I? thought Jacko, suppressing a flush, determined not to gloat. 'How did he take it?'

'Badly. He's talking of quitting.' Talk. All Keeling ever does, thought Jacko. All mouth and ski pants. They'd probably polish his bruised ego by making him a uniformed superintendent and another dodo would get to the top by default. 'Which means you're in charge.'

In charge. He'd never been in charge of a murder. Always part of the team, often No. 2 but always answerable to someone. Waves of apprehension began to pound through his pulses.

'With an inspector as a suspect, you'll need a bit of rank. Acting chief inspector, as of now.' He still toyed with the elastic band. 'All right for manpower?'

'We've a dozen on the team, all dedicated. All I need.' A shrug, trying to be carefree. 'It's brainpower we want.'

'We're in trouble then.' He unwound the band and threw it playfully towards him. It landed harmless on the carpet. 'If you ever need a leg-up, I'm here.' Waves again, calm this time. 'How do you read it?'

'I've never been sold on the mugger theory. Wrong sort of weapon and taking Davis's notebook, not his credit cards, never made any sort of reason. I think you got it right at that first briefing. Rule out a chance street crime and the answer is in his background.'

'Your friends, the Frosts?'

'We've still got to find Leroy's donkey jacket man who's probably George's six-footer. And that slovenly woman with the head scarf, smelling of stale fags and scent. There's a call on his answering machine talking about some deal struck three days before he was croaked. And we still don't know which murder Davis wanted to talk to French about. There's some mileage in that family.'

Scott opened a second file on his desk. 'After his acquittal Lance Frost was checked out for a rape on another force's patch. He was alibi-ed and eliminated and they got someone else. We got a complaint of harassment from his mother. Handle that with care. Get a firm link before you act. They're trouble.' Jacko nodded. 'What about the Fixters? Can we lift their suspensions?'

'Give me a few days. I want to put George Marshall's nose to the test.'

Scott frowned when he told him how. 'He's very anti-police, I hear. Handle him with care, too.'

Jacko smiled. 'As if he was my old grannie.'

'What about Golden Jim?'

'There's not much we can do until surveillance pick up something. We need to nick and hold him in custody. People around him won't talk unless he's out of circulation. Caroline fancies him but she's a dog-lover.'

Scott laughed through his stuffed-up nose. 'How are you getting on with her?'

'Fine.' Not enough, he told himself, make amends. 'She's terrific.'

He nodded, satisfied. 'Good luck, then.'

Jacko rose stiffly and looked down on him. His eyes were glistening, his nose was red, his normally shiny complexion was mottled. He looked very ill.

'Why do they do it?' He patted the Udden and Bullman file.

Jacko had thought this through, last night on the way home. 'They want a pat on their head from their chief inspector and have beer bought them by admiring juniors. They want to be known as the ones who deliver and never mind if the goods are soiled. Every profession has them. We've had them for years. Now we catch them because we want to catch them. It's bad publicity, I know, but this job won't be worth a light if we stand back and do nothing.'

Scott looked up. 'And why do we do it? Why do we beat our brains out, day in, day out?'

Jacko turned and walked slowly to the door. This he had not thought through but he found a story, one from his store, untold for years, which somehow summed up his philosophy, the *raison d'être* for the hours he worked, the aches and pains he suffered, the meals he missed, the shit he took. He turned at the door to tell it.

This clerk was sent to the circus, see, during a population census. He got all the details from the ringmaster, the lion-tamer, the trapeze artist and all the stars on their big money, living in their luxury caravans.

As he was leaving he spots this tiny bloke wearing a filthy smock.

'Excuse me,' he says. 'I need your details for my census. What is your job here?'

'Elephant-purger.'

'What's that entail?'

'Well, sir, elephants in the wild have very regular habits but in captivity they become very constipated. My job is to force down a gallon of cod liver oil, and, if that doesn't work, I have to pull on their tails until they're purged. That's why I'm always covered in shit.'

'What do you earn?' asked the clerk, taking a pace back from the appalling smell.

'Ten pounds a week, sir, but I have to give half back to sleep with the camels and eat with the monkeys.'

'Don't you realize,' said the clerk, horrified, 'that you could sign on the dole, get thirty pounds a week for nothing, live in a nice council flat and stay in bed all day? Why don't you do that?'

'What!' said the little elephant-purger, aghast. 'And give up show business? I love the lousy job.'

Scott didn't laugh. But he smiled philosophically.

11

Brown eyes, deep, dark and dead, found his face as soon as he introduced himself. 'Come in.' George Marshall, back broad and erect, led the way into the lounge of his home, a converted corner shop. He held his neck stiff which, Jacko had noted as a small boy, is the way of the blind who have no need to look about them.

A black and white collie, which barked and ran to the door when the bell rang, shepherded Caroline from the rear of the procession.

'Make yourselves at home.' A wave of the hand in no particular direction. Both sank comfortably into soft armchairs. The dog sniffed the scents of their pets, seemed to prefer Caroline's to Jacko's and curled up at her feet.

'Tea's on.' George had disappeared into the kitchen. Jacko looked around. The room was cosily overcrowded with a three-piece, a drinks cabinet and a desk where a sideboard should be. On it stood two high-tech phones, a radio, a typewriter and documents in untidy piles.

'Find us OK?' A call from the kitchen, a countryside voice, slow, rolling, vowels extended.

'Easy,' said Jacko. 'What's your secret?'

George, white shirt-sleeves rolled up to the elbow, carried three steaming mugs, hooked to his index fingers and clamped together. Both only had to half raise a hand to have their mug thrust into it. He walked back to collect a bowl of sugar which only he spooned in. He talked as he walked. 'Nearly every town has a London Road. Once you get that firmly fixed in your mind, you can work out the points of the compass. I just make a mental note of roundabouts and Maggie tells me where the traffic lights are. Simple, really.'

He had settled in a chair beside the desk. 'This is the third or fourth time and I'm not sure I can add . . .' He looked up as Maggie entered in a flowered apron. 'Tea, love?'

Undecided, she addressed Caroline. 'Will this take long?' A hint of inhospitality there so, quickly and with a smile, she added, 'Ruff hasn't had his walk yet.'

Caroline showed the initiative that Jacko had come to rely on. 'Mind if I come?' That way, they would be questioned individually without the risk of prompting each other into giving details they didn't really recollect.

The word 'walk' had brought Ruff to his feet, wagging his tail, running back to the door. Caroline took a few more hurried sips and rose, leaving the mug half drunk on the desk.

'I've been through it three or four times,' said George when they were alone. 'Nothing's changed.'

'Anyone on our side ever put you in the picture?'

A headshake. 'Your lot like to keep people in the dark.' Nothing in his ruddy face signalled an attempt at black humour.

The drivers of the three cars he'd heard had all come forward, Jacko reported. So had the couple leaving the pub. 'They didn't see a thing.'

'That's often the case with sighted people.' A humorous smile now which Jacko returned, pointless, superfluous.

He briefed him fully on the statements of all witnesses and George had nothing much to add.

'Fancy a scotch?' He got up suddenly, rubbing his hands. He walked in slippers to the corner cabinet, put a hand straight on a whisky bottle on the bottom shelf. He felt for two glasses on the shelf above and put them on top of the cabinet. He poured two drinks without a drop spilt.

Here am I, thought Jacko, a grown man, so frightened of waking up in the dark that Jackie bought me a teddy bear on honeymoon. There he is, in a pitch-black world, confident, in control.

His research into George Marshall had been thorough. He was a full-time local politician of the left, sometimes critical of the police. He was hot on civil liberties, a big campaigner for equality. Jacko raised the real reason for his visit with caution. 'I'd like to ask you a favour.'

'What's that?'

'We'd like to put your nose to the test,' and he gave him a lengthy explanation of why and how.

'Of course I will,' said George. 'Cheers.'

Both raised their glasses briefly, sipped and rolled the whisky on their tongues.

'Been in the force long?'

'Twenty-six years.'

'You'll have seen lots of changes then.'

'Not all for the best.'

'What's gone wrong, do you think?'

And they were arguing, reminiscing, laughing and drinking a second double when Ruff tugged a wind-blown Caroline into the lounge almost an hour later. Lord, she thought, an acting chief inspector half-pissed in the middle of the morning.

She stood over Jacko, holding out her hand for the car keys. She patted Ruff, said goodbye to Maggie and led her chief to the door. He turned to face George who had followed.

'Thanks a lot. I enjoyed that.'

'Me, too. See you soon.' He stood on the step and seemed to watch them drive away, his useless eyes fixed on their car until they were out of his hearing.

Jacko lapsed into a long silence. Caroline thought he was dozy from booze. But he was thinking of his grandma and he closed his eyes so that Caroline could not see the tears welling in them.

12

He opened the flaking front door with a wet brush in his hand and an annoyed look on his face, an old master disturbed in mid-masterpiece.

Jacko stepped into a hallway covered in dust sheets. 'Smart,' he said, looking round.

His eyes finally rested on Mike Fixter. Two months had brought change. His face had aged and lined. His body had slimmed a stone. No home cooking, Jacko guessed, no drinks with the boys.

He was dapperly dressed for decorating – grey slacks, scarlet Aertex shirt which had avoided the magnolia on his narrow brush. 'Just cutting in.' Jacko nodded knowledgeably, not a clue what he was talking about.

Fixter crouched to lay the brush across his paint kettle, wiped his hands on a spirit-soaked rag and stood again. He showed Jacko into a lounge where the woodchip walls were fresh buttermilk. 'Once it's shipshape, it's up for sale.'

Over then, thought Jacko, sadly. Divorce is a painful road to walk. He'd been down it.

Fixter eased himself into a chintzy chair. 'I gather you're in charge now.'

Jacko sat back on a matching sofa. 'Headquarters thought it ought to be a squad only operation.'

'And I gather you've suspended two of my old team.' A thin voice, chilled. Jacko nodded.

'And now you've come to do the business on me.' Sullen, truculent.

'If there's any business to do,' a single nod, '. . . yes. If not, no.' He pulled out his notebook. No pleasantries, no gossip exchanged, the way it was with squad and divisional detectives.

He handed him three news clippings, pinned together, with 'Soccer Star's Shame' on top.

Fixter knew Golden Jim, though he didn't play snooker or gamble at his casino. 'I nicked a couple of his bouncers for GBH on a drunk they were throwing out. They nearly killed him. Golden funded their defence.'

'He and Davis rowed over that story but Golden claims they'd kissed and made up. What do you know about him?'

'He's behind a lot of things but we've never nailed him.'

Me neither, thought Jacko. 'Was he into dog-fighting?'

Fixter turned to the second cutting, shaking his head. Big Vyn Baldwin and the dog-fight gang were not on his patch.

He turned to the final cutting, the main reason for Jacko's visit. 'God,' he groaned. 'Not the jewel in the crown of my career, is it?'

He read rapidly, confirming that he knew the details all too well. 'You're keen on this, aren't you?'

'Why do you say that?'

'I remember you mentioning it at the evening briefing before . . .' An anguished look came and went. 'I remember Mr Keeling pooh-poohing it and I don't figure it, to be honest. Completely different *modus operandi*. The court case was seven months earlier, the girl's murder fifteen. None of that could have been in Davis's current notebook, which, I gather, you're also keen on.'

'Tell me about it anyway.'

'It's a long story.'

Katie Burrows had been a bit of a rebel, by all accounts. Torn jeans, blouse knotted at the front by its tails, dangling plastic ear-rings, hair dyed blonde and set in spikes.

She might have looked sophisticated, tough even, but she was just fourteen when she was killed. She'd never mentioned Lance Frost, a tall, thin, odd youth of seventeen. They lived on the same estate, fifties, council-built, on the edge of the city.

He'd just transferred with moderate CSEs from comprehensive school to sixth form college to study catering. He lived with his mother, Rita, small, plumpish, fiftyish, and her second husband Harry Morris, a toy boy, fifteen years her junior. Her first husband, an oil worker with a Middle East company, died from cirrhosis of the liver when the boy was twelve.

Neighbours regarded Rita as volatile, quick to hand out a piece of her mind, Harry as henpecked, Lance as eager-to-please.

None of them knew that at the age of fifteen Lance had been caught flashing on a footpath in a park. A nurse complained: 'He jumped out from behind a rhododendron bush, his penis exposed and erect. He didn't say a word, just jumped up and down, babbling like a baboon.' He ran when a jogger approached; not fast enough, his flight slowed by pubic hairs trapped in his zip. He was brought down in a flying tackle before he could reach his lime-green cycle with cow-horn handlebars.

A constable went to his home to deliver a formal caution and a lecture to keep it in his trousers in future. Routine, everyday police business.

Rita switched shifts at the garden centre where she worked so that either she or her husband Harry would always be at home to keep an eye on him. He was made to do all his homework before he went out, was banned from the park and given a nine o'clock curfew with extra chores when he broke it. Firm parental control, impressive in this age, Jacko thought.

On a wet Saturday evening in October, eighteen months ago, Katie Burrows left home to swap Madonna tapes with a schoolmate. 'Where's Katie?' asked the friend when she phoned an hour later. Her frantic parents phoned other friends. None had seen her. They reported her missing.

By then Detective Inspector Mike Fixter, the duty DI, had already been summoned from a quiet evening with Chrissy. A gang of boys had found a young girl, deathly still, at the edge of a lake in the park, her body on the bank, her face looking up at them through two feet of water.

It was Fixter who broke the news to the Burrows. 'May God forgive him,' said her church-going mother. No anger, no demands for revenge, just grief and forgiveness. Fixter shook his head at a poignant recollection.

Next morning, playing it by Keeling's book, he asked the Press Office to call a media conference, outlined the sketchy details and appealed for witnesses who had been in the park.

Within two hours of the bulletins running on the two local radio stations, he had three sightings of a lime-green bike with extra-large handlebars.

He ordered the cycle's description to be circulated to all stations. A constable phoned up. 'I had to caution a youth with a bike like that for flashing in the same park.' Two detectives drove to Lance's home. His mother was at work. His stepfather accompanied him to the station.

For half an hour he was uncooperative. 'Not me. I was watching TV.' Then he started to cry; real tears, sobbing and shaking.

He asked to see Harry, waiting outside. Fixter and his sergeant left them alone for ten minutes. When they got back in the room Harry had been weeping, too. 'I have told Lance to tell you the truth.'

Lance pulled himself together and made a statement under caution. He claimed he went into the park, with nothing particular in mind, just to ride around. He bumped into Katie, whom he knew from his old school, and they started chatting.

He suggested a kiss and cuddle and she agreed. He felt her breast with no objection but when he tried to slide his hand in her waistband she screamed, hit him and ran off. He caught her up by the side of the lake. In a panic, he held a hand over her mouth to stop her shouts. He said she went quiet and he left her. He denied any attempt at strangulation or drowning.

Fixter knew he had not got the whole truth. The speed of the arrest was, in fact, a handicap. By then the post-mortem examination had not been completed. That was finished in the afternoon. The Home Office pathologist certified death from shock. The girl, a virgin, had been forcibly held under the shallow water and sucked mud into her lungs.

He returned from the mortuary with plenty of questions to ask. Why, if she consented to heavy petting, was her bra still in place? How did Lance explain the bruising at the side of her neck? And wasn't the real truth that he'd been flashing, realized she could identify him and killed to silence her?

By now his mother and a solicitor were at the station. He wouldn't add to his statement. The forensic scientists found fibres from the girl's pink sweater on Lance's sleeveless body warmer and semen in his underpants which proved sexual activity of some sort, even if one-sided and self-induced.

He was charged with murder and spent seven months in jail awaiting trial. Fixter expected him to go for manslaughter either on the grounds that he didn't mean to hurt her or that he was suffering from diminished responsibility.

He'd heard that Terry Davis had been snooping around on behalf of Lance's solicitor and thought he might be looking for details of other flashing offences to boost a medical defence.

A surprise awaited Fixter as he sat in the foyer of the Crown Court amid tropical plants rampant in pots topped with plastic pebbles. Lance pleaded a straight not guilty with no offer to plea to manslaughter. Fixter was the last witness to be called by the Crown. By then the evidence of the witnesses who had seen the green bike had gone largely unchallenged. The only question he was asked was about the time he had allowed Lance and his stepfather to spend together in private.

Lance left the dock and walked with a prison guard to the witness box and took the oath on the bible.

'Did you kill this young girl?' asked his QC.

'No, sir.'

'How did she die?'

'It was my stepfather, sir.'

A gasp went round the court. His QC turned, frowning, to his junior counsel, then to the solicitor who half rose from his bench behind them. All three heads closed in huddled conversation. He turned back to Lance. 'Why?'

'He saw my bike at the park gates. I was inside, snogging with the girl, then petting and she played with me. We came out of the bushes and he spotted us and shouted. I knew I was in trouble. I shouldn't have been in the park. I just ran. He chased us. He caught up with her at the side of the lake. I didn't see whether he pulled her down or what. I just turned and saw them struggling on the grass. He kept shouting "Slag." I ran to my bike and went home.'

His stepfather returned a short while later. By then his mother was home from work. Nothing was said in front of her.

Next morning, after his mother had left for work, he told Lance, 'I taught her a lesson.' They agreed to keep it secret from his mother. By lunchtime both of them were at the police station.

'Tell the jury in your own words why you made that statement,' asked the QC, waving exhibit No. 1.

'My stepfather told me what to say when we were alone. He said I would get away with it if I made it out to be an accident. He said there was no chance the police would believe him because he was twice my age and married.'

'Why did you lie to the police?'

'For the sake of my mum, sir.'

In the public gallery Harry Morris was looking around, dumbstruck. His wife sat still, watching her son intently.

The prosecution barrister abandoned a cross-examination based on Fixter's unasked questions designed to restore Katie's honour. He fought a rearguard action to salvage a crumbling case.

'Why didn't you tell Mr Fixter this straight away?'

'Because I was frightened and wanted to keep my family together.'

'Isn't it a pack of lies to secure your release?'

'It's the truth, sir.'

The jury were out for less than an hour before bringing in their not guilty verdict.

'Just on Lance's say-so?' asked Jacko, incredulously.

'Think about it. The petting explained the forensics. His statement admitted his presence at the scene, but not the killing. They sprang this defence after we closed our case so we couldn't call Harry, who wasn't alibi-ed anyway. And the judge summed up strongly in Lance's favour.'

Jacko thought about it. To have convicted Lance on such confusing, conflicting evidence would have given reasonable jurymen and women sleepless nights for the rest of their lives. Even Fixter, in his bitter disappointment, could see that. The jurors couldn't be sure. They didn't really know what had happened.

A dejected Fixter saw Harry Morris standing in a daze beneath the Lord Chief Justice's plaque on the wall in the foyer while his wife hugged her son. Terry Davis took them out of a side entrance to avoid the journalists waiting on the red-bricked walkway outside for any quotes or photos they could snatch. They had to fall back on demands from MPs for a full inquiry and a tearful interview with Katie Burrows' family wanting justice for their dead daughter.

Fixter was taken off the case and Chief Inspector Keeling put in charge. Lance refused to add to his court statement. Morris hotly denied it all. His clothing was examined. It had been washed several times in the seven months that had elapsed since the crime. Nothing was found to tie him into Katie's death. The case was quietly dropped.

Within a month the Frosts had split up and moved. Mother and son had gone to live in a market town fifteen miles away where they had adopted the name of Vinter. Harry Morris was living and working in a suburb of a city twenty-five miles to the north.

Jacko sat for several silent moments digesting the long story, fluently told with hardly a break, so fresh in his memory were the stunning facts, mind-boggling. Jesus, what a cock-up. So near and yet . . . I'm bloody pleased that job wasn't down to me. He looked at Fixter, who seemed to be awaiting his reaction. He'd rushed it, hadn't copper-bottomed his case. But Jacko offered a sort of sympathy. 'Who could have anticipated a turn of events like that?'

'It's Katie's family I feel sorry for. Imagine how they feel with their daughter's killer still roaming about.'

A twinge of shame now, at such a self-centred response, but it was quickly dismissed. Stand back. Take the overview. Difficult for Fixter, though, having it explode in his hands and probably his promotion prospects with it. 'Seen or heard of the Frosts since?'

'We had a request from South Midlands just before Christmas to do a movements check on Lance after a rape in a park. My old sergeant Danny Edge handled it. They got a different bloke a few days later. All Danny got was a flea in his ear.' A pensive pause. 'Why are you so keen on this?'

'Because Davis told his reporter pal he had some info on a murder. This is the only murder we can trace that he was involved in, either on the force or as a private dick.' Jacko had caught Fixter's depression. 'Unless there was something

110

in his notebook we don't know about.' Snap out of this. 'What does Lance look like?'

'My size, much thinner.' George's six-footer perhaps? Jacko queried himself. 'He's a raving nutter,' Fixter added. 'A bundle of nerves. That nurse he flashed is right. He scratches himself like a baboon, too. He's a loner, no real chums, a big mother complex.'

'What's she like?'

'Trouble. Past fifty and looks it; small, skinny, pinched face. She's like a lioness with her cub.'

'A smart dresser?'

'The reverse.' The slovenly woman? Jacko continued his self-questioning, then aloud: 'Does she wear a head scarf?'

Fixter started to flick his head to one side, then stopped. 'It was autumn when we picked up Lance and the trial was in the summer.'

'Does she smoke?'

Fixter nodded and Jacko felt a tingle of excitement. He asked what Lance had been wearing. Dirty trainers, blue jeans, black polo neck and the grey body warmer on which the fibres had been found, replied Fixter with instant recall.

'Nothing like a donkey jacket or a three-quarter length car coat?'

'No, but Harry Morris had one. He was wearing it when he came to the station. Keeling had it tested. Nothing.'

Acidic juices gnawed at Jacko's stomach linings. 'How tall is he?'

'Your size. Around five ten.'

'What sort of man is he?'

'Protests he's innocent. Very offhand with Keeling, apparently. Can't say I blame him. Lance killed the girl and his mother manufactured his defence. They dropped him in it.'

With Terry Davis's help, thought Jacko. Where did he get the idea from? He mentally assigned himself to read right through the crime books on his shelf.

'Which may explain why Harry left them,' Fixter was saying. 'He could have been next. Lance is dangerous. I'm sure of it. So is Rita in a manipulative fashion.'

'Maybe we'll get him second time round.' Jacko slipped his notebook into his pocket.

13

Chrissy Fixter came down to the door in a lime silk dressing gown that had swept the stair carpet behind her. It was eleven o'clock. Caroline Parker had been up and dressed for five hours.

She got a close view, as she followed her up, of long black hair that covered the head of a Far Eastern fire dragon embroidered on the back of the gown.

Nice bum, Caroline noted, but with no more than the mischievous interest that Jacko had shown when he saw Chrissy at the station.

The first-floor room was a neat collection of wood and wicker. The friend who had given her sanctuary had built a warm nest with spring bulbs bursting into bud in moss-covered bowls. Only a half-filled ashtray and a mug with the grey dregs of cold coffee marred its cleanliness.

Chrissy turned and Caroline studied a face capable of beauty. High cheekbones, moist white skin, even white teeth but eyes more tired and unfocused than Jacko's after one of his late nights at the Fairways. 'Is Mike all right?'

'I think so. My acting chief inspector is with him.' She wanted to say overacting chief inspector. This morning he had made everyone in the incident room stand and salute. She took off her mac and hung it over the back of a basket chair.

Chrissy sat down before her, hung her head so that her hair covered her shaking shoulders and started to weep. Now look what you have made her do, Jacko, Caroline thought irrationally. She picked up the ashtray and mug and retreated into the kitchen to give her privacy. When she returned with two hot mugs and a clean ashtray, Chrissy greeted her with a smile.

Caroline sat beside her on a cushion-laden wicker sofa and shook her head when offered a Silk Cut. She dug into her shoulder bag, as though delving for her own brand, but came out with three newspaper cuttings.

Chrissy held her cigarette between two fingers, with Bette Davis' elegance, well practised, as she read of the Soccer Star's Secret Shame. She knew Golden Jim by name but had never met him. 'Terry never took me to his club or the casino. We only used his local.'

'He did take you to the Grand.'

'Only once to drop off an envelope. We had the one drink with his reporter friend.'

'Did he tell you what was in it?'

She blew out a thin jet of grey smoke. 'A job for Golden Jim. That's all.'

'Did he talk about his work for him?'

'I knew he had a contract and there was some doubt about it being renewed. He was scouting around for other work – security consultancies, that sort of thing.'

Caroline took the cutting back and handed her the dog-fight exposé. She read it, shaking her head. 'I didn't know about his involvement in this until they ran the story after . . .' She couldn't bring herself to say murder or even death so went back on herself. 'Until afterwards.'

'Did he ask you at any time to provide him with details from the computer on car numbers?'

'No.' She looked close to tears again, of anger this time. 'I've told you before. No one wants to believe that, but no.'

Caroline had fabricated and rehearsed this next line. 'Girl to girl, a neighbour of mine's dog was bowled over by a car. The driver had to stop because so many people had seen it. He gave false details but someone had taken his number. The dog had a broken leg, the vet's bill was high and she's hard up. She could have got the details with a formal application but that takes weeks. I got them for her. Something on those lines?' A conspirator's smile.

'No.' Chrissy's face had set, lined, unattractive. 'How many more times?' She pulled hard on her cigarette. The lines vanished. 'Honestly.'

She read the Frost saga through a cloud of drifting smoke.

113

In those days, she had only known Davis as a colleague. Their affair began three months later. In the spring, Terry told her he had been hired by solicitors acting for Lance Frost.

'We were actually in bed . . .' She looked away. 'I told him, "I don't want to know about this, please." Look at it from my point of view. Mike for the prosecution, Terry for the defence. It was too heavy.'

'Was the subject raised again?'

She ground out the cigarette, sighing. 'By Mike, constantly. He was very confident he'd get a good result and gutted when things turned out the way they did. He could hardly talk that night. He thought he'd made such a mess of it that they'd put him back in uniform.'

'Did Terry ever mention the topic again?'

'I didn't see him for several days. He rang once to say he was baby-sitting the family to keep other reporters away. When I did see him he was full of himself. He said he'd earned as much in a week as he did from Golden Jim in six months.'

That's right, thought Caroline with a start. There were no payments out of his bank account to the Frosts. He kept the whole five thousand himself. Why should they go through all that publicity for nothing? What was in it for them if not the money? 'Did he ever explain what part he'd played in preparing Lance's defence?'

'He said he'd seen Lance twice in the remand wing with his mother.' She half reached for another cigarette but changed her mind. 'He said that Mrs Frost was a real shrew but he admired her in a strange way.' Her face registered remembrance. 'He did say – and this was some time after the trial – that his job had been research but don't ask me what sort. I didn't push for details. In the circumstances it was hardly a topic for pillow talk, was it?'

'Did the subject ever come up again?'

'Vaguely. On New Year's Day.' The last time she saw him. She closed her eyes. They hadn't seen each other over Christmas, because of family commitments. They met up for a drink soon after six because Mike was due home at eight. She asked if his problems with Golden Jim had been sorted out.

'No,' he said. He didn't seem worried. 'There's something in the pipeline.' He didn't say what and she didn't ask but soon

114

after he said, 'I wonder how the Frost family celebrated their Christmas.' A long silence.

'Is that all?'

'Yes. I just said, "Search me" or something and started to talk about something else.'

'Was he fishing for something?'

'I don't know. If he was, he was wasting his time. I don't know what became of them. Mike never mentions them. It was as though he was trying to block the case out of his mind.'

They had one more drink, chatting about mutual friends on the force. They made their tentative date for the Tuesday. They wished each other Happy New Year and parted with a peck on the lips. That was the last time she saw him.

Her tears flowed unabated now and Caroline tried to ease her agony. 'Never mind. You've still got a job.'

'Some hope.' A muffled reply through a small grubby handkerchief.

'Why not? You've committed no offence. You've passed no confidential info.'

'Who'll believe that?'

'I do.'

She looked up and wiped her eyes. 'Even so . . .'

She was right, of course, Caroline knew. If her husband had been screwing a WPC they'd be telling that joke in the canteen about him:

'Do you ever speak to your wife during intercourse?'

'Only if she gets through on the girl's bedside phone.'

What makes it right for men and wrong for women? she asked herself. Who are they to judge us? If the chief sacked men for bits on the side, he'd lose half his force. But Chrissy would carry the can. They won't sack her. They'd offer her awful postings. They'd make it difficult. 'Your husband's experience makes him irreplaceable whereas . . . Best interests of the service, my dear.'

Chrissy was smiling at her. Oh Christ, do something, say something, Caroline was urging herself. 'Come on. Get yourself under the shower and put some clothes on. We're off for a drink. This time yesterday my chief was half-pissed. If it's good enough for him it's good enough for us.'

Over the first drink, Chrissy gloomily told her that all she'd heard from her husband was via solicitor's letters and a divorce was a certainty. No face-to-face, no attempt to sort things out. Male pride, Caroline diagnosed. She'd come across it many times when she'd snubbed advances. They were like spoilt children.

Over the second drink Caroline put what Jacko had dubbed the Marshall Plan to her. 'Yes,' said Chrissy, trustingly.

Over the third, fourth and fifth, just chat, like two blokes on a spree, and a sozzled Caroline got a taxi back. Jacko had the grace to let her claim the fare on expenses.

It would, Jacko speculated, have made a nice picture for Jason French's paper. *Standing on the corner smelling all the girls go by*, the caption could have read.

But only fifteen other people were in the know – George Marshall and his wife, Chrissy Fixter and Caroline who lined up the other eleven women, all shapes and sizes, taking part in the parade.

Chrissy opted to go seventh and walked briskly, as though late for a train, into the railway station foyer. George stood, back to the wall, four senses on full alert. 'No,' he said, positive. 'She smokes all right but the sound's all wrong. She picks her feet up, doesn't slouch in her shoes. Definitely not her.'

They went through the motions with the remaining five. Five nos; twelve in all.

Caroline stayed behind to say goodbye to Chrissy. Jacko strolled slowly back to the police station with George on Maggie's arm. I wonder if this old bugger, this scourge of the police force, knows what he's just done, he mused with an amused smile.

They climbed the steps into the incident room where Caroline caught them up. George sniffed his way through the contents of Leroy's first-aid box, Fixter's bathroom cabinet and Chrissy's vanity box. Three nos.

Then he started on a boxful of tubes and small pots Jacko had spent most of the morning buying at chemists' shops. Half-way through his neck straightened. 'Something here.'

He bent his head again, turning a white tube in his hands,

nose over the nozzle. 'Close. Some of the same ingredients are in there, I'm certain.'

He handed the tube to Jacko who studied the label. *For embarrassing itch*. He smiled, a long, slow smile of self-congratulation.

Nothing else came close and the four of them took a steady walk to the Barley Mow where they stood drinking against the busy bar.

'Well?' said George, a touch regal.

'Well, you've given us a lovely lead. We know now what kind of ointment we're looking for. Thanks a lot.'

'And that girl?'

'What girl?'

'Come on.' An irritated voice and face. 'I'm not stupid. There must have been a suspect on that parade. I failed to pick her out, didn't I?'

Go on, tell him, Jacko told himself. He's big enough to take a joke. 'You've eliminated her – and her husband.' And without giving their names he told him of Davis's WPC lover who'd been at the railway station about the same time they were collecting their car and of her policeman husband who'd been just across the road in the pub when the attack took place.

'She was on that parade and you confirmed she's in the clear. It can't have been her husband either. They've both been on suspension but they can go back on duty as far as I'm concerned. You've done them a favour.'

'Good.' George put his pint glass on the bar. 'I'm very fond of policemen.' Jacko gave him a questioning look which he obviously sensed. 'You find that hard to believe, don't you?'

He drew himself erect, shoulders back, on his soap box. 'You see, a long time ago, forty years almost, when I was fifteen, a policeman was very, very kind to me. I've never forgotten him. I was packed off to this residential school in North Wales. Hated it, I did. Apart from pining for home, they ran a strict ship. I had a bit of sight left, just a bit, and I ran away.' He smiled to himself at the memory.

'I had enough money to get to Crewe on a bus but not enough for the train home or to eat. I was wandering about in the pouring rain, penniless. Lord, was I scared. This bobby on the beat found me. Kindness itself, he was. He took me to his station, dried me off, shared his grub with me. He let me phone a neighbour and speak to my mum. He stayed with me, long after his shift was up, until they collected me from school. He gave me a ten bob note out of his own pocket and he told me that any kid with my problem who could find his way that far was bound to find his way in life. "The biggest crime in life is giving up." He told me that. Never forgotten it or him. Never will.'

Caroline sniffed and Jacko bit his lip.

'So don't misundertand the speeches I make. Every time I hear about policemen being heavy-handed, I ask myself, "How would that bobby at Crewe have handled it?" He's my yardstick. You have a lot to live up to.'

They parted with handshakes (George added, 'See ya') soon afterwards because, as Jacko told Caroline, there wasn't a lot to say after that, was there?

14

With two armfuls of files, Jacko retreated to the archives' quiet room, set aside for reading documents. He speed-read the trial transcripts, dipping in here and there, to cross-check Fixter's memory, decided it was vividly accurate and sped on.

He concentrated on the Keeling report, noting the addresses where Lance and his mother lived together and Harry Morris lived apart from them.

He studied Harry's indignant denials. 'I didn't set foot in the park. I knew nothing about the girl's death until the CID called. We had no discussion about it at home. How could we when I knew nothing about it? Our only discussion was at the police station after he broke down. I told him to tell the truth because he needs treatment. He's a sick boy.'

Morris was without an alibi for the time Katie Burrows died. He claimed to have driven round to his mother's but she wasn't in. Jacko flicked to the mother's statement.

Harry was a dutiful son, she said, who often popped round for an hour on a Saturday. Three Saturdays before, however, they had argued.

'I mentioned I thought Rita ought to loosen the apron strings on Lance. She treats him like a small child. Harry flared up and said I didn't understand the problems they were having with him. He told me it was none of my business and stormed out. He'd never spoken to me like that before.'

The following two Saturdays she expected him round, thinking the row would have blown over. He didn't come. On the third Saturday, she popped to a neighbour's for five minutes. She thought to herself, Why bother to stay in if he can't be bothered to come round?

So she was out when he claimed to have called. 'But he

must have called. Otherwise, how could he know I was out?'

Good question and Jacko pondered it. They could, of course, have primed each other but then, again, sometimes the most genuine alibi of all is not having one.

He looked at photos of the deserted death scene, the park lake with a crack willow at the water's edge, tranquil and colourful enough for a glossy calendar, and the death mask of Katie Burrows, taken in the infirmary mortuary. Her eyes were closed tightly. Her mouth hung slightly open. Her young face was grotesquely distorted with shocked disbelief, as if she was asking him, Why me? He shook his head, as if replying, I don't know, darling, but there's only one way of finding out; the basic way: read, question, listen, think.

He browsed through Keeling's review of the pathologist's and forensic findings. *The victim was found lying on her back on the grass at the edge of the lake. Her head was in the water, face up. The scene had been heavily trampled by the boys who recovered her. No identifiable footprints could be isolated. Her head had been immersed in the shallow water by means of hands placed each side of the neck. The bruising indicated the right-hand grip predominated. As both Frost and Morris are right-handed this detail is of no help in establishing which of the two was responsible.*

He read on and found himself agreeing with Keeling's cumbersome conclusion: *Notwithstanding the fact that Harry Morris is unalibi-ed at the crucial time, without an admission from him and scientific evidence against him, a charge is insupportable.*

He flipped through the Chief Constable's mollifying letters to complaining MPs and Katie's family with half-hearted curiosity which was left somehow unsatisfied, and he sat for several thoughtful seconds working out why.

Then he walked back to the library counter. 'This is all?' The clerk, a fussily efficient woman, nodded, not fully following. 'You see, there was a check run on Lance just before Christmas. I can't find it.'

'Oh.' An understanding beam. 'That will be in the active log.' She disappeared behind a bank of grey filing cabinets and came back with a single sheet of paper which she turned towards him.

It was headed with a cross-reference to the files he had just

120

examined with columns for date, a code for the type of crime, nature of inquiry, the originating force or division and initiating officer.

There were two entries on the log. The first mid-December. The code was R for rape. SM stood for the South Midlands force. The inquiry was to establish Lance's movements. The initiating officer was D/Sgt Edge D., Fixter's sidekick, who recorded, *Eliminated*.

The second entry was dated 2 January with a code for an indecent assault on a female on Western Division. Again *Eliminated* had been recorded.

He read it three times – in puzzlement, then astonishment and finally wonderment.

He turned and walked away, a bounce in his step, getting somewhere, going places. He looked down, smiling, at the final entry made on the day after Davis's last drink with Chrissy and six days before he died, re-reading it again and again as he walked the carpeted corridors to Scott's office.

The initiating officer: D/C Udden, J.

Caroline Parker was dispatched from the incident room when the desk sergeant rang up to say suspended Detective Constable John Udden was in the front office.

'Dazzle him, darling.' Jacko blew her a kiss and she practised an over-the-shoulder pout as she sashayed away from him, trailing a fragrance all the more sexy by its faintness. What a woman, he thought. He had put the idea to her with trepidation and she had been cross but only because he'd doubted her commitment. 'I want the truth as much as you,' she'd snapped.

She tucked her white open-necked shirt tightly into her black skirt as she descended the stairs. She led the way back, allowing Udden an eye-level view of her flexibly firm buttocks. 'He won't be long,' she said in the Deputy's office.

'What's he want?' Udden appraised her bird-like features, cautious.

'Just to pick your brains.' She slid left leg over right knee, smiling primly as she tugged on the hem of her skirt.

She ran her eyes over him. Blood-red slip-ons, white socks

('Never trust a man in white socks,' her mother had said before she knew about her sexual preferences), light fawn slacks, multi-coloured shirt, battered brown bomber jacket with cuffs rolled up to reveal a fake Cartier wrist-watch, announcing to the world, Look at me – I've been out east. Plonker, she thought.

She gave him her sweetest smile. 'Keeping occupied?'

'Job-hunting.'

'Will it come to that?' Brown eyes concerned.

'You tell me.'

'I'm just the office girl on this job.' A dejected shrug, put upon. 'My chief hogs everything.' Jacko and Scott, listening in over earphones in the incident room, grinned at each other across a desk.

'Weren't you on my spot of bother?'

'Out of the office that night, thank God.'

Ambiguity missed, he answered the original question. 'There's an outside chance but I'll be OK.'

'Good.' Very sincere.

They told each other how long they had been on the force, Caroline conjuring up a boring, admin-bound CV. 'Just a general dogsbody. Still, I'm off next week, skiing. Never been before.'

She listened as he told of the places he'd skied and the sports shops he patronized for bargain price equipment. 'I'll introduce you.'

'Would you?' She uncrossed her legs. 'I'll hurry up the LFM.' A puzzled look. 'Chief Superintendent Scott. We call him the Little Fat Man.' She switched off any trace of a smile and so did the listening Scott, to Jacko's undisguised delight. 'He's not in your sort of shape.'

'No rush.' He rubbed his back on the padded rest of the chair. 'Afterwards, a bite, perhaps?'

'Lunch duty.' Downcast.

'No, after you've looked at some ski stuff. I can get you cost price.'

'Really? The trouble with being stuck on admin is that I never make contacts like that.'

He casually cited a travel agent and three clothes shops that would 'do a deal' and three eating places, including Golden Jim's casino.

'I've never set foot inside one,' said Caroline, genuinely honest.

A world-weary sigh. 'I get up quite regularly.' Not with her, you won't, thought Jacko, acidly. 'I do a bit of moonlighting there which might lead to a permanency if . . .' A shadow passed across his face.

'Good thinking. I had to type up a report for the BOF.' Another questioning look. 'Chief Inspector Jackson, the Boring Old Fart.' She pulled an unimpressed face and so did Jacko; Scott clamped the earphones tighter while his head rocked in suppressed laughter. 'Terry Davis seemed to be doing well out of it.'

'Not half.'

'But . . .' A pause, ponderous. 'His work there seemed more humdrum than mine.'

The Little Fat Man and the Boring Old Fart looked away from each other, concentrating now.

'Oh, well.' Udden replied hurriedly, not thinking, walking blindly into the trap. 'You've got to have your potboilers but he did some pretty interesting stuff, too.' She arched an eyebrow. 'He was on those dog-fighters and the Frost case for the defence. He was still busy on that.' A pause. 'Poking around.' Salacious smiles

The link, the firm link and a thrill charged through Jacko. He nodded to Scott who removed his head-set and got up from the desk they were sharing.

'. . . and the beauty of it is you don't have to take orders from the likes of . . .' Udden was still talking when Scott walked in.

Caroline sat straight, in awe of Scott. Udden slouched lower in his chair, indifferent.

'There's a bit of background you might be able to help us with.' Scott laid a file on the desk, which he sat behind.

Udden drew himself up, playing to his gallery. 'Shouldn't you be cautioning me?'

Scott looked baffled. 'It's only a witness statement, top wack.' He relented. 'Still, if you insist . . .' He spoke the words of the formal caution with a hand resting on the cream phone. 'You can call your solicitor.'

Udden hesitated. 'What's it about?'

Scott withdrew his hand and opened the file. 'The Katie

123

Burrows case.' A puzzled silence. Astonishing, thought Jacko, still listening in, how people remember the names of the killers, seldom their victims. 'The girl in the park; the green bicycle job.'

'Before my time on CID.'

'I appreciate that. The file's still open because it was never resolved. We keep tabs on Frost for obvious reasons. For instance, we ran the rule over him on a South Midlands rape at the end of last year but he was in the clear.' Udden, alerted, was listening intently. 'I see you checked him on January the second. What was that about?'

'Just a routine query after an indecency.'

'Who initiated it?'

'Mr Fixter.'

A headshake, slow, positive. 'Not according to him. We've checked with him and the files.'

He looked at Caroline who wet a thumb and flicked through her notebook to the page she needed. 'The case file you quoted indicates an indecent assault on a woman walking through a park. Her assailant was arrested next day. This case was solved before you made that query.'

Udden looked, desperate, from one to the other. 'What's this about?'

'We think it could be about your old friend Terry Davis.' Udden lent back. His jaw, his vulnerable spot, sagged, a giveaway. 'Was it?'

He lowered his head. A long silence. His eyes came up but not his jaw. 'What's in it for me?'

'How do you mean?'

Silence. Then, 'I help you. You help me.'

Scott folded his hands on the desk, as if undecided. Udden grew bolder, chin up. 'I've got a fighting chance on the James ABH. I'm pleading self-defence, reasonable force. I might get it down to common assault. It's not a jail job. It's dismissal but I have other plans.'

'That's a fair assessment.' Scott nodded agreement.

'But if that planting evidence charge goes against me I'm looking at two years.'

'True.'

'So . . .' He looked from Scott to Caroline and back again.

'You somehow lose that dope business and I'll help you all I can. I could be useful.'

'A deal, you mean?'

Udden shrugged. Scott lent forward. 'OK, we'll do you a deal. You assist us and we won't charge you . . .' He stopped, agonizingly, looking into space for the right words. '. . . under Section Two of the Official Secrets Act, the particulars being that on or about January the second this year you disclosed information to one Terence Davis, he not being a person authorized to be in possession of such information, from our intelligence records. How's that, Miss Parker?'

'About right, sir.'

'Balls.' Udden shouted it. 'You've no fucking evidence.'

'Oh, I don't know. We've got evidence of your relationship with Davis. Under caution, you have falsely blamed an inspector for originating an inquiry you can't explain. What do you think, Sarge?'

Caroline fingered her nose, thoughtful. 'It's not cast-iron but alongside the James conspiracy it makes a strong case. His defence would seek to split the indictment but I think we could resist on the grounds that both individual cases show a common course of criminality.'

'How long if we make it stick? Four?' Scott strummed the desk, impatient.

'Precedent suggests six, sir.'

He glared at Udden. 'Think of the headlines. "DC on Spy Charge." No sinecure jobs after that with Golden Jim.' He paused, letting it register. 'It's up to you.'

Silence, suspenseful, a minute at least. His Achilles jaw sank to his chest. 'OK.'

Udden had been closer to Terry Davis than he'd ever dared to admit. 'I'd have dropped myself right in it if I'd told the truth.'

Scott nodded. Off-duty associations with ex-members of the force who had left on disciplinary grounds were actively discouraged.

They had paid for that trip out east before Davis's enforced resignation. 'I couldn't cancel without losing a bomb. The travel docs and my bank statement will back that. I couldn't go all the way with him to Kuta and then drop him when I got back. He'd been a good mate for years.'

Yes, he knew about Chrissy Fixter. 'He told me he was giving her one. I stayed out of it. I didn't tell a soul. There was no way I was going to tell Mr Fixter. I wanted to stay in CID. It would have been like you telling the Chief Constable that your mate Jackson was screwing his wife. Can you imagine that?'

With difficulty, the eavesdropping Jacko conceded, but then Udden clearly hadn't seen the Chief Constable's wife.

Yes, he knew that Davis had been hired by Lance Frost's defence lawyers. 'He didn't say why. On the QT, I tipped off Sergeant Edge. He didn't seem bothered. He thought Terry was helping to get Frost's medical antecedents together.'

Yes, he said, squirming, he'd been the source of Davis's information from the national vehicle computer which led to the dog-fight gang. 'He said he was going undercover and, if anything came of it, he'd share it with me. Honest to God, I never got a penny. All I wanted was info. He claimed to have an informant close to getting the time and venue of a fight. My idea was to pass it on to Mr Fixter so we could do a bust. It would have been a feather in my cap.'

And, yes, he admitted, Davis did approach him for the new address of the Frost family. 'I played snooker with him on New Year's Day. He said he wanted to get in touch with them again. He'd been round to their old home but they'd moved. Could I help? I said I wanted a result on the dog-fighting first. He said it could break at any time but Frost was more important.'

'Why?' Udden had asked in the bar at the Gold Spot as players circled the tables below them.

'I know what happened in the park and I think I can prove it,' said Davis, nursing a gin and slimline.

'Does it matter? We can't charge him with the same offence.'

'It would get those leftie MPs off Mike Fixter's back,' Davis answered, obliquely.

Udden knew the case still troubled his inspector. Next day he used the sex incident as a cover to get the addresses from force intelligence.

'Addresses?' Scott queried, urgently.

'Lance and his mum's and Harry Morris's. They've split.'

He phoned the details to Davis at his home and they arranged to meet the following Tuesday for snooker.

'By then the dog-fighters had been plastered over the paper. I was seriously upset. He said someone had blown the operation. I was getting bad vibes. I thought he was stringing me along.'

They talked about the Frosts. 'He said contact had been made and it was going well. He expected to have something for me within the week. I still don't know whether to believe him. I half think he was bull-shitting me. Looking back I think he was full of crap, just using me.'

Udden left the Gold Spot after one soft drink and joined Fixter and his crowd at the Royal Mail. 'Davis said he had half an hour to kill and hung on. Honestly he didn't say who or where.'

An hour later Udden was in the car-park with Fixter and the rest after Mrs Marshall had raised the alarm. 'I stayed with him at the infirmary until they lost him.' Slower now, struggling. 'It was an awful sight. His Adam's apple was hanging out. I had to go through his clothing. Christ, what a mess.' He dried up.

Scott prompted him. 'Tell us again what you found.'

'No money. That's why I pegged it as a mugging. He had forty or fifty on him when he bought the drinks at the Gold Spot. I saw it.'

'Wouldn't a mugger have taken the credit cards, too?'

'I thought the attacker had been disturbed and had to make a quick getaway.'

'What about his notebook?'

'It wasn't on him. I wouldn't destroy evidence.'

'Do you suspect there might have been anything in the notebook that could have incriminated you?'

'Now, look.' Udden was regaining his composure.

'It's got to be faced.'

Udden faced it, brow furrowed. 'My name and address could have been in it. And the addresses I'd given him of the two dog-fighters and the Frosts and Morris. That's all.' His thoughts progressed to a conclusion that snapped his head upright. 'Surely, you don't think I killed him?'

Scott watched him, unremitting. 'You did have a motive.'

'But no opportunity, sir. I wanted to tell Mr Fixter all of this on the night. But how could I? It was more than my job was worth.'

Now his future was worthless, thought Jacko. A sharp stab of pity, just as quickly blunted. This was the man prepared to swear he'd found drugs on an honest, innocent kid. He's worthless.

Scott went over and over it, again and again, a pitiless savaging. And Udden did what Leroy James had never done. He started to beg. 'Why won't you believe me?'

'Why should I, you little shit?' Scott went over it one more time.

'How did we do?' he asked Jacko, when he strolled back into the incident room.

'I was going to give Caroline ten out of ten but she called me a boring old fart.'

Caroline looked down in faked penance. 'She's quite right, of course,' said Scott.

Jacko looked at Caroline; a long look, eyes running over her, admiring her. Worth twenty out of ten, he conceded but only to himself. That was some performance for a dyke.

15

'She'd been some mother,' Caroline said, as Jacko drove, stopping and starting, down the bustling main road that runs through Leicester's Asia Minor.

'Best dressed little boy down the street ... And the best behaved.' Head down, she was quoting from a thick background file which four of their team had meticulously compiled.

Rita Johnson was pregnant when she married Bryan Frost; her stomach heavy when she moved into a terrace on the council estate. They didn't fly his body home when he died in the Kuwait oilfields where he worked.

Rita got a job within weeks of Lance starting school. She worked outdoors, all weathers, hoeing and pruning in nursery beds, shouldering plastic bags of fertilizer on delivery runs. 'Only a slip of a thing but as tough as old boots,' her foreman had said.

Caroline turned a page in the file resting on her knee. Widowed Mrs Frost met Harry Morris at the garden centre where he sometimes called to collect the rustic poles and fencing his employers, the National Coal Board, bought to pretty up approach roads to pits. 'Early thirties then, fifteen years younger than her; an average, likeable chap. From what the team can gather he'd never had a steady woman before. They just upped and married one Saturday at the register office with Lance as witness. On the Monday both were back at work.'

She looked up. 'Pull in after the lights.' Jacko did as he was told. He was used to doing what he was told by Caroline these days. She unbuckled her belt, got out, went into a newsagent's, then a florist's shop with spring flowers, all colours, fresh and dazzlingly beautiful, spilling out on to stalls on the pavement.

She came out with a big bunch of red tulips which she carefully placed on the back seat.

'Your turn for sweet talk today, Jacko.' The journey resumed, soon picking up speed on the dual carriageway.

Lance was still called Frost and neighbours never got used to calling Rita Mrs Morris. They noticed a change in her soon after the marriage. She'd never done much more than pass the time of day. Suddenly she was often rude or seldom spoke. She transferred from weekday to weekend work. Some thought she no longer needed a big wage with a hubby to support her. Others thought she was grieving over the death of her mother who'd been very close.

'Obviously,' said Caroline, skipping a few pages, 'none of them knew the truth – i.e. that Lance had been caught flashing in front of that nurse within two months of his mum's marriage.'

Lance, confined to camp, put on a spurt in his final year at school and got better grades than his teachers had expected. Neighbours were less surprised than his teachers. Caroline quoted one: 'The older he got, the stricter she became. He had no pals. Hardly ever allowed out. Homework, homework. All he ever did. If he did go for a bike ride, his mum waited for him at the garden gate.'

Hoping, no doubt, thought Jacko, that he didn't return with his bone in his hand and a police dog in panting pursuit.

At a big roundabout they left the dual carriageway, following the signs to Melton Mowbray through several villages.

Katie's murder and Lance's quick arrest stunned the estate. When the shock subsided, the gossip began. 'Always such a loner . . .' 'She was becoming a little madam . . .' 'Never had a proper father . . .' 'She was always glad-eyeing boys . . .' 'The way he used to stare made my flesh creep . . .'

'Know the sort of thing?' asked Caroline, looking up.

Jacko nodded. He knew. Tittle-tattle; worthless. A few pages were skipped.

Rita left her job soon after Lance's first court appearance. Every weekend she and Harry visited him in the remand wing. 'A model prisoner,' reported an assistant governor. 'Volunteered to work in the kitchens. Excellent at pastries. Played pool and darts, not very well, but he mixed. Never displayed any sexual misbehaviour or aggression.'

Because, Jacko suspected, there were no young girls in jail to excite him.

Over the page with wettened thumb. A second shock engulfed the estate with his acquittal and the publicity that surrounded it, particularly Jason French's piece. The collator had dissected it line by line. Beneath the headline was a big photo of mother and son, cheek to cheek, smiling. At the bottom of the page was a single column photo of Katie Burrows, in bridesmaid's dress. *Victim*, it said underneath. Alongside, a similar-sized photo of Harry Morris, carnation in his lapel, cropped from his own wedding photo. *Accused*, it said below.

All the quotes, apart from two sentences, came from Rita, intermingled with details from the court proceedings. She talked, gushed, really, Mills and Boon style, about her nightmare months, her love for both Lance and Harry and of how she was torn between the two. 'I still cannot believe what Lance has said about my husband. To me he is a gentle caring man without an ounce of evil in him. I tell myself that Lance must be mistaken; that it is all a bad dream from which we will soon awake.' Do people actually talk like that? Jacko asked himself

There was only one quote from Lance. 'I have had my say in court. Now I just want to get on with my life.' There were no quotes from Harry and no up-to-date photo of him. 'French said over dinner in the Grand that he was miffed,' Jacko recalled. 'So miffed, by the sound of it, that he refused co-operation altogether.'

Caroline nodded and read on. 'Neighbours only saw him once more when he collected his clothes and tools and drove off in his old VW. And workmates only saw him when he collected his reduno cheque. He didn't buy them a farewell drink.' He stayed a month with his mother until he found a job and digs in West Bridgford on the south side of Nottingham.

Lance and Rita returned home on the Sunday French's paper ran his piece. She never went back to work and ventured out only to shop. Lance was seen out and about on his bike. He told one inquisitive youth he planned to join the army. 'Didn't seem as if he had a care in the world.'

It was all too much for some neighbours. They circulated a

131

petition asking the council to evict them. 'It isn't safe for our daughters to go out,' a delegation told their ward representative. He went to see Rita who accepted a council house exchange.

Within a couple of months they had moved to Melton, a peaceful place, a town with a feudal feel, hunting capital of a hunting county.

They settled in on a sixties estate. Lance had gone to a new college to complete his catering course. They'd adopted the name of Vinter. No one locally knew of their past.

Caroline closed the file on her knee and they travelled in companionable silence, each lost in their own thoughts, until a roadside sign appeared, announcing they had reached their destination.

Jacko was carrying a picture in his mind. Of Katie Burrows. Not the photo of her as a bridesmaid in taffeta, little lace gloves and a floral headband which the paper had carried, but her death mask with that haunting question on her lips. Why me? Be patient, darling.

Feeling as if he were visiting the sick, he pushed the bunch of flowers into unreceptive hands as soon as she opened the door. 'Police. May we come in?' He didn't wait for an answer, sliding, crab-fashion, in front of her. She involuntarily opened the door wider to admit Caroline in her white mac.

She stood, nonplussed, in the hallway, clutching the flowers by their stems, buds pointing at Jacko's midriff.

'It's just a routine matter.'

'What's the idea of . . . ?' She clamped the tulips to her flat chest.

'We thought we'd make out we're family friends.' A scowl, his opening gambit not working yet. 'Don't want the neighbours talking, do we?' A curt nod, a slight breakthrough. 'It's just a loose end.'

The scowl returned. A setback. 'We don't want to discuss it any more. We don't have to and . . .'

'Oh.' A light laugh, brittle, anxious. 'It's nothing to do with Lance. It's you we've come to see.'

She shut the door and clicked on the latch. Caroline pointed at the flowers. 'Perhaps they ought to go in water.'

132

Mrs Vinter (aka Mrs Morris, Mrs Frost and the former Miss Johnson) turned, holding the flowers upright. Jacko followed her through the hall, eyes on down-at-heel flat shoes. A few steps, slovenly steps. Good old George.

A tall, thin figure ducked from behind the lounge door. When they reached the room, Lance was bent over the TV set turning down the sound on a matinée western.

'Hi,' said Jacko, very chummy. Lance gave a shy nod as he straightened and backed across the bronze-coloured carpet into a square armchair.

Rita put the flowers on a table, its polish dulled. 'Sorry to disturb you,' said Caroline. Both visitors stood, making no move to take off their raincoats.

Jacko looked at the TV screen. 'Good film?'

'Seen it before,' said Lance, quite pleasant. 'Sit down.' They sat on a couch, quickly. In, thought Jacko, relieved, we're in, off and running.

Rita, a blue dress buttoned at her flat chest, hovered above them, hostility on her small face, worn and lined, a grannie's face. Whatever Harry, her toy boy, had seen in her, it certainly wasn't beauty, Jacko thought.

He craned towards her. With so many names to pick from he'd decided to play safe and call her by none, certainly not Rita. 'I'm Inspector Jackson and this is Sergeant Parker. We're on the Terry Davis case.'

'I fail to see . . . You see . . .' A stammer, off guard. 'What's that got to do with me?'

'Probably nothing.' An exhausted sigh. 'We're having to call on everyone he worked for – sporting clubs where he did security, the paper he did a bit of freelancing for.' A pause. 'Everybody.' Another pause. 'And he did work for you.'

'That was a year ago.'

'Ten months.' Jacko corrected her with a cheery smile. 'Seen him since?' She shook her head. 'Heard from him, then?' He inclined his head towards the hall where a phone stood on a stand beneath coats on wall pegs. Another shake.

'Still.' A shrug, easygoing. 'It's possible you can help.'

'About what?' She remained on her feet, determined, it seemed, not to sit, to make them feel unwelcome.

'You know about his death?'

133

'Only what I read in the papers.'

'And you can't always believe them.' A little laugh, harmless, merry, and Caroline thought she detected the slightest of smiles on Lance's face, unshaven, ginger stubble a shade lighter than crew-cut hair.

'In what way?' Rita rephrased her question, insistent, wanting it over, wanting them out, making no secret of it.

'He had a few enemies . . .'

'I find that hard to believe.' A schoolmistress's tone, clear, firm. 'I found him a very nice man.' Relaxing a bit. 'Anyway, I thought the paper said he was the victim of a mugger.' At last, she sat down on a chair by the table.

'Well, he certainly made a lot of enemies debt-collecting and on a dog-fighting case he worked on with Jason French, the journalist.' A slight start, hardly noticeable. 'I gather you know Mr French?'

He looked away to Lance, lounging back now, a hand scratching a knee of his dark jeans. 'Nothing to do with your case but Terry was in a dicey line of business. We can't assume it was a mugger, can we?' An understanding headshake.

'It's a pity', said Rita, tartly, 'that you didn't take as much care with Lance's case.'

'Sorry?' Head cocked, encouraging more.

'You wrongfully arrested him. Held him for seven months. We're forced out of our home. Haven't you read about us?'

'Only in passing.' Very casual. 'We're solely on the Terry Davis case.'

She lent forward. 'On top of that, we're still being hounded. A chief inspector questioned us for days even when the trial was over, trying to get us to confirm our evidence; then a sergeant trying to blame him for a rape in a town he's never been to. It's getting too much.'

'Mind if I take this off?' Caroline rose suddenly. 'I'll pop it in the hall.' She was pulling her raincoat from her shoulders as she walked towards the door, stopping to collect Jacko's Bogart mac.

Rita was caught in agitated indecision, unable to make up her mind whether to go with her or keep watch over Lance. Jacko made it up for her, addressing her son. 'Settling down?'

'It's OK.' An uncertain face.

134

'Got a job?'

Rita broke in, a whining voice. 'And no one has the courtesy to explain or apologize.'

When Caroline returned, Girl Guide badge on view in her jacket lapel, Jacko had his book out, noting the name of Sergeant Edge who had quizzed Lance about the South Midlands rape. 'I'll have a word with him. Now, can we get back to Terry Davis? According to his records, you saw him on and off between March and May of last year?'

'On and off.' She was giving nothing.

'How did you meet him?'

'How do you mean?'

'Did your solicitor engage him or did you pick him out of Yellow Pages, get a personal recommendation or what?'

'I don't see how that helps.' A holding answer, playing for time.

'It helps us to establish how he found work and then maybe we can trace other clients.'

'Personal recommendation.'

'From whom?'

'Oh, no.' A firm headshake. 'We're not involving other people.'

A peacemaker's shrug. 'Over those two months, how did he seem? Did he express any fears for his safety? Talk about any enemies?'

'Never.'

'How did he get on with Jason French? Were they buddies or what?'

'What are you getting at?' Scowling again, on guard.

'It's known as cross-checking.' Jacko spoke with emphasized patience. 'Mr French was in town on the night he died. He was only five minutes' walk away.'

'Is he a suspect?'

'Everyone within five minutes' walk has to be eliminated.'

Rita laughed, without mirth, ugly. She tilted her small, thin body back, lifting the balls of her feet so that only her worn heels remained on the flowered carpet, manual worker's hands on her knees. 'That's one you can't blame on him.' Lance laughed, just as harshly, sticking out his long legs, stuffing his white hands deep into the pockets of his jeans.

Jacko smiled weakly. 'I was coming to that. It's routine to ask everyone who knew him where they were when . . .'

'In.' Loud, triumphant.

'Watching *The Graduate*', said Lance, smiling.

'Some looker, Anne Bancroft,' said Jacko, just testing.

'I fancy Katharine Ross myself.' A cunning smile now, a smart-arse's.

Rita watched them, uneasy. Caroline's eyes found the black video machine beneath the TV set.

'You've got remarkable memories,' said Jacko, evenly. 'Most people have to sit and ponder to remember where they were almost three months ago.'

'Not if they'd been through our ordeal.' Anger. No, more, torture, in Rita's face. 'You learn. When I read about Terry in the *Mercury*, I knew you'd be round. I'm not as daft as I look.'

Jacko met her gaze. 'I don't think you're daft at all.'

His eyes broke away to the western on TV where Van Heflin was catching the three-ten to Yuma. The room joined the screen in silence. Caroline eyed the silver carriage clock on top of a brick fireplace that housed flickering gas-fired logs, but failed to locate any ashtrays.

'Great film this, Lance,' said Jacko, enthusiastically. 'Ranks with *Gunfight at OK Corral* and *High Noon*. Go to the cinema much?'

'Not here. When I was in Leicester, quite a bit.' Rita was watching over him, the lioness Fixter had spotted in her, about to defend her young.

'What do you like?'

'Most things.'

'Not sex and violence,' she pounced. 'Not horror films if that's what you're getting at.'

Jacko ignored her. 'Detectives?'

'*Dirty Harry*, I suppose. Seen all of his.'

'Good, that scene where he gets the pyscho in the sports stadium.'

'Yer. He had it coming, didn't he?' His satisfied, delighted look disturbed Jacko.

Caroline took a full packet of cigarettes from her shoulder bag and lent across Jacko to offer them towards Rita. She fiddled with leathery hands to free one. Jacko, thinking through a new

136

question-line, absent-mindedly helped himself as Caroline's hand passed his chest. She offered the packet towards Lance, who shook his head. She took one herself.

Rita stood, went into the kitchen and returned with a glass ashtray and a yellow lighter. She put the tray on the arm of the settee and drew her chair closer to share it. With her left thumb, she flicked the lighter wheel down three times before yellow and blue flames spurted, offering it to Jacko ahead of Caroline. He nodded as smoke tickled his throat, his first cigarette in months.

He swapped critiques with Lance on paperback books standing on a sideboard, thrillers mainly, a few James Herberts, nothing that matched anything on Terry Davis's shelf.

Lance, losing interest, dug his hand deep into his right trouser pocket and he seemed to sooth an itch at his groin with unseen fingertips. He withdrew his hand when he saw Jacko staring.

Oh, dear Fixter and that nurse, thought Jacko, a wave of excitement surging within him. His head was light from his first shot of nicotine for a long time. A thrill, overpowering, swept downwards to his intestines, clamouring dementedly for release.

He put his cigarette in the tray and stood. 'Mind if I use your loo?' Caroline looked up in surprise and Lance in a sort of sympathy, understanding, certainly. 'Top of the stairs on the right.'

He took them, two at a time, quickly, lightly, a man with a mission, in a hurry. He locked the door of the bathroom, half-tiled and white. He lifted the lid of the toilet, heavy-handed, so that it banged noisily on the pot casing. Then, three quick paces to the hand basin, on with the cold tap, a half-turn to face himself in the cabinet mirror. He eased the twin doors open noiselessly. His tense face vanished.

On the top shelf, alongside a crêpe bandage and an unopened tin of smoker's toothpaste, he found what he sought and he felt a pang of disappointment. The well-squeezed tube was not the shape or colour of the sample George had examined. It had a blue band running round it. He turned to the label. Among the list of complaints for which the antiseptic offered relief: Sweat rash. He had to squint to read the small print. Two of the ingredients were the same as in the ointment George had identified.

He shut the doors as quietly as he had opened them. The excitement still surging through him forced him back to the toilet where he unzipped his grey trousers. He stood, feet apart. A quick squirt only, little more than a dribble. Oh, sweet George. The relief. Such relief.

He zipped up and pressed the flush. Back to the sink, normal strides now, and held his hands under the running water, then dried them on a towel hanging over the side of the bath. He went down the stairs, forcing himself to slow down, trying not to run.

He sat and picked up his cigarette, tapping off half an inch of ash before putting it back to his mouth, inhaling deeply, enjoying it, needing it.

'Now.' Businesslike, turning to Rita. 'You noticed no animosity between Mr French and Mr Davis?'

'No.' She lent forward to flick ash into the shared tray.

'Was it your idea to get in touch with the paper or Terry's?'

'His. He thought we might recoup some of the money we lost. I had to give up my job, you know.'

'Was it worth while?' A neutral smile, fishing.

'We've no complaints, have we, Lance?' They traded secret smiles.

Jacko asked how often they had seen each other. Half a dozen times at her former home, she said, relaxed now, calm, twice on prison visits to Lance and for a couple of days in a hotel after the trial.

'When did you see him again?'

'I've already told you. We didn't.' On edge again.

'So how did you settle up?'

'We were legally aided. Our solicitor settled all the bills.'

'What about payment for the newspaper article?'

'All arrangements over that were settled at the hotel.' She's clever, Jacko acknowledged. Stir her up. 'We can't find any evidence in his records that he shared his payment from the paper with you.'

'This is none of your business.' Hard words, quickly softened. 'We're more than satisfied with the outcome.'

Another thrust, keeping up the pressure. 'How did your husband get on with Terry?'

'I don't follow.'

'Well, you two seem to have got on well with Terry. How about Harry?' A clouded face, a storm brewing. 'We'd like to chat to him. When will he be in?'

'Can't help you about that.'

'We can always pop back.'

'Don't you dare.' The storm broke. 'Don't you *dare*.' She raised her shoulders, shortened her scrawny neck, swayed forward. Lance sat up, alarmed. 'You're here under false pretences. You're checking up on us.'

'We're checking up on the late Terry Davis.' His calmness, laid-back almost, only fuelled her anger.

'You're using his death to get back at us. You won't admit defeat, will you? You, Fixter, Keeling. You're all the same.'

'I've not mentioned the Katie Burrows case.'

'It's there, isn't it? Always there.'

'Well.' Shrugging, unruffled. 'Technically, it's unsolved.'

'Exactly. And that's why you're here. That's the real reason, isn't it?' Her fists were clenched tightly on her knees.

'Oh, Mum.' Lance spoke like a reprimanded child trying to appease an enraged parent. 'They're only doing their jobs.'

Rita unclenched her left hand and raised a finger at him. 'What did Terry say? What were his last words? "It's all over. You don't have to speak to anyone, if you don't want to."' She rounded on Jacko, bristling, voice raised. 'And we don't want to.'

Jacko needled her still. 'Lance doesn't seem to mind. He's over eighteen. He's got a vote and he's got a right . . .'

'Don't.' She repeated the word, almost shouting it. '*Don't* you come into my home lecturing me. What about our rights?'

'We have every right to speak to Mr Morris if . . .'

'Then make your own arrangements. What he does is up to him. As far as we're concerned you must get in touch with Mr Hoyle in future.'

She gave Jacko the name and phone number of a law firm. Not the one, he noted, who'd handled the murder charge.

She stood. 'And now we have friends due and, as you said when you came in . . .'

'There are a few more . . .'

'Then see Mr Hoyle.'

'But . . .'

139

'Have you a warrant?'

'This is just supposed to be a friendly chat.'

'Then I must ask you to leave.'

Jacko and Caroline rose, she following Rita into the hall to collect the raincoats. Jacko turned at the door. 'Thanks.' Lance, white-faced, nodded, blinking rapidly, worried, frightened even, by his mother's outburst.

Rita opened the street door, temper finally in check. 'I'm sorry we can't be more helpful but we've had enough.'

'That's all right.' He passed in front of her, following Caroline out. 'We'll get to the bottom of it.'

The door was shut in his face.

'Some sweet-talking guy you are,' said Caroline, handing him his coat. Jacko said nothing, playing it all back, trying to work it out. To his simple layman's mind, Rita had seemed almost pottier than her potty son.

'Close.' Scott closed the file which told him that voice printing proved Lance Frost made the phone call to Davis's answering machine and George Marshall had positively identified the brand of ointment in his bathroom cabinet. 'Very close.'

Jacko clasped his hands on top of his head, his thinking position. 'Caroline's adamant there was no donkey jacket on the clothes rack, though. Is it worth a warrant?'

Scott looked down on the brown file, pensive. 'What if he's got rid of it? What if he's got rid of the spiked glove he used on him? What if he screams for his new lawyer – and he will – and says nothing?' The very questions a moody Jacko had been asking himself, not getting satisfactory answers. 'What if Mum sticks to the story that they were watching a film?'

He knew the answer to that one. 'She will; bound to, cunning bitch. She's in on it. She probably went with him. She's the slovenly woman.'

'OK. They're lying about having no contact with Davis but they'd explain that in the witness box by saying they panicked when you called. They'd started a new life and wanted to put the past behind them. They phoned Davis because he hadn't paid them their cut from the paper's fee but they never met face to face.' He'd made up his mind. 'No. Prove a meeting.

You need to corroborate George Marshall's testimony. He's not enough on his own. Build your case. Take your time.'

But how? Jacko asked himself. And how much time do I have? He's a child-killer who's killed again to silence a man who knew too much. Who next? His stepdad? His ultra-protective mum? How long before he strikes again?

16

Caroline went prepared to do most of the talking. Jacko had been against it. Lawyers, he said, were more secretive than Freemasons; professional ethics and all that, a waste of time. But she argued that the trick when seeking a solicitor's off-the-record guidance was to detect the signals they were transmitting. As usual, she won.

Clive Seaton was around thirty-five, junior partner at a law firm in New Walk, a delightful part of the city with the restful feel of the finest London square. He had a thick ginger moustache, deep brown eyebrows, very shaggy, and beige hair. The Lord must have been off-colour when he painted him, thought Caroline, looking at him across a paper-strewn desk in his tome-lined office.

She knew, she said, talking quickly, that Terry Davis had done some work for his firm because the invoice was in his files. Used him before the Frost case? A shake. Or after? Another shake.

She dug into her shoulder bag and handed him a copy of Davis's report which detailed his two long interviews with Harry Morris and his mother. 'Two days' work, £140?'

Seaton read it, refreshing his memory. 'That's about the going rate.'

She knew there was no mileage in asking outright why Davis had been checking up on Morris. He'd plead confidentiality, though he no longer represented Lance. 'His sole duty, according to that,' a nod at the invoice in his hand, 'was in connection with Mr Morris. Prison records show that Davis twice visited Lance while he was on remand and his mother confirms that.' Seaton frowned. 'Yet he never billed you for work on those two days. Am I right to assume those prison visits were not made on your instructions?'

He picked his words carefully. 'It would be very rare for a private investigator not to submit an account for commissioned assignments. They're not charity workers.'

She dug into her bag again and produced Jason French's story. 'There's nothing in Davis's records to indicate that your firm was involved in negotiations over this.'

He took the cutting and read it, moustache twitching disapproval. 'Our advice was not sought or given on this matter.'

Caroline moved with caution on to the trial. 'Lance pleaded not guilty to murder and I can well see why. The statement he made to Mr Fixter puts him in the park with Katie Burrows but doesn't admit to putting her head in the water.'

'You've seen the statement.' He was telling her nothing.

'That statement was not contested in cross-examination. You didn't, for example, accuse Mr Fixter of undue pressure or fabricating it.'

'You've seen the transcript.' Still nothing, blood out of a stone.

'Mr Fixter reports that when Lance blamed his stepfather in the witness box his legal representatives seemed a little, well, wrong-footed, shall we say?'

Seaton thought hard, trying to find a formula to help without betraying an ex-client. Finally, a sly smile. 'Shall we say we have no complaints about Mr Fixter? Shall we say that we find Mr Fixter reliable and truthful in every respect?' Find. Caroline noted the present tense.

The only way of tackling the last bit, Caroline decided, was to ramble. 'If I remember my law course, the only possible pleas in a case such as this are . . .' She counted them off on her fingers:

'Guilty, I did it.

'Not guilty to murder but guilty to manslaughter. I didn't mean to seriously harm her but I accept that putting her head in the water was a reckless thing to do.

'Not guilty to everything; it was a tragic accident.

'Not guilty. It wasn't me, guv. She was alive when I left her so someone else must have done it.

'Or . . .' She stuck up her thumb, all four fingers folded, used. 'Not guilty to murder on the grounds of diminished responsibility – i.e. I'm potty.'

Seaton was smiling broadly, won over by her cheek and charm. 'I'm sure you'll also remember from your law course that you need medical reports to run that last defence.' He lifted his shaggy eyebrows. Got it? Caroline had got it.

'Don't you get it?' Caroline asked Jacko, across the desk in the incident room.

'Not really.' A confused face obscured by a cloud of cigarette smoke. One at Rita's and he was back on twenty a day and rising.

'It means his lawyers expected him to say Katie was alive when he left her. That's all. Fingering Harry Morris came as a surprise to them. If Lance had planned to plead an accident, they would have withdrawn from the case because he'd have been telling them one thing and the court another.'

Jacko nodded, still uncertain.

'Also,' Caroline babbled on, 'diminished responsibility was never a runner as a defence. Which means the shrinks found nothing wrong with Lance.' A pause, giving Jacko time to grasp it. 'Which means there's no proof that Lance is mad.'

He groaned. 'One thing's for sure. I'm going mad here.' He picked up a book, which had a forest of marks, torn from newspapers, between its pages. In alphabetical order he had speed-read Davis's shelf from the Black Panther to the Yorkshire Ripper via the Moors Murders in two versions. Dipping into the 'W's he had ground to a halt over *The Last Word* by Auberon Waugh, had gone back to the beginning and slowly read an account of the trial of ex-Liberal leader Jeremy Thorpe.

'This other ex-MP was a major witness and it came out he had a deal with a Sunday paper to double his fee if the verdict was guilty. OK?' Caroline nodded.

He opened the book at a pre-marked page and read slowly. '"In other words he had a direct financial interest in securing a conviction."' He turned to another page. 'A juror interviewed afterwards is quoted as saying: "By this means he was wholly discredited as a credible witness."'

'How does that apply to Lance's trial and acquittal?' Caroline's turn to be puzzled.

'It doesn't. The deal with Jason French was signed after Rita had given evidence. That played no part.' He snapped the book shut. 'But it explains the unsigned contract we found in Davis's files, the one French knew nothing about.'

'How?'

'Say Keeling, in his inquiry after Lance was freed, found some evidence against Harry Morris. A witness who put him in the park. A hair on his donkey jacket that had survived laundering. Say Keeling charged Morris with Katie's murder.'

Caroline nodded, following.

'The plan could have been to leak a copy of that contract. To make sure his defence knew that Rita and/or Lance had a financial interest in securing a conviction. The defence would produce the contract in front of the jury. Their evidence would be discredited. Harry Morris would walk free.'

'You mean' – Caroline was double-checking – 'they were plotting to con the jury to get Harry off if he was ever charged?'

'Yep.' He stubbed out his cigarette, angrily. 'Brilliant, eh? Davis kept the five grand from the paper as payment for arranging Lance's defence. And Harry's. Two separate trials for the same murder. Two acquittals.'

Caroline whistled softly. 'So the unsigned contract was really a failsafe in case Harry was charged. All four – Lance, his mum, his stepdad and Davis – were in on it.' A moment's silence hung heavily. 'So who killed Katie Burrows?'

A slow headshake, bemused, baffled.

Caroline stirred, unhappy. 'I think we ought to make a move. Killing a corrupt ex-cop is one thing but either Lance or Harry murdered a totally innocent girl and is walking about free to tell and sell the tale.'

'For Christsake.' Jacko reacted sharply, out of character in Caroline's company. 'These are devious bastards. If we go blundering in, we'll cock it up again. How's that going to protect innocent girls?'

'Sorry.' A slight blush.

A sigh came out with a whistling sound. 'Don't think I don't worry about it every night.' A forgiving smile. 'Let's forget all the protests of innocence. What do we know about Harry Morris?'

* * *

He parked his dirty white Montego at the end of a long road which Harry Morris walked, regular as the clock on the nearby Trent Bridge pavilion, at five forty-five every weekday evening.

He knew who he was looking for – mid-thirties, appearing older with grey creeping like weed into his black hair, always in white overalls with dust from sanded wood ever-present on his shoes.

He rolled down the window to let out cigarette smoke and studied a coloured photo the team had dug out. Chin too pointed, brown eyes set too deeply, shifty.

Harry had lived down this road for nine months, five minutes' walk from the carpentry shop where he worked. His job was to fit new mahogany doors and strip old ones of paint down to original pine.

This decade, Jacko reflected, may have brought heartache to steelworkers, shipworkers and miners, to inner-city comps and school-leavers and the crew of the *Belgrano* but, by Jesus, these are great days for doors. A twisted smile, cynical almost.

Harry used the firm's van and Jacko had already seen his old yellow VW parked outside Mrs Dodds' when he drove by on a recce.

He had one room and run of the house, turn-of-the-century with Edwardian bays, in West Bridgford, a self-contained town, bedsit land, on the south bank of the River Trent.

The fact that he lived in lodgings told Jacko a lot about Harry Morris. Single men these days rented flats or, better still, bought their own place as an investment. An age that had brought independence to women had forced them to cook, clean, iron and generally fend for themselves, adequately, if not wholly happily. Grown men in lodgings were mummy's boys, in Jacko's experience. Not necessarily chauvinistic, unable to cope. A man too much under a woman's control was a weak man, in his view, a weakness that could be damaging and lead to assaults on the young and helpless, for vengeance, to prove manliness.

He'd been for pulling him in. Caroline had argued against. 'Why alienate him? We got no confession heavying Rita and Lance, did we? String him along. Gain his confidence. Use him as a Trojan horse to penetrate the family's secrets.'

He let the cigarette drop into the gutter when he saw the approach in his mirror of a dark-haired man in green padded windcheater over white overalls.

He wound up the window, got out, slammed the door, turned, timed to perfection. 'Mr Morris?'

'Yes.' He stopped. Dull brown eyes appraised him, deepening, suspicious. 'Who wants to know?'

'Jackson, CID.' Then, matey: 'Howdo.'

'Whatyerwant?' A growl, low, threatening, like his dog at the Co-op milkman.

'It's about Terry Davis. We're talking to everyone who knew him.'

'Talk to Mrs Morris, then. She knows him best.' He half turned as if to start walking again.

'Already have. It's just a chat. Over a pint, if that's convenient?'

Harry turned fully back to face him. 'I know your chats. I had two days of them with your Chief Inspector Keeling. I'm up to here with them.' His right hand came up and he made a slicing motion, palm down, over the top of his dark hair.

'It's not about Katie Burrows.' Morris's face flickered, frightened. 'It's about Terry Davis. How did you get to know him?'

'My solicitor has told me to say nothing.'

'About Katie Burrows, maybe. This is about Davis. If we thought you'd killed Davis, you'd be inside and under caution. I just want a chat.'

'That's what Keeling said. Two days.' Morris gave a V-sign. 'Two days he kept me locked up.'

'I could have pulled you in from work or from your digs. I thought you might have had enough of formalities.'

'Formalities.' His eyes widened. 'For-fucking-malities. My own family betrayed me, helped some scumbag reporter do the dirt on me. I'm put through the hoop for two days. I'm sick up to here' – another slicing motion – 'with formalities.'

He turned and walked away, briskly, shoulders rounded. Jacko kept in step. 'It will be over when we've cleared this one up.' Harry thrust his head forward and down, not listening, cocking a deaf 'un. 'Don't you want to be in the clear?'

He looked round. 'Heard that before. Thanks all the same.' A snort, like a horse blowing. 'I'm in the clear as far as Davis or anyone else is concerned.' He started nodding, repeatedly, rapidly. 'But I'll tell you what. I'm shedding no tears. That bastard was behind it all.'

'Tell me about that, Harry. That's the sort of thing I need. In private, up at the local nick if you don't fancy a pint.'

'Are you arresting me?' He looked straight ahead, walking faster, his face jaundiced, as yellow as his old VW, getting closer with every step.

'No.' Jacko put a hand on his shoulder, part restraining, part comforting.

'Get your grubby hand off me.' He twisted his shoulder, walking all the time.

'Right then, Mr Morris. We'll do it at the station.'

'Not without a warrant, you won't. You want to see me, then fix up an appointment with my solicitor.' He gave him a name, not Seaton's or Lance's new lawyer's. 'I'm saying nothing. I helped in one inquiry. Look where it got me.' He looked sideways.

They walked ten yards in silence. 'Give me half an hour. I'm trying to help you . . .' A dozen yards to the sound of their own fast steps. '. . . to get to the truth.'

Harry slowed, only slightly. 'You didn't get it on Katie Burrows, though. You had her killer and you let him go. A maniac's walking the streets. That's your fault, not mine.'

'And Davis's. Tell me, what part did he play in Lance's defence?'

His yellow face seemed to scab over, inflamed, festering. No response.

'I know better than anyone on the force that Davis was a total shit, capable of anything. What did he do to you?'

Alongside his car, he veered right, pushed open a brown gate in a low brick wall, turned and closed it against Jacko's stomach. 'Piss off.' A hiss, hot breath on Jacko's face. An about-turn. Three strides up the short path, two steps up to the brown door.

Jacko watched it close. He started to fumble in his trouser pocket for his cigarettes, fingers dwelling for a scratch, probing fingers, seeking to relieve his stress.

Mrs Morris opened the door wearing a trusting smile. She'd let him in before he'd showed her his warrant card. 'You really ought to see this.' Mummy's boys' mums are all the same, he reflected.

She led the way, hobbling, into a lounge with a view of an ancient chestnut on a green surrounded by three-storey blocks of flats built in sandy-coloured brick, easy on the eye, bright in the spring sunshine.

He was shown to a sage green couch, pine arms, which pulled out into a bed. She sat on a chair, soft with diamond fabric and padded wings, strategically placed three short steps from the TV in the corner.

A small, silver-haired woman, around seventy, with specs, she eased out a leg, making herself comfortable. 'Now then?' A local phrase, an invitation to state his business.

'We're looking at the Katie Burrows case again in the light of the death of Terry Davis.'

Blood pressure flushed red and blue through temple veins. 'I hope you're not going to blame Harry for that as well.'

'Oh, no.' Very sincere, soothing. 'No one has ever accused Harry of anything.' The flush receded. 'Except Lance.'

The veins reappeared. 'That little monkey. After all he did for him.'

'Yes,' said Jacko, stirring it, pouring in the poison. 'He certainly caused a lot of trouble. It must have been a great strain for you both.'

She nodded her head so abruptly that her spectacles, framed in transparent plastic, leap-frogged the bony bridge of her nose. She prodded them back as she spoke of the visit Davis made to her clean, cosy first-floor flat.

'Let me think.' Her leathery brow wrinkled. 'About a year ago. March, it would be.' The date tied in with his invoice to Seaton's law firm.

Jacko nodded, content with her memory. 'He said he was working for Lance's defence. I helped all I could. I wished the boy no harm.' She glanced away. 'Then.'

His questions seemed harmless, mainly sounding out her opinion. The truth, she realized now, was that she didn't know Lance all that well. 'In fact, I'm still discovering things about my own son.' A sorrowful look, pale blue eyes wandering out of the window towards the chestnut tree.

'Tell me a bit about him.' Gentle now, coaxing.

Harry was five years younger than his sister, who was happily married with two teenage daughters of school age. Their photos were on the sill of the picture window (not step-grandson Lance's, though, Jacko noted). His father had been a faceworker who'd died from lung dust disease in his fifties.

Harry followed him into the coal industry as a surface carpenter. 'Most weekends he went watching football with his pals and he played himself on Sunday mornings.'

'A handsome chap, by all accounts,' Jacko lied, casually. 'Many girlfriends?'

'A few.' A disturbed look. She glanced away, a giveway. She's lied, Jacko detected. 'He was more interested in sport.' She looked back wearing a truthful smile.

He'd been born in a three-bedroomed terraced house, which became too big, too cold for his lame mother. She'd had her name down for a council flat for years. Eventually arthritis stiffened her left knee and ballooned her fingers and made her a priority case.

When she was offered this one-bedroomed flat, he moved into digs. He was past thirty, living away for the first time. 'He always said it wasn't home.' A trace of pride in her voice. 'He often stayed over and slept on that put-you-up.' She nodded at the couch where Jacko sat. 'And he seldom missed coming round for Saturday tea after the match.'

Ah, Saturday tea after the match, Jacko thought with a fond smile. John West salmon or Curtis's pork pie. Never varied. 'When are you going to start bringing him to the match,' his own mother had asked when his son was barely two soccer seasons old. She could hardly wait to lay another plate and discover if her grandson was a tinned salmon or pork pie man. Mrs Morris reminded him of his own mum, honest and independent, loyal and loving. He liked it here, felt at home, at ease with her, safe. He sat back and let her talk, eyes never leaving her.

Harry, she went on, stopped calling so often when he started courting – her word – Rita after they met at the garden centre. He started going straight back to his digs after the match to change and take her out for a drink. 'I knew she was a widow, quite a bit older.'

He brought her for Sunday lunch and, later, Lance. 'Twice

her size. His father must have been a big 'un. Rita was well into her forties then. Worried me a bit, the age gap, you know. But . . .' A tiny shrug, not her business.

The wedding was at the register office. 'Everything was fine for a couple of months, then suddenly . . .' She entwined her deformed fingers.

It started when Harry began showing up again on Saturday, always with Lance. He told his mother Rita had switched from weekday to weekend work and he was keeping an eye on him.

'Good Lord,' said Mrs Morris, 'he's fifteen. If he wants to go to the match he should go with his own crowd. You did at his age.'

Harry made excuses about hooligans causing trouble but Mrs Morris could tell that Lance wasn't interested in football.

Over the next year or so, she noticed him changing from a normal chatty boy into a nervy youth. 'Harry kept saying everything was all right. It wasn't. There was such tension; you could cut it with a knife. He and Rita weren't going out. She never seemed to let Lance out of her sight. It wasn't natural.' A headshake, condemning a style of parenthood foreign to her. Jacko nodded in mute agreement.

Throughout the cricket season, Harry and Lance continued to call. 'Unless he'd got a private job.' She stopped, suddenly, a harassed look, as though she'd said too much.

Moonlighting, she means, Jacko decided. 'Off-duty policemen do it all the time.' He smiled, encouraging her.

'Even then, he took Lance with him.'

Two or three weeks into a new soccer season Harry turned up for tea on his own, explaining Lance was with Rita who had the weekend off. Mrs Morris seized on it for a heart-to-heart.

'Don't you think it's about time she let him off her apron strings?' No messing, this mum, Jacko judged, straight to the heart of the matter.

'You don't know the problems we're having with him.'

'What problems?'

'Adolescent problems.'

'Good Lord, Harry. He's a strapping lad of seventeen. Girls are bound to take his fancy. What's wrong?'

'Don't interfere, Mother.' It was the first time she could

151

remember him calling her Mother. 'Rita knows what's best for her own son.'

Being accused of interfering riled Mrs Morris into a row which ended when he got up from the table and shouted, 'It's me who should be off your apron strings.' He left without their usual bye-bye kiss.

There was no Harry, no Lance for the next two Saturdays. On the third, the night Katie Burrows died, she waited in till after six, then popped to Mrs Bell downstairs.

Next day Harry did call, ashen-faced, trembling. He sat her down, held her hand and broke the news of Lance's arrest for murder. She didn't fully comprehend.

'I don't believe it.'

'He's a very sick boy.'

It was on that visit that he told her he had called the night before. He'd spent the afternoon with Lance, erecting a shed and fencing, a moonlighting job. Just before six, Lance disappeared on his green bike. 'Harry was anxious to find him before Rita came home from work. He came round here in case Lance had dropped by. Harry must have come, don't you see? Otherwise, he couldn't possibly have known I wasn't in. I've never been out on a Saturday teatime in years.'

She looked at him intently, holding his eyes, telling the truth, seeking his support. Jacko nodded, pretending belief, but put the issue on hold. Harry could have conned her into telling him about her trip downstairs, the same way I am conning her now, he thought.

'Wish I'd never gone. Then I could stand up and say he was here, that he couldn't possibly have been in the park. There wouldn't be this dreadful suspicion. People round here still think it might have been him. They don't say so, not to my face, but I know they are thinking it.'

She sucked in her small mouth, slack facial skin tightening against her frail cheekbones. Jacko thought she was about to weep. 'We don't, though, do we?' He spoke at just above a whisper.

No, no, she said and she shook her head twice, adding, 'And we know it was Lance, don't we, who killed that poor girl?' And Jacko nodded, stringing her along; no qualms about it, a job being done.

She composed herself, anger at the injustice of it overcoming sorrow. 'Harry stood by him all that time. And how did he repay him? By telling those lies at his trial.'

During that seven month wait, Terry Davis had made his call on her. 'I only told him what I've just told you.'

Jacko speculated. 'And Davis told Lance in prison that Harry had no alibi so he shifted the blame?'

Yes, yes, yes, she said, nod, nod, nodding. He'd sized her up now. She anticipated every statement, every question before he'd finished them. If she agreed, she said yes and nodded simultaneously and repeatedly. If she disagreed, she said no and shook her head in unison. She was a lady who knew her own mind and couldn't wait to express it. An annoying trait in most people, engaging in her.

All this she told Terry Davis, who'd sat where Jacko was sitting, a year earlier.

Then came Lance's allegations against Harry at his trial. 'Didn't believe it then, still don't. I know my son.' No doubts, no questions, end of story.

All this she went over yet again with Chief Inspector Keeling, who sat on that same sofa making copious notes within a day of Lance walking to his freedom after destroying his stepfather.

Keeling acted fast; had to, Jacko recognized, before Harry had time to rehearse his mother in a false alibi. And, with MPs demanding a police scapegoat for the débâcle, he'd be under the same pressure from the Chief Constable as Udden and Bullman were from him. But, Jacko was soon to realize, he'd acted too fast, like Inspector Mike Fixter before him.

In the ten months since, Mrs Morris had learned much, much more, unmined information, gold dust to a detective.

Harry came for tea on the Saturday after the trial. 'Stayed a month sleeping on that put-you-up. Looked like a ghost.' She didn't press him. Bit by bit, over the months, it came out.

'He went with Rita, Lance and Terry Davis to some hotel from the court-house. He couldn't believe some of the things she was telling the paper. Absolute rubbish. All for money. He wanted nothing to do with it, thought it was poor taste. He left them and came home.'

In that month Rita came to Mrs Morris's flat three times. She

153

didn't bring Lance. Mrs Morris popped down to Mrs Bell's to let them talk in private.

'He told me afterwards that she wanted him to go back to them and start afresh. He couldn't face it. Not after what Lance had done to him. Didn't want to share the same roof.' He quit his job at the colliery and found work and digs. 'He wanted to be away, where he wasn't known.'

On his Saturdays off he went to watch Forest, ten minutes' walk from his digs, standing alone on the terraces, not caring who won. They weren't his team, wearing his colours, carrying his hopes, and Jacko understood this, for he never felt emotionally involved in any game that didn't feature his home town side.

Harry began making the half-hour trip to Filbert Street to watch Leicester again, calling for tea afterwards. He said he kept in touch with Rita at her new home. 'I think he still carries a torch for her. Silly boy.' A mother's face, scolding, yet understanding. 'I don't think there's much chance for them while Lance is still with her. He needs treatment, doesn't he? Stands to reason after what he did.'

'What else did he do?'

'That adolescent trouble, Harry talked about. Remember?'

Jacko nodded.

'He was caught in a park, it turns out. Peeping Tomming or whatever they call it. A nurse reported him but decided against bringing a case, provided he got medical help.' A shudder, disgusted. 'Rita packed him off to a psychiatrist who said there was nothing wrong with him. Growing pains! I ask you. He should be struck off, that doctor. All he suggested was that an eye be kept on him while he grew out of it. That's why Rita changed her shift so she could be at home weekdays and Harry looked after him at weekends.'

She tipped her tiny body forward, looking over the top of her spectacles, confidential, a bit of hot gossip to impart. 'And do you know what was really upsetting Harry that Saturday when we had that row?'

Jacko shook his head.

'Lance had been up to his old tricks again two or three weeks earlier.'

Jacko frowned, thrown for a moment. Again? There was

154

no second flashing offence on Lance's record. 'What happened?'

'A policeman caught him and took him home.'

A policeman? Impossible. For a second offence of indecent exposure there'd have been a court case: force policy.

'Rita was beside herself. Her precious boy up to rude things. She punished him.' A disapproving headshake. 'I don't hold with that. He needs treatment, not punishment.

'So, you see . . .' A quiet smile of vindication. 'Harry wasn't really upset with me. Things were getting on top of him. That's why he raced round here on the night that girl died when I was out. He was terrified what would happen when Rita came home from work and found that Lance had disobeyed her. She can be a real tartar. Still . . .' A shrug, forgiving. 'I suppose she had her plate full with a son like that.'

The Saturday before the murder Harry hadn't called for tea because, he later explained, he'd taken Lance to an away game. And the Saturday before that both had been on a moonlighting job.

Harry only mentioned it – and then in passing – the week after Terry Davis's murder had been all over the front page of the *Mercury*.

Mrs Morris repeated for the umpteenth time how sorry she was that she'd ever set eyes on Davis, letting him wheedle his way into her confidence, betraying her trust, destroying her son.

'Don't worry, Mum,' said Harry. 'He asked for all he got. He was a con man. Do you know whose bungalow we fitted for free with a new kitchen that first Saturday I missed coming round for tea?'

Jacko had worked it out before she gave Harry's answer.

The bobby who'd caught Lance flashing again, and hadn't reported him, kept quiet in return for having that modern, trendy kitchen fixed up in his bungalow.

Terry Davis, the corrupt bastard.

17

Next to family and workmates, what's worth getting out of bed for of a morning? Jacko asked himself, snug beneath the salmon pink duck-down duvet on an off-duty Saturday.

There's walking with Mark, his son, and Lucy, his dog, down the overhung footpath over the stile into the cornfield which dipped away and up again to a small copse screening the power station behind which the sun set, calmly on some nights, stormily on others, always reluctant to bid him goodnight.

There's reading, from Hemingway whose work came alive for him in Paris through O. Henry and Runyon to le Carré whose books Jackie gave him. 'Ten out of ten writing,' she'd called it.

There's music, from Haley, through Donegan's railroad songs and the Beatles to Mozart, again Jackie's gift, and he rather fancied dying to the Adagio from the Clarinet Concerto, a low, slow, beautiful note to sign off on, he sometimes thought.

There's a night out with the boys and girls, lots of lager and a late curry, the latest jokes, the latest gossip and digging deep into his store of happy memories.

The morning after lots of lager and a curry was a reason for staying in bed, along with weeding the garden, do-it-yourself, church weddings, shopping for suits, queuing at a supermarket check-out for half an hour when you've trolleyed round in ten minutes, washing the car – and autumn. He smiled to himself . . .

'You can stick autumn up your –'

'Don't be so rude,' Jackie had said the night before, back-handing him hard on a shoulder.

'Up your jumper.' And his right hand led his body towards hers on the sofa, fiddling to create a gap at her waistband, sliding

156

upwards, fingers spreading. Caressing her breasts, compelling her to turn, as it always did, eyes closed towards him.

He had timed it to perfection. Three glasses of cheap claret that went with the French bread, pâté and cheese on the coffee table before the TV set and her willingness peaked. One more and her speech would have thickened, her eyes misted. One after that and she would have become argumentative before fading away into sleep.

He made his move after three. It was the first time they had romped, eventually naked, on the sofa since the sound-asleep Mark had been born.

'Did you use to heavy pet like that in the back row of the cinema?' she asked as they held each other, talking awhile, as they always did after lovemaking.

'Nar,' he said, roughly. 'We used to tear out the seats to "Yes, I'm the Great Pretender".' He sang, off key, into her ear. *'I played the game but to my real shame –'*

She cut him short. 'There's no romance in your soul. Fancy not liking autumn.'

He flopped back. 'All autumn leaves are fit for is the compost heap. It's all right Walter Huston droning on about them turning to gold. He doesn't have to rake the sodding things up. Now spring . . .' He hooked his hand round her waist and she curled up to him again. 'Spring is to be celebrated.'

Spring was the season of yellow, his favourite colour, the sight of succulent new grass, the smell of linseed oil on a scarred cricket bat.

Spring was the time of year when all that was magical had happened to him. He'd got to know the Little Fat Man three springs earlier and found the joys of working within a fine team under a fine leader. He'd found Jackie and Lucy that same spring when he'd given up hope of being a part of a family. And a year later Mark had completed that family.

Spring was to be celebrated and they'd celebrate tonight with a party, the sort he liked, with his workmates, listening to shop talk.

His love of parties was shared by Jackie. Last year she drank a bottle of wine as she cut the sandwiches and washed the salads. By ten she was sound asleep under a pile of coats in the spare bedroom. She'd missed his regular sidekick manhandling an

157

ice-cream sign on a concrete base on to their porch roof while his young wife, who'd played in the brass band at her school, stood on the front lawn, blasting the sleeping estate with the opening bars of the 'Coronation Street' theme.

This year Jackie was inviting a few neighbours and her own workmates from the secretarial agency. 'You're such an incestuous lot,' she'd said. Her real motive, he knew, was the belief that civilians would bring with them a civilizing influence.

Wide awake now, as bright and breezy as the spring day outside, looking forward to it. Tonight they'd all get pissed. 'And what's wrong with that, I'd like to know?' he sang to himself as he threw off the salmon pink duvet.

The lounge was heaving when Caroline arrived with a redhead called Rosie who wore a green tie knotted at her eye-catching bosom and an open-necked white shirt.

Caroline looked stunning in a midnight blue trouser suit which, Jacko told her, made her look like the second violinist on Skeggy pier. 'Hope not. It broke its back and floated off on a storm.' She eyed him, full of mischief. 'Still, I'd rather be playing "Lilac Time" to a shoal of haddock on the Dogger Bank than listening to your boring stories.' They laughed. They laughed a lot these days, like big brother and small sister, poking fun when together, missing each other when apart.

Jacko turned to Rosie. 'All these weeks under my command and she still loves me.' He kissed her then, for the first time, lightly, on the lips and she put her hands on his shoulders to receive it.

Soon he was called away to the garage where real ale drinkers had run out of glasses. Cut glasses were blown free of dust and removed from the safety of the cabinet. Even an inscribed pewter mug, a christening gift for Mark, was pressed into service. Bone china ornaments became ashtrays and, soon, the rose bed at the back a relief loo.

In a quiet moment in the kitchen, Jacko found himself alone with Jackie. 'You don't think that Caroline and Rosie are . . .'

'Good Lord.' A sharp tone, reprimanding. 'Do you think that crosses anyone's mind when you go partying with the boys?'

A thoughtful silence. 'I still think it's a pity.'

158

'Why, for God's sake?'

'Because it means she'll never be a mum and she'd make some lucky kid a great mum.'

She smiled at him then, understanding, forgiving, for she knew that in his simple mind he had paid Caroline the greatest compliment he could give any woman.

The kitchen filled as fast as it had emptied and they threaded their way, hand-in-hand, through the hall to the lounge where they danced – he in a red and white striped shirt, the colours of his home town team, she looking like a sky diver in a yellow jump suit.

When the music stopped, Jacko left her chatting to Caroline who was fretting about leaving her dog on its own all night. 'I have to leave the light on for her.'

'It's the same with my geriatric John Travolta' – and Jackie went on to share a bedroom secret which Caroline swore on her dog's life never to repeat.

Jacko blinked in the brightness of the hall as he stepped out of the lounge, lit by one forty-watt candle bulb. He cadged his second cigarette from Tony from Television who was arguing about policing inner cities with the collator in front of a small knot of listeners.

Jacko had been subjected at previous parties to his finger-pointing harangues over civil rights during the coal strike which Tony, a combative debater, very articulate, had covered. This time he went straight in on the attack. 'It's OK you media liberals harping on about us. What about cleaning up your own act?'

'What yer on about?' growled Tony, who was inclined to lose his carefully modulated on-screen voice in drink.

'For starters, paying criminals money to tell their sordid stories.'

'Went out with the ark.'

'Oh, really?' Mocking, goading. 'What about the girl murdered in the park eighteen months ago?'

'He was acquitted.'

'That makes it right, does it?'

'It makes it legitimate. If he's acquitted he can't be a criminal so he can be paid for his story.' Simple logic.

'What would it be worth to him?' Carefully, but casually, Jacko was checking a theory.

159

'Two or three thousand to a daily; twice that from a Sunday where the competition for exclusives is fiercer.'

'And what would your self-righteous colleague – the reporter or freelance agent – pocket from that blood money?'

'If it's a staff reporter, nothing. It's all in a day's work. A freelance? Ten or fifteen per cent.'

Jacko scoffed. 'Still goes on though, doesn't it? Signing up prosecution witnesses so they have a financial interest in securing a conviction. It's corrupting justice.'

'Christ,' said Tony's wife, a radio reporter, dark, attractive. 'That went out with the Thorpe case. Who are the police anyway to question us when . . .' And so another finger-pointing debate began, while in other groups gossip and stories were being exchanged, the stuff of a good party.

Jacko left them arguing and circulated, a lager with this school, a scotch with that crowd. It was well past midnight before he knew it. He had gone through his mischievous and noisy stages and was now in need of meaningful debate. In a shadowy corner over the heads of a thinning crowd of dancers he saw Caroline standing alone, a pint glass of real ale in her hand. He drifted towards her. 'Where's Rosie?'

She nodded towards the couch where he had performed (with some distinction, he congratulated himself) the night before. She and Jackie were dozing on each other's shoulders. No encore tonight, he realized.

He slid down the wall and sat on the leaf-patterned carpet, legs outstretched. She sat beside him, legs entwined. Elegant as a model, he thought, until he saw her brown eyes roaming independent of each other. 'You're pissed.'

'Pissed off, too.' He gave her his hurt look. 'Not with you,' she added, hurriedly. 'It's a great party.' She guzzled noisily. 'With our case.'

He sighed. 'Let's see if the booze helps us to think it through.' He addressed the carpet, speaking slowly but, unusual in drink, softly. 'Either Lance or Harry killed Katie. Davis and Rita briefed Lance on what to say in the witness box. Davis kept all the paper's fee as payment. I'm sure of that now.' He jerked his head towards Tony's crowd. 'If Harry had been charged on Lance's evidence, they would have signed a blank contract and leaked a copy to his lawyers to run the tainted evidence

160

defence. We didn't charge Harry and Davis was done out of a big pay day he was counting on.' Caroline gave a tired nod, about to drop off to sleep.

'Nothing more happens for the rest of that year,' Jacko continued. 'Come Christmas Davis has money troubles, compounded by his row with Golden Jim. With a tax bill coming up his bank account needs a quick injection. What has he got to sell Jason French?'

Caroline blinked her roving eyes into focus. 'The truth about what happened to Katie Burrows in the park. He gets their new address from Udden, drives to see them and talks Lance and/or Rita into a financial deal for the story which he notes in his book.'

'Makes sense.' Jacko smiled grimly at a bitter memory, which he shared with her. A shopkeeper was found battered to death. He was a junior officer on the inquiry. His chief questioned a local villain who'd been seen running away and got a confession. The trial judge ruled the statement had been improperly obtained when the accused was confused and tired. With his confession inadmissible, he was acquitted. A few months later he sold his 'I got away with murder' story to a Sunday paper.

He was re-interviewed. The team knew he couldn't be charged with murder again but thought they might get him for robbery. 'I was drunk when I told the paper that,' he said. 'I told them a pack of lies to get some money because I was broke.' The killer was still walking the streets.

'They were about to pull the same stunt.' Caroline was wide awake again but mumbling. 'Davis phoned French. They arranged to meet on Tuesday at the Grand. The plan was to take Lance and his mother with him. They knew French. They'd had dealings with him before. They could get the whole thing sorted then and there.

'Over that weekend, Lance and/or Rita rethink. Cold feet. Whatever Davis is offering, they decide, isn't worth having their new identities blown and moving on again.

'Lance phones Davis at home. We know that for a scientific fact. He confirms the time and place to meet on Tuesday. Instead of going to the Grand, Davis is lured to the car-park. One or other rips out his throat. It has to be Lance. The six-footer wearing his ointment left the scene some time after the slovenly woman. Mum must have been lookout-cum-getaway driver. He takes his notebook which contains that incriminating statement and his cash to make it look like a mugging.' She sat in silence, finished.

Jacko nodded across the room to Scott, engaged in abusive debate with Tony. 'The Little Fat Man says identifying that ointment isn't enough. Thousands must use it.' He fought off a desire to scratch an imagined itch.

'What about Lance's message on the answering machine?'

'He could make up any story to cover it.'

'Why lie to us about not having any contact?'.

'They'd say they didn't want to get involved in Davis's death. They were frightened of further publicity, fearful it would shatter their new lives. They'd accuse us of a vendetta. These days a jury might buy it on that evidence.'

'It isn't much, is it?' Caroline shuffled her bottom, looking downcast.

'It's one hell of a good start.' Jacko tried to sound enthusiastic, optimistic. 'We just need a bit more.'

'Is it worth a search warrant?' asked Caroline.

'The LFM reckons that if they've got rid of the weapon, the donkey jacket and the notebook, we're further away than ever. We mustn't let them know we're this close.'

'Are we ruling out Golden Jim?'

'His motive's only good if Davis knew about his involvement with dog-fighting.'

Caroline looked down again, unhappy in the knowledge that there'd been nothing on the phone surveillance for weeks. 'What do you make of Harry Morris?'

Jacko's turn to look unhappy. He wasn't sure. He'd been dominated by Rita, certainly. He could have been used by her to get rid of Davis. But he wouldn't talk and his lawyer wouldn't help and he couldn't work out whether that indicated guilt or just desire to wash his hands of the whole messy business. He answered with a question. 'Heard of *folie à deux*?'

Caroline had, on her law course. Madness of two. But she realized he was going to tell her of another case and she liked listening to his stories, learned from them. So she said, 'Only vaguely.'

They'd been called one morning to an old ramshakle house,

Jacko began. An appalling sight greeted them. A toddler in bed with his throat slit. His parents were rushed to hospital with overdoses from which they recovered. Instead of blaming each other both claimed full and sole responsibility. 'I didn't want him to grow up in this evil world,' said the mother. 'God told me he was too good to live,' said the father. They were kept in different hospitals. The mother, whose prints were all over the carving knife, sank into a deeper depression. The father, parted from her influence, got better. The judge detained both without imposing a time limit on their stay. The father was let out within two years, cured. The desperately ill mother took much longer.

'We could be dealing with a similar family here, one infecting the others. Harry's made the break. He may be our way in.'

'How?' asked Caroline, sounding sober now.

'We have to look at the methods other detectives have used to crack cases that seemed impossible.' For example, he went on, a smart super was sitting in his office one day when a woman came in and announced her runaway husband had killed his first wife twenty years before.

'Imagine that, twenty years ago and no witnesses.'

'How did he go about it?' She listened, enthralled, as he told her. When he finished, an excited Caroline asked, 'Can't we do that?'

'First,' he said, quietly, 'we have to decide which one of them to use as bait.'

The lights were out now, couples necking, not always with the partners they'd brought. The Beatles were on the record player and they stood up to dance as the party got its second wind. It was the first time he'd smooched with a lesbian, knowingly anyway, and she was one hell of a good mover.

The success of Jackie's scheme for introducing civilians for their calming effect can only be judged by the end results. Apart from Scott and Jacko wrestling on the floor, egged on by encouraging juniors, and a bleary-eyed neighbour telling a revived Rosie to a Sinatra song for Swingin' Lovers that he longed to shin up her green tie and sink his teeth into her gorgeous tits and being told that, if he tried, she knew an excellent dentist who made first-class dentures, and a quarrelsome teacher with radical views asking if plainclothes

163

officers carried truncheons and being told that, if he bent over, he'd soon find out, and Caroline advising Scott's wife, a marriage guidance counsellor, that if her husband spent a bit more time at home he might be less grumpy at work, and the collator being given a hand job on the back patio by a forty-year-old divorcee who explained she was a high-speed typist when he complained it hadn't lasted very long, everyone seemed remarkably well behaved.

Just before three the last taxi took away the last guests and Jacko shut the door with an exhausted sigh. He forced himself to go from room to room, ignoring the wreckage which included a damp patch on the leaf-patterned carpet, a crack in a smoked glass panel in the cabinet and a ham and pickle sandwich on brown stuck to the matt ceiling in the kitchen, in a desperate search for a cigarette, any brand, in tossed-away packets.

He found what he was looking for in the kitchen and he smoked it as he emptied the piled-up ashtrays into a metal bin which he put outside the back door.

He looked up at the stars, silvery, frosted. Never again, he told them. He'd said exactly the same thing after last year's party.

18

Brrrr. Brrrr.

'*And then we will stop and talk to a cop, Down Main Street.*'

He was Gene Kelly tap-dancing down Main Street with Vera Ellen, his schooldays' fantasy woman.

Brrrr. Brrrr. '*He made an arrest way back in ninety . . .*' Brrrr. Brrrr.

'Aren't you going to answer that bloody thing?' A voice from the kitchen, Jackie's, always grouchy with a hangover.

Oh, Christ. He rolled off the couch. The after-lunch nap had not stilled the pounding in his brain and had worsened the foulness in his mouth. Brrrr. Brrrr. He shuffled into the hall, puffing, blowing. Brrrr. He picked up the phone.

'Hold on to your helmet.' Caroline's voice, urgent, disgustingly bright. 'Control's had Mrs Dalby on.'

'Who?'

'From Animal Alliance. Asking for me. Are you in the land of the living, Jacko?'

'Just about.' The mist was beginning to lift.

'This is the verb. "Please inform Sergeant Parker that Champion is at Northfields right now."'

Northfields? A frown faded as he recognized the name of Golden Jim's place. 'Give her a ring.'

'I've tried to.' Caroline sounded irritated. 'Continuously engaged. She's probably rounding her activists for a rescue mission.'

A pause for thought. None came.

'We need to act, Jacko.'

'We need a marksman with a tranquillizing gun, handlers, warrant . . .'

'That's being fixed but it will take time which we may not

165

have. There's nothing to stop us having a quick look-see while it's being organized.'

Tempting, but dangerous, Jacko thought. Still, thinking it through, he won't have the black brute running free. He couldn't pass up the chance of finally nailing Goulden. For something. For anything. Temptation overcame danger. 'Pick me up.'

No answer to their bell-ringing and door-knocking. None of the small leaded windows ajar. No cars in the adjoining double garage with ivy creepers that could not hide the ugliness of the breeze blocks.

No barking dog. No one mucking out in the stables, five each side of a wide sawdust path, some with the heads of horses, chestnuts, greys and a black, poking out, chewing, bored.

They turned at a heap of steaming straw and retraced their footsteps on the soiled sawdust, stopping to look inside three empty stables. Nothing. Not even clean straw. Like a ranch in a ghost town, he imagined, eerie, sinister. He primed his ears and eyes. Nothing registered.

They reached a fork in a shrub-lined, pea-pebbled path. Right was back to the house, limestone, long and low, a handsome view from here, looking out on to a grass-encircled bed of blood-red wallflowers mixed with yellow tulips.

Left was a barn, recently renovated, brickwork pointed, woodwork a fresh green. 'What's that?' asked Caroline, white mac billowing behind her on the bitter wind.

'His hospitality suite, he calls it.'

Without further words she walked towards it, pebbles scrunching beneath her flat black shoes, Jacko tagging on behind, dragging his shoes, kicking up tiny stones, no bounce in his walk.

She thumbed down a latch on a door, domestic-sized, and pushed it open cautiously. He stood looking over her shoulder. In front of them, a snooker table, sheeted down, strip-light in a long shade above, unlit, carved legs on a big square carpet. On the whitewashed wall behind, a rack of cues, a scoreboard and a cork board, notes and messages pinned to it. Two fruit machines, old-fashioned, lever-operated, against the wall to their right. Wooden stairs with a handrail to their left. Caroline's eyes ran up them. 'His bar,' said Jacko.

Both strolled in, very slowly, looking around, feet tapping on buffed-up lino, silent steps on the carpet round the snooker table. She walked beyond the table and browsed at the notes on the cork board. Jacko stopped in front of it, thighs against it, gripping the firm cushion with his fingers.

Across the ceiling above them, flapping, scurrying sounds. Pigeons in the loft, he guessed, or rats. Louder now, nearer, faster.

Caroline turned. '*Jacko.*' A shrill scream that emptied her lungs, and her screwed-up face had the lopsided look of a stroke victim. He swung round.

Down the wooden stairs it was coming. Jet black with a glint of silver at its arched neck. Ugly, agile. Ears high, tail low. 'Shit.' A glance over his shoulder at Caroline, motionless, brain-dead. Back at the dog. 'Easy, boy.' A tight voice, quaking.

The dog slipped as it turned towards him on the polished lino, scratching, scrambling. On to the carpet, nails digging in, graceful rhythm restored. 'Ea . . .' The word died at birth in his desert-dry throat.

Lower in its stride, then rising like a game bird, into the air. Flying, dipping down, swooping; a monstrous black bird of prey, homing in.

Your throat. Protect your fucking throat. He threw his right arm across it. Front legs, ramrod straight, hit him square on the chest, bowling him backwards on to the table, legs dangling over the side.

A vice gripped his forearm. Steel spikes bit through brown waterproof, white lining, white cotton, white skin, red muscle to white bone. A scream, more terror than agony. Mind-numbing shock masked expected pain.

His left hand weakly squeezed its neck but found no loose skin to hang on to, to grip, to pull. He hooked his arm round its so-smooth body, pulling it closer, hugging it, rib cage to rib cage, trying to crush it. Three stones pressed down, winding him.

His ears, the whole room, were filled with a low rumbling sound. Not a snarl, a growl like his own dog with an old sock. The fucking thing's enjoying itself. A petrifying thought. His sleeve ripped and another thought, idiotic this time: My missus will kill me when she sees this mac.

Caroline bent under the light shade, swinging like a hurricane lamp. Her legs were next to his, kicking out as though in death throes. She clambered astride the dog's back, glossy coat stiff to her touch. Knees pressing hard on either flank, she pulled two-handed on the silver chain round its hard, muscular neck. Its head came back slightly and Jacko got a fleeting, frightening view of its broad skull and black round eyes set far apart.

Hot breath, foaming saliva and brown bits of his sleeve spurted from its clamped-together jaws, working, chewing all the time. Oh, Jesus, it's going to eat me alive. 'Caro . . .'

It shook its broad shoulders, muscles bulging, in a sort of casual shrug, and rotated its neck, twisting his arm. He screamed. He felt the pain now, ripping like lightning down to his fingertips, up to his shoulder, across his chest into his heart, which seemed to swell, about to burst.

Caroline's trapped fingers, whitened and deadened fingers, let go.

The dog opened its mouth fractionally. Sweet relief. Then clamped it jaws tighter and tugged. A dozen incisors followed four fangs into his flesh as it took firmer hold. He sensed it trying to pull his arm away for a strike at his throat. Panic, blind and furious panic, overwhelmed him.

Eyes screwed shut, he punched left-handed at the side of its head. Knuckles cracked against bone. The dog didn't flinch.

He pushed up on shoulder blades and buttocks, arching his back. Roll free, he commanded himself. Push the fucking thing over the edge. Fall with it, if you have to. Do something, anything. The dog seemed to body-slam him with its deep chest, knocking the breath, the fight out of him. I'm fucked, finished.

Caroline – just a blur of white to him now – vaulted back on to the table, a snooker cue in her right hand. She slid it through the steel link collar. Gripping the cue with hands close together, she pulled.

Its chin jerked up. A second's breather for Jacko. No relief from the pain charging up and down his arm but time to catch breath. A ray of hope, half a chance, good girl.

Crack. Down, hope smashed, as the cue snapped in the

168

middle. The half with the tip fell on to the carpet. The butt of heavy, hard wood, stayed in her hand. She slid it back inside the chain. Another tug, harder, longer. Its head came back again.

Another breather, longer this time. Hope chased away the panic and the pain. The dog was snarling, higher, hideous, in a real fight; not fun any more. 'Turn it.' A gasp, begging.

'I'm trying.' A breathless answer with her left hand down, right hand up. Its head jolted left. Its black nostrils flared and flapped to find air. 'And again.' Another gasp, beseeching.

One hand further up, the other further down. Its grip on his arm weakened, just a little. He felt for its eyes, to gouge at them, to rip them out. It shook its head, maddened.

'It's coming. Again.' Hope, real hope.

With every ounce of strength, every muscle at work, Caroline tilted on her left knee and pushed up her right shoulder. An anti-clockwise turn, further than the previous two. Her chin flopped to her chest, exhausted. She held it there, right hand directly above left.

Its jaw dropped, only slightly. Blood flowed through his arm, tingling, back into his fingers. 'Again.'

She took her deepest ever breath, raised her head so high that it hit the swinging shade above her, and turned it again as though closing the hatch of a submarine; as tight as she could.

The jaw fell open. Blood and bile mingled with the saliva spreading over Jacko's face, covering its pure white skin, far, far whiter than Caroline's bloodless hands.

Its black eyes skinned over. Its breathing became short and shallow. Caroline's hands were crossing now, right over left.

The dog gulped and belched and fouled the air. Its long pink tongue fell out between its bloodied teeth. It shuddered and rolled limply off Jacko on to the table covering, dark and moist with blood and sweat.

Caroline fell with it, knees still gripped to its sides, and rolled with it, rolling on, on to her back, looking up at the swinging light, spent.

Jacko coughed and hacked up phlegm. He felt his breathing and pulses beginning to slow from frantic to merely fast. He turned on his left elbow, back to Caroline, and pulled his right arm across his chest. The raincoat was shredded from the elbow down. He couldn't tell the brown bits from blood, the lining from skin.

Caroline opened her eyes and looked towards him. The dog lay between them, on its side, facing her. Its coat was glossed over, its muzzle smeared red and white. Its mouth hung open, locked. A slow stream of white and brown and red bubbled out, hot as lava, eyes as lifeless as black buttons.

'I think I've killed it.' Her voice was small and a long way away and he could hear her sobbing.

He wanted to turn and hug her and hold her but all he could manage was, 'Thanks.'

19

Katie Burrows smiled down from the walnut Ladderex. Her hair was hidden beneath a white cap. She wore a black swimming costume. Her bare shoulders were smooth, more developed than the rest of her. One hand was raised in salute. Rings rippled round her. She was treading water.

Just like Scott had told Caroline to. 'The old fart will be back in a week. Take charge while he's away.' A vote of confidence, certainly; but she missed him, wished he was back.

She looked away from the framed photo when Mrs Burrows returned to the lounge with two cups and sat beside her on a small settee.

'Sorry to have to put you through all this again.' She'd come in a vague hope of finding a connection with the Frost family that had been missed in the original investigation, to help decide which bait to target for their trap, but she had feared the meeting would be painful. Instead, she'd been made very welcomed and they looked like Palm Court regulars, sitting there, demurely sipping their tea.

Caroline explained they were looking at her daughter's case again in the light of the Terry Davis murder. 'We think he and Lance got their heads together before the trial and that knowledge cost Davis his life.'

Mrs Burrows dwelt at length on the strength her Baptist beliefs had given her. 'I do forgive whoever did it because I know God wants me to. That doesn't mean he gets away scotfree. There has to be repentance and justice.'

All Katie's clothes, records and old toys went to charity. Only her old rag doll, in a blue and white striped shirt, was kept, she said, in her wardrobe so she'd see it every day and sometimes touch it, and on those occasions when the missing was too much she would hold it and hug it and cry.

All this she told Caroline, not seeking sympathy, just sharing a burden. Visits like this, talks like this, are why police officers can never be liberals; why they work with manic obsessiveness to catch child-killers. To cage them, to prevent other mothers suffering what Katie's mother had been through, was going through still and would go through for the rest of her life.

'There isn't a day when I don't think of her. Making the beds, washing the pots at the sink, walking to the shops. She is always in my thoughts. Sometimes I am stricken with guilt over little things – not letting her have the kitten she always wanted, for instance. My husband is still consumed with it. He didn't offer her a lift in his car, you see, to her friend's house. He doesn't talk about it any more but sometimes I can see, actually see, it preying on his mind. Many nights we have cried in each other's arms.' Mrs Burrows' grey-blue eyes sparkled. 'Few people let me talk about her like this. They mean to be kind, I know, but . . .' A slight sigh accompanied a slighter shrug.

Caroline guided her on to Mrs Morris (aka Frost) who used to live five hundred yards down the main road past the park.

'I can't recall seeing them till the trial.'

She folded her hands on her lap. 'We knew Lance Frost was saying those things about Katie. You know, what was supposed to have happened in the bushes between them. Mr Fixter told us it would come out in court but his statement would be disputed and the record put straight.' She looked up, eyes saddened. 'It never was. No one spoke up for Katie in court.'

'The trouble with courts,' said Caroline, sincerely, 'is that they are concerned with proof, not truth. Truth is sometimes the real casualty of courts.'

'We could just about have lived with a not guilty verdict.' Anne Burrows didn't seem sure. 'I mean, if there was doubt, that was the jury's duty. The judge made that plain. What we never got over was the way Frost and his mother acted afterwards, raking it over in that newspaper. Not a word of remorse about Katie. Just her own nightmare.

'We wanted the case reopened because the killer is still out there. Either Frost or his stepfather. We had someone called Keeling round. All we got a few weeks later was a letter

172

saying there was insufficient evidence to take the matter further.'

Caroline decided on the truth. 'That's the way it stands at the moment. There's only Frost's word against his stepfather. On the Davis inquiry, we're convinced Katie is the key.'

'There's still hope, then?'

'Oh, yes.' She lied this time, thinking, Not unless we can decide on the bait.

Her mind drifted on a wave of depression. Nothing. She'd unearthed nothing. Her eyes went back to the photo in the swimsuit on the Ladderex. 'Good at sport, I see.'

Mrs Burrows followed her gaze. 'Swimming, certainly. A proper water baby. She could swim as far under water as I can on the surface.' A light laugh, proud.

Caroline's mind drifted to the pathologist's findings, floated on to the conclusions in the Keeling report and washed up with that meeting with Mrs Frost and Lance and the cigarette that ended Jacko's abstinence. I wonder, she wondered.

A blustery breeze snatching at her white mac, Caroline went through black spiked gates into the park. She passed the bushes where Lance had either exposed himself or had hand relief, depending on whom she wanted to believe.

Alongside the shrubbery was an asphalt path which she left to walk on the wet shaggy grass, still awaiting the season's first cut, down a slope to the edge of the lake.

She stood alongside an old willow tree, its new leaves defying the cracks in its thick trunk, and looked into the brown water.

She closed her eyes on the scene in disappointment, then opened them wide. Stupid bitch, she told herself sharply. This is the water level after winter's rain. Katie died in autumn after summer's drought.

She drove back to the incident room, read and re-read all the reports and statements and studied the photos with a magnifying glass.

She closed her eyes, in blessed relief. Oh, Lance, she sighed, you've conned us. She reached for the phone and dialled a number she knew by heart. 'How's the Little Fat Man making out with Golden Jim?'

'Not good, I'm afraid.' Jacko sounded gloomy. 'He was at a clay shoot, miles away. Scores of witnesses plus a photographer. He claims he's never seen the dog, knows nothing. Says it was dumped while he was out and he was set up by a rival. What did your friend at Animal Alliance say?'

'She got the info from a man who gave a number which turned out to be a phone box. She passed the tip straight on, as promised. Later she found her phone on the blink. They kept the call connected so I couldn't get through to her.'

Jacko groaned. 'We were set up and walked right into it. His nark must have tipped him about our phone tap and he wants us off his back. The way things stand we're not even going to get him for having a dog without a licence.' A gloomy sigh. 'To complete a perfect day we've had a complaint lodged against us. From Rita and Lance via their solicitor. Harassment and incivility.' A moment's meditation. 'Next time we go, we'll need that warrant.'

'That's really the reason I'm phoning.' She told him of her visit to Mrs Burrows and the park and her study of the documents.

A long silence, then, 'I think you've identified the bait.' He was sounding his old bright self again.

Caroline held on to her sodden, rakish trilby to save it joining two squad officers in the wind-whipped lake where they worked in thigh waders. Hands and arms red-raw with cold, they located the thick roots that spread underwater from the crack willow. They traced the outlines by driving white stakes into the mud, stirring the water into the colour of milky coffee.

Jacko, in flat cap and green wellies, crouched on the grass, using his left hand to push white pegs into the soft earth. His waxed jacket bulged at the chest where his bandaged arm rested in a sling. Rain was running down his neck.

Caroline studied a stiff white square of cardboard, as a general would a map. It had six coloured photos stapled on, covered with cellophane to keep them dry. They were pictures of this scene, as it had been after the four youths found Katie Burrows.

Now and then she pulled out their statements from a plastic folder to correct by an inch here and half an inch there the directions she was calling out to him.

174

The pegs outlined the spot where Katie had been found, back on the grass, head face up in the water. Now the lake was a foot wider and six inches deeper. The two officers waded to the edge to complete the outline with stakes. At last Caroline was satisfied.

'No one suggested this at the time,' said the pathologist, defensively.

'That was because no one thought of it then.' She gave him an appeasing smile. 'All we're asking is this. Given the water level then, bearing in mind her lung capacity, her body measurements and the purchase she might have got from the nearest root, taking all that into account, is it possible?'

'Very possible.'

'Agreed,' said the forensic scientist from under a huge colourful umbrella he was sharing with the doctor.

All of them walked to their cars parked outside the spiked gates.

Caroline helped Jacko off with his wet jacket which she tossed on to the back seat. He sat in the passenger seat, lighting a cigarette with cold hands. She held the steering wheel but made no attempt to start the engine. 'Well?'

He blew out the smoke through tight lips, making a rustling sound. 'I think you've solved it.'

No pleasure purred through her; no satisfaction, only doubt. 'But how are we going to prove it?'

He inhaled and exhaled three more times as he told her how. 'It means double-crossing all of them.' He shook his head, uncertain.

'You've got to do it, Jacko.' She looked sideways at him, smiling encouragement.

He nodded, reluctant. 'OK. Let's get it over with.'

Mrs Morris was surprised but pleased to see him again so soon. He let her do the early talking, getting her loneliness out of her system. Oh, you poor thing, wet through, take off your coat, have a cuppa. What happened to your arm?

Then he dominated their conversation, talking fast, the way he always did when he was conning someone, especially someone he liked. Get it over quick and get out.

One of Terry Davis's crowd, he said. All evil men.

She nodded and said yes.

It can't go on forever, can it? Harry, in self-imposed exile, cut off from his family, the finger of suspicion forever pointing at him?

No, no, no, she said, as she shook, shook, shook her head.

So it's best, isn't it, to sort this out once and for all, get Lance the treatment he needs, release Rita from the burden of looking after him, give her and Harry a chance to get back together, if that's what they want, and allow Mrs Morris to go to her grave with a song in her heart when her time came, so to speak?

Yes, yes, yes, she nod, nod, nodded.

So, you lovely little lady, here's what we'll do. OK? She said yes and nodded.

20

The white cotton cloth was already on the square table by the window.

Surprise was pursued by anger across Harry's face. 'What the hell . . .?'

'Now.' His mother spoke firmly. 'Mr Jackson is here at my invitation.'

He let the *Mirror* slip out of his hand on to the flowered carpet by the chair in which he was sitting. 'You talk to him then.' He started to rise.

Mrs Morris pressed a hand on his shoulder, pushing him down. 'You'll listen.' A command. 'For my sake.'

Jacko coughed to clear his throat. 'We had a long chat, your mum and me. I've told her we've gone back through all the evidence. Harry, we know it wasn't you. In either case. I wanted someone from the police force to say that in front of your mother.' He stood, awkwardly, at the lounge door. 'To put her mind at rest.'

Harry stared at the blank TV screen. 'This is a liberty.'

His mother waved a gnarled finger. 'You should be grateful to him for turning out on a Saturday, with a bad arm and all.'

She motioned Jacko in, took the waxed coat and pointed to his place on the couch. 'Now you'll stay for tea.' An order, not an invitation.

He perched himself on the edge of the couch. His tie, red imps on grey, hung clear of his sling. 'How did Lincoln do?'

Harry retrieved the paper. 'Lost.' He asked after Leicester and reeled off birthday numbers he used weekly on the treble chance. Harry answered everything, added nothing. There were few score draws among them. 'I'll still be working next week then.' A weak laugh, not returned.

Mrs Morris, blue pinny over pink dress, limped through a sliding door from the kitchen carrying a plate filled with thin slices of ham. No John West salmon or Curtis's pork pie, Jacko noted, with a pang of disappointment. 'Can I help?' He started to get up.

She waved him down and set the table with crockery, cutlery, a jar of pickles, bread and butter, cake, completing the task with a tea tray on which sat a steaming pot.

'Sit here.' She pulled out a straight-backed chair from the table with a view through the window of the chestnut tree casting spidery shadows on the grass.

'Harry.' He rose and sat at Jacko's right without looking at him. His mother sat opposite. She cut the ham before handing Jacko his plate, then spooned pickle on to it, treating him as the invalid he felt.

Harry ate in silence while Jacko talked to his mother about the joys of parenthood and the afternoon walk he had taken with his son and his dog.

He nibbled the slab cake politely (at home Jacko was a great wolfer) and Mrs Morris talked about some of the scrapes Harry had got into as a boy. He disputed and corrected one story. 'I didn't cry then. That was when I was caught scrumping in that orchard.'

Soon he was joining the chat. Jacko told him a DIY carpentry story. About how he'd spent days making a garden cold frame, stepped back to admire his work and put a foot through the glass lid. Harry laughed, for the first time, and Jacko felt the lines that had corrugated his stomach all day smoothing away. It's going well, he told himself. Don't push it. Nice and easy does it.

Mother and son did the washing up between them while Jacko brought them the plates and cups in one hand.

Mrs Morris reclaimed the TV chair. They sat side by side on the put-you-up, Harry pulling the bottom of his thick fawn sweater down to the crutch of brown cords where his hands rested as he pushed out his legs, making himself at home.

A stranger's silence fell, threatening. Now or never, Jacko decided. He half turned towards him. 'Your mum and me are agreed that your family and friends and her neighbours ought to know that you're innocent.'

Yes, yes, Mrs Morris nod, nodded.

178

Harry gazed at his brown shoes. 'You can't charge Lance again so I don't see how.' His mother kept her head and mouth still in indecision, looking anxiously at Jacko for an answer.

'Let's find a way via Terry Davis. Let's have a chat man to man.' He turned further, so that only his left buttock remained on the cushion. 'Off the record. I can't make notes anyway.' He lifted his bandaged arm. Harry smiled. 'Level with each other. You tell me the lot. I hold nothing back from you.'

'Then I'll be going.' Mrs Morris started to pull herself out of the chair.

Harry looked at her in alarm. 'No!'

'Please stay.' Jacko spoke hurriedly. 'I don't mind, if Harry doesn't.'

She was out of her chair, untying her pinny. 'I've promised Mrs Bell downstairs a game of Scrabble.' She hooked the pinny over the back of her chair, staking her continuing claim to it.

She hobbled to the door where she turned. 'Just you be truthful, Harry. If not for yourself, then for my sake.'

Jacko watched her close the door on them. That, he decided, was as good a performance as Caroline's with Udden. Twenty out of ten.

His old mum had been spot on. Harry still had a thing for Rita, rated her, carried the old torch.

Jacko listened patiently to the potted history, never rushing him. About Lance's father, the drunken spendthrift. That first Saturday night date, a sing-along at the miners' welfare. His blooming relationship with Lance. The way he'd helped with his homework, teaching him squares and angles. The steakhouse meal over which they'd told him they wanted to marry.

'Lance was a bit, well . . .' He hit the right word. '. . . clingy, but he seemed pleased enough.'

A month of magic, the best of his life, then . . . He took his right hand out of his pocket, flicking thumb against middle finger which slapped noisily against the palm . . . Disaster.

First her mother died and she'd been devastated. Then Lance's trouble. 'You'll know about that.'

'How did she react?'

'Badly. Wouldn't you? A policeman brought him home and

told us what he'd been up to in the park. It was a bombshell. Never any hint before. No dirty mags, nothing. She kept him off school until the policeman came back and said the nurse wasn't pressing charges.'

'And then?'

'She marched him off to a shrink. She was so ashamed she didn't even want her own GP to know.'

'What was his verdict?'

'Immature personality, he said it was, seeking a bit of attention after the upheaval in his life. Our marriage, he meant. He asked us, well, if Lance may have seen us, well, sort of, at it. In bed, like. He told us to watch out for that in future and give him a lot of our time.'

'Did Rita accept that finding?'

A headshake. 'No. She had this bee in her bonnet. Thought he was a budding psycho or something.'

'Why?'

'Down to her father, that. He was a mental nurse at one of those state institutions. He died long ago but she remembered his tales. She became convinced that indecent exposure is the first symptom of something much more serious. Turned out to be true, didn't it?' Jacko nodded, gravely.

Rita, he went on, put into practice what she learned from her father. Psychopaths need discipline, he'd told her. She imposed a curfew, drew up a rota of chores, withdrew privileges when he stepped out of line.

Gradually the routine was relaxed as Lance did better in school reports. 'Thought we were over the hump.'

Then, a fresh disaster.

Within a week of him starting college to study catering, a uniformed PC – Terry Davis – came to the door. He had Lance's green bike in one hand. In the other, its rider, by the collar.

Harry came home from the colliery to an unforgettable sight. 'She was holding his head in a bowl of water in the kitchen sink, shouting at him. I pulled her off and he came up gasping. When I calmed her down she told me he had been flashing again. I asked her what the hell she was playing at. She said her father told her that psychos were frightened of water. They used to put them in the punishment block in strait-jackets and hose them down. God knows what sort of hospital he worked at.

'There wasn't going to be a court case, she said, but she wasn't going to let him get away with it, unpunished. That's why she had given him a ducking.'

'Did she explain why there was no court case? You see, we can find no record of that incident.'

A sly look, knowing. 'You wouldn't, would you? Rita said we owed Davis a favour for not reporting it. His kitchen. Two days' work it took and not even a cup of tea.'

Slowly, with the patience of a craftsman, he came to the day of Katie Burrows' death. 'We'd spent the afternoon replacing a shed up the road. Come five thirty, I start packing up. Lance is nowhere to be seen. I thought he'd gone home ahead of me. To get Rita's tea, one of his chores. There was no sign of him or his bike at the house. Knowing how Rita would react, I was getting worried. I drove here in case he'd popped to see Mum. No one was in. I toured around, looking for him, then headed home just after seven, fearing the balloon going up.'

'He was there. I expected a mouthful from Rita but not a word was said. Next day Lance was preparing the veg for the roast when your detectives called. They said they were investigating the death of a girl in the park and were arresting Lance on suspicion. He went as white as a dove.'

The detectives said Harry could go with Lance to the station. They took the boy into a room. He waited on a bench outside. An hour or so later Inspector Fixter came out and said Harry could talk to him . . .

Lance looked like a question mark the way he sat in his chair, long legs wrapped round each other, bent forward, head in his hands.

Harry stood before him, cradling his head to his stomach. 'What is it, son?' He'd never called him son before; always Lance.

'I'm scared. This will kill Mum.' He was sobbing.

Harry lowered his head so his chin rested in Lance's hair, damp with fear. 'I'll look after her.'

'That's my job, too, you know.'

'The best way of doing that is to be truthful. What happened?'

'We were messing about in the bush, me and this girl. Something frightened her and she ran off. I wasn't doing it again. Honest.' He looked up with tear-filled eyes. 'But she's young and I thought I might be in trouble. So I chased her to the side of the lake. And . . .' His rounded back trembled and he buried his face into Harry's jacket, mumbling. 'I can't remember. They say she's dead. What's going to happen?'

Harry crouched to bring up Lance's face, holding it gently in his hands. 'Tell them the truth, son. If you can't remember or don't know, say so. Don't make anything up. We'll work something out.'

He called back Inspector Fixter and sat silently in a corner as the statement was taken under caution.

Harry got a message to his wife at the garden centre. A van dropped her at the station. 'She was furious. She wanted to know why I hadn't called her earlier, why a solicitor hadn't been sent for, what sort of statement Lance had made. She saw him alone and came out in hysterics. When I got her home I had to call a doctor to give her sedatives.'

Terry Davis re-entered their lives in the spring. 'I didn't know he'd left the force to become a private investigator. Rita told me he had volunteered his help. He said he wanted to interview me for background. When I got to that bit about Lance and me being alone in the police station, he wanted to know if I'd take a lie test or hypnosis. He thought something may have been said that I'd pushed into my subconscious. Absolute crap and I told him so. In any case, I said, Lance would verify everything.'

On to the trial now. 'It was like a film, some courtroom drama, me sitting there, not realizing it was me they were talking about. It was all I could do to stop myself jumping up and screaming, "Lies!" I was in a daze afterwards. Stayed one night at the hotel with the paper, then came here.'

He couldn't face reading what Jason French had written straight away. Weeks later, in exile, he took the article ('Such shit') to a solicitor. 'He said all they'd really done was rehash the court stuff which was covered by something or other . . .'

'Privilege,' said Jacko helpfully.

'. . . which meant there was nothing I could sue over. I wasn't after compensation. All I wanted was a retraction. All I want is the truth to come out.' His face was drained, empty.

'Seen Terry Davis since?'

'No thank you.' A pause between each word; each word emphasized.

'How about Rita and Lance?'

Lance never, Rita often, he replied. Apart from her three visits here before he ran himself out of town, she'd been round to Mrs Dodds' digs complaining about those neighbours and their petition . . .

'What do you expect?' He had addressed her with a bluntness never displayed in their life together. 'Accept the transfer and start afresh like I'm trying to do.'

'Can't we be together?' Her face was masked in misery.

'Not while Lance is at home. How could he do that to me?'

'It was an accident but he didn't think anyone would believe it. He just made it up on the spur of the moment. He hadn't even told his solicitor.'

Since the move to Melton, Harry had driven through the rolling hills of the Vale of Belvoir to see her. 'Just for a drink.' Diplomatic code, Jacko noted, to tell him conjugal rights had not been reclaimed.

'How's Lance?'

'Well, according to her, but I don't believe it. He missed two terms of college while he was in prison but he's getting good marks at his new one, she says.'

'Any chance of a reconciliation?'

'Not while Lance is there. I wouldn't feel safe under the same roof. I know the truth, see.'

'What if he gets a job away from home?'

A faraway look told Jacko that this was the dream that lulled him to sleep at night. Reality returned with a single, slow shake of his head. 'Doubt it. She claims he's going out on his own but I can't see her allowing that. She's bound to be keeping an eagle eye on him. He's dangerous. He shouldn't be walking the streets. I'm surprised you've never acted.'

'We can hardly give him a fair trial and then lock him up when the jury disagrees with us. That might upset some civil-righters, don't you think?' A bleak smile.

They'd had a drink together the week before Christmas, he went on. 'Gave me a kiss, in fact.' A faint smile. They sent each other lovey-dovey cards. Rita didn't add Lance's name to hers. He'd only seen her once since.

183

'She phoned Mrs Dodds' one weekend and asked to borrow the car. Lance had a driving test fixed and needed some practice.'

'Can he drive?'

'Should be able to by now. I was giving him runs round a disused airfield before he was arrested and she bought him a course of six lessons for his birthday.'

'When was this phone call?'

'Just after Christmas.' A vague reply without thought, then thought through when Jacko asked again. Second time round he was very precise.

'The first weekend in January. I'd just got back from a fortnight off here with Mum. At my firm you take part of your holidays over Christmas and New Year because people don't want you messing up their houses then. She phoned on the Sunday just after I got back in the evening to Mrs Dodds' for work next day. She asked if she could borrow the car on the Tuesday.'

The day of Davis's death and Jacko had to quell his excitement.

'I didn't mind. It sits in the road all week because I use the firm's van. She said she was coming to Nottingham by bus to do some shopping and would collect it about six.'

Closer still and Jacko consciously immobilized his face to hide the thrill he was feeling.

'I told her to be careful because it was getting foggy. She dropped the car off outside Mrs Dodds' the next afternoon while I was at work.'

'That Tuesday evening after you'd seen her off.' Jacko spoke slowly, trying to steady himself. 'What did you do?'

'Dunno. Watched telly, I suppose.'

The thick sod hasn't even worked out an alibi, Jacko thought, and any lingering doubt about Caroline's theory vanished. 'Not *The Graduate*, I hope?' A bright smile, amused with himself.

He shook his head, puzzled.

Jacko tried again, serious this time. 'With Mrs Dodds?'

He pondered. 'On my own. She was away into the New Year in Edinburgh.' It came back to him via his stomach, the way it does with spoonfed men. 'First week back I was living on take-outs. Why?'

Jacko held up a silencing hand. 'One more thing and I'm all yours. When you moved to Mrs Dodds', did you take all your clothes?'

'Most of them.'

'Including the donkey jacket you wore when you worked at the pit?'

'Haven't had it on in months.'

'Where did you last see it?'

'Hanging up in the shed.'

'What shed?' Jacko wasn't leading him. He had to be sure.

'At Rita's. Our old place. Why?'

'Did you take all your tools?'

'I may have left a few odds and ends.'

'Such as?'

He thought. 'A nail bar, a couple of crowbars. Offcuts from jobs, perhaps.'

More. Come on, Harry. Give me more. 'And?'

'Well, only a few rusted nails and screws.'

'Leave any work gloves behind?'

'Only a very old pair.'

Jacko fell back with such force that he moved the couch with their combined weights on it. He felt for his cigarettes.

He drew in smoke greedily and let it go sparingly. 'Lance killed Katie. No doubt about that. He didn't make a completely clean breast of it to Inspector Fixter because he couldn't face up to what he'd done. You're right. He is dangerous. No doubt about that. No one is really safe.' He was laying it on, thick, fast.

'Rita's right, too. That's the way psychos operate. They start flashing. They can't stop, can't help it. When the urge comes, they must do it there and then, whatever the risk. That's a well-known medical fact.

'Katie probably recognized him or his bike so he had to kill her or face Rita's wrath again.

'When the remand hearing appeared in the *Mercury*, Davis, kicked out of our force by then, recognized him as the flasher who'd provided him with a kitchen, buckshee.'

He tapped ash into a tray, slowing. 'There are two possibilities here, Harry, and I have to tell you in all honesty I don't know which is right.

'First, blackmail. Davis knew more than any policeman about Lance's flashing. It would have strengthened the case if he'd shopped Lance. Maybe he approached Rita for hush money.' He waited, frowning, thinking. 'But then all Rita would have to have done was tell us and we'd nick him for accepting bribes. I'd have done it with pleasure. I'd been after him for months.' The more Jacko thought about it, the more he seemed to be going off this idea.

'Second, he came on as the Samaritan, offering help for a quick buck. Not many private eyes get on murder cases. Mostly it's dirty divorces and debt-collecting. I don't know.' His creased-up look confirmed his doubts.

'While he's playing the private detective he rumbles that you haven't got an alibi. He tells Lance this when he visits him in prison.'

Harry shook his head, dissenting. 'Rita went with him. She'd never allow –'

Jacko broke in, firmly, brooking no argument. 'They're not together all the time. She'd wander off to get tea and biscuits from the visitors' canteen. On these visits, in her absence, Davis told him exactly what to say.

'When Lance did as coached, he takes everybody in court by surprise – his mother, his lawyers, the judge, the jury and, above all, you. Davis must have known what he was going to say because he sold the story to the paper in advance of the trial. I can prove that. And I can prove he kept all that money himself as his payment.'

Jacko stubbed out the butt, a tricky task with his wrong hand, and he caught the flesh alongside his thumb nail. He licked away the pain, looking at Harry. 'So far so good, for Lance anyway. Right?'

Harry's eyes were on him, engrossed. Jacko looked away again. 'Come the New Year and Davis is broke. Believe me, we know that for a fact. He needs money fast so he wheels out Lance again for Jason French.

'We know how he got their new address and we can prove that, too. He drove over to see him, door-stepping till Rita went out shopping. He offers Lance a deal – fifty-fifty, say –

on anything they made out of the paper. All he had to do was put his name to an "I Got Away With Murder" story. This he did in Davis's notebook.

'They make a tentative arrangement to meet and then see French. Over that weekend Lance suspects he's been conned. He didn't make a penny out of the first story. Why should he out of this? He realizes, too, that Davis knows the whole truth about what happened in the park. He may even have admitted it to him. It dawns on him that for the rest of his life he's going to be blackmailed. He decides Davis has got to go.

'His mother has no transport. You have. He talks her into borrowing your car.'

'Never.' A headshake, emphatic. 'She wouldn't do that.'

'She wouldn't know what he had in mind. She sits with him for one spin. Then he says, "I've got this college mate who's qualified. Let me practise some more." He drops his mate off and sets sail. Alone. He lures Davis into the car-park, rips his throat out, takes his notebook with the incriminating statement.'

'I can't believe that.' A headshake, rejection, conflict coming.

'Wait, Harry.' Index finger raised, eyes sidelong, cunning. 'It gets worse. Not only did he borrow your car, he was wearing your old donkey jacket. We have a witness to that.' From a pocket he took a tube of the ointment he'd seen in Rita's bathroom. 'Seen anything like that before?'

Harry nodded, speechless.

'Who uses it?'

'Lance.' Hardly audible.

'A skin irritation?' A nod, dumbfounded. 'Now how did I know that?' A smirk. 'Because a very good witness told me. He smelt it on him.'

Harry groaned quietly.

'It gets worse still. Why was I asking you what you left behind in the shed? Because the pathologist says his throat was ripped out with one, most likely, two steel-spiked gloves. Or could they have been your old gloves with nails and screws driven through the fingertips?'

Harry closed his eyes and dropped his head.

'What you've totally missed is this, Harry. He was in your car,

187

wearing your coat, using your cast-offs as a murder weapon. If anything had gone wrong, who would they have been traced back to?' A pause, potent. 'You.

'And who has a motive for killing Davis because he helped blacken his name?' Pause. 'You.

'And who was sitting alone at Mrs Dodds' watching TV with no alibi?' Jacko didn't answer his own final question. No need. Harry clamped his hands to his face. 'He was sticking you in it again, Harry.' A low tone now, concerned. 'I'm very worried for you. You're the only one left who knows the truth.'

Harry stared through his fingers. 'You don't think . . .' He was unable to articulate the unthinkable.

'I don't know. But I do know we must stop him.'

'How?'

Jacko told him. Half-way through Harry began shaking his head. 'I can't do that. It would kill Rita.'

'Let me finish.' His head was shaking firmer still when Jacko did finish.

'You're asking me to act the Judas.'

'I'm asking you to help me stop the killing.'

'I'd rather die.'

'Lance might be rather keen on that. And who after you? Your mother? Rita?'

'What about Rita?'

'Look.' Jacko moved his head close to his, speaking very softly. 'I know you're fond of her. When the truth comes out she'll be badly hurt, true. But, given time, when she sees Lance making progress, she'll come round. Hospitals aren't like they were in her dad's day. There've been big changes. We don't lock them up any more and throw away the key. It won't be forever.'

'It's asking a lot.' He was wavering.

Jacko moved in for the kill. He looked at the window-sill, to the photo of his sister's two children. 'How old are your nieces?'

'Sixteen and fourteen.' A mumble through the gaps in fingers pressed to his face.

'How would you feel if one of them was walking through a park one night while Lance was riding around on his bike and . . .' He went no further. They sat in silence for a full minute.

'Would you tell me what to say?' Hesitant, confused.

'You'll be word perfect.' Calm, confident.

'It can't be at Mrs Dodds.'

'We'll find the ideal place.'

He looked at Jacko, hands together in front of his face, the prayer position, pleading. 'You won't arrest her?'

'Why should we? No jury will convict a mother for protecting a sick son. That's what he is. That's all she's done.'

Harry lowered his head. 'OK, then.' Tears were leaking between his fingers.

21

This tape begins at nineteen thirty hours.

Over his earpiece came the 'Coronation Street' theme, a dispiriting dirge he hated.

The street bell rang above the wailing cornet's solo. Caroline closed the broom cupboard and locked the door from the inside. Just a quarter-inch of light, dim but comforting, ran along the gap at the bottom.

He sat beside her, both on kitchen stools among the buckets, brooms, an ironing board and a tape machine on the floor by his feet.

Enough light to survive on, he told himself. He breathed slow and easy, bending forward to rest his right elbow in its sling on his knee.

Heavy footsteps departed down the stairs. The sound of splashing traffic came and went as the door was opened and closed. Muffled voices, contralto and baritone, filtered up. Two sets of footsteps now, faint at first, louder as the lounge door squeaked back into its frame.

'Needs a drop of oil,' said the contralto as though contributing to a debate in the Rover's Return.

'There's a fair bit needs doing,' said the baritone. 'Let me just . . .' A click and Ivy Tilsley was switched off in mid-sentence.

'What do you think?' asked the baritone, crystal clear now.

'Nice.' Approval in the contralto's voice. 'What made you move?'

'I couldn't stay at Mrs Dodds' for ever, could I?' Silence. Tick, tick went the kitchen clock.

'Sit yourself down.' A newspaper rustled, then the sounds of cushion springs contracting. 'Sorry to drag you here, Rita. The car's kaput.'

'Don't worry. I wanted to see your new place.' Tick, tick. 'What's the problem, Harry?'

'I didn't want to tell you over the phone.' Conspiracy in Harry's voice. 'I'm being chased up by the police over Davis's death.'

'That's nothing to worry about.' Very placid. 'They're bound to be seeing everybody.'

'You, too?'

'And Lance. A couple of weeks ago.'

'Did they ask about my car?'

'What about it?' A questioning edge hardened her tone.

'They're linking it with Terry Davis's case.' Shit, thought Jacko, he's missed a line out of his script.

'They're questioning everybody Terry knew. It's routine.' Tick, tick. 'You worry too much.'

'Worry!' He growled it. 'Of course I bloody worry. I've been branded a murderer. I've lost my job, my home . . .'

'You can always come back to us. I've told you that before.' Softness there, caring.

'And Lance? No thank you.' He pecked it out.

'What happened in the park was an accident. I've told you that before, too.' She spoke sharply, offended.

'And was Terry Davis an accident?' A measured question, well executed.

'What do you mean?'

Several seconds, several ticks.

'What about the car, Harry?'

'What?' He'd lost his thread. Get a grip, son, Jacko urged.

'The car.' A prompter's voice, urgent.

'Oh. They questioned me for two hours. I'm sick up to here with them.' Jacko imagined him slicing his hair with his palm.

'What did they want to know?'

'Where I was. Where the car was.'

'What did you tell them?'

Tick, tick. 'Rita, I worked it out.' He was speaking very deliberately, as though reading lines. 'You borrowed the car that night.' Tick, tick. 'For Lance.' Tick, tick. 'You phoned on the Sunday and collected it on the Tuesday, that Tuesday.'

'Well, we didn't go to Leicester.' She was sounding flustered. 'We just drove around Melton.'

'That's not the impression they gave.' A good ad-lib line that, thought Jacko, approvingly.

'What did you tell them?' Consternation overpowered the curiosity in her voice.

'That it was parked outside Mrs Dodds'.'

'Good.' Satisfied, relaxed.

'But they said they'd be back.'

'They always say that.' A light laugh. 'Register a formal complaint. We did. It frightens them off. Haven't seen hide nor hair of them since.' The clock's solo lasted several tense seconds. 'How about a coffee?'

A cushion's springs were released with the rustling sound of fabric unfolding. Dull footsteps past the locked cupboard door. A loose floorboard groaned. Sharper steps on kitchen lino. Water hissed into a kettle which was clicked on. Pots scraped on a shelf, then clanked on contact with a plastic work-top.

'How many more rooms?' Rita's raised voice was caught by the lounge microphone fitted among the brass rings on the closed blue curtains.

'Just the bedroom and bathroom.' Harry's voice was recorded on the mike behind the kitchen radiator which was picking up the ticking of the round quartz clock on the wall.

The lounge door squeaked open and the mike in the bedroom behind a framed photo of Leicester's tree-lined New Walk transmitted the sound of the bottom edge of a door rubbing against a thick carpet.

The clock ticked off ten seconds. The sounds were repeated in reverse through the black padded headphones which the collator wore as he crouched over a recording machine in the back of a big white van parked in the busy street outside. In the van, dressed in grey overalls, were four squad officers – two men, two women.

Shuffling steps covered the lounge carpet, then burst into life on the kitchen lino. 'Very cosy,' said Rita above the gathering rumble of the heating water. Spoons clinked in mugs. 'Maybe you'll invite me for the weekend.'

'What about Lance?'

'He's old enough to take care of himself.' Suction pads popped on the door of a humming refrigerator. 'Better than you, by the looks of this.' A milk bottle rattled against a steel bar.

'I haven't had much chance to shop yet. Anyway, there's a pizza place, a curry shop and a chippy round the corner.' As good as his dear old mum is our Harry, thought Jacko.

'What you need is home cooking.' Tick tick. 'Lance is top of his class, by the way.' Tick, tick. 'Come on, love. Cheer up.'

A deep sigh. 'I've got this awful feeling it isn't over.'

'Of course it is. They're whistling in the dark to keep their spirits up.' Jacko shook his head, smiling. 'If they do come back, what will you tell them about the car?'

'What do you want me to say?'

'I'd appreciate you not mentioning I borrowed it. It will only cause trouble for Lance.'

'Why should I protect him? After what he did to me.'

The kettle clicked. A spoon stirred. A lighter flicked. A gas flame hissed. 'Here,' said Harry, 'use this.'

'Thanks.' Tick, tick. 'It was an accident, you know. What was said in court wasn't his idea.'

'Whose was it then?'

'Terry's. He told him to blame you. It was the only way out, he said. No one would believe it was an accidental drowning. He should know. He was a policeman.'

'And Lance did as he was told, like a good boy.' Sardonic.

'We wouldn't have let you go to prison, you know.'

'Really!' A sneer, not a query.

'We had a plan to get you out.'

'Escape?' Don't overcook the sarcasm, Jacko fretted.

'No.' Impatient. 'Out of trouble, if they'd charged you.'

'What!'

'We had your defence all worked out.'

'Big deal. Six months in custody and then trot out the same story. What was I to do? Blame Lance? It wouldn't have worked twice.' Tick, tick. 'Let's go back into the lounge.' Shit, thought Jacko. You should have kept her talking.

Footsteps echoed on the lino. The carpet deadened them. Snap. The line of light at the bottom of the door went black. Jacko closed his eyes and opened them. The blackness remained. The door jerked against its lock in front of his face. A shudder shot through him. A knot in his stomach tightened. His injured arm started to throb.

'What's this?'

'The broom cupboard. The lock's knackered.'

The deadened footsteps faded. Cushion springs compressed. A couple of minutes were spent chatting about Harry's mum, Lance's college and Mrs Dodds. He's blown it, thought Jacko, agitated. Calm came again when Rita returned to the subject left in the air in the kitchen.

'We wouldn't have let you go to jail, you know.'

'Why not? You only have to watch "Rough Justice" on the telly. They jail innocent people all the time. Mainly on false testimony.'

'Not with what we had worked out. It would have meant trouble for me.' Tick, tick. 'I would have stood by you.' Tick, tick. 'I want you back, Harry.'

The veins inside Jacko's bandaged arm bulged. His blood begged for a shot of nicotine. He lectured himself: You can last half an hour without a fag. He questioned himself: Isn't that, is it? Face up to it. You need one for its glow, its light, its redness. Anything but this total blackness that's burying you alive. He began to breathe rapidly.

'I'm frightened, Rita.'

'There's nothing to worry about.'

'There's Lance to worry about. What's he doing tonight?'

'Swotting for an exam. He's all right.'

'He's dangerous.'

'Nonsense.' A shout, jarring Jacko's eardrum.

'He killed Katie and now Davis.'

'Rubbish. Absolute rubbish.' The sound level on the collator's dial flicked towards red. 'How can you even think that?'

'And he was planning to drop me in it again. He borrowed my car . . .'

'I borrowed your car.'

Jacko felt the sweat running in beads from his forehead, seeping through his thick eyebrows and under his spectacles. Salt stung his eyes. Sticky riverlets ran down his cheeks. Another set sail from the nape of his neck, down the plains of his back into the valley of his buttocks. His left hand dug deep in his trouser pocket, two fingers prodding the lining into his groin. I've got to have light. I need light. I must see light. He swayed on the stool.

He felt Caroline's small hand grip his elbow, then slide down

194

the arm. He took his hand out of his pocket to meet it. She threaded her fingers between his and lifted both their hands, twisting them, so that the back of his felt the coolness of her smooth cheek.

Think of grandma, he instructed himself. Think of George Marshall. Every second of every day in total darkness, like this. Hang on for them. They have given you so much. Be patient for Katie. You're about to get the answer you promised her. And for the boys and girls in the squad who have sweated blood for you. Hang on for Scotty who trusts you. Hang on, son, hang on. The coolness of Caroline swam through his veins like a lazy river, calming him, caressing him.

'He needs treatment. Then maybe we could –'

'Where the hell did you get that idea from?' The needle in the van outside went up again. 'You were there when the doctor said there was nothing wrong with him.'

'Yes, and look what's happened since. First Katie Burrows, then Davis.'

'Davis was a charlatan. You know that.'

'Katie wasn't.'

'She was a slag.'

A shocked silence. Then, incredulous, 'Rita, she was fourteen.'

'And a slag. The bushes were her idea.'

'Lance is having you on.'

'She egged him on.'

'You say that because you want to believe it. You can't face up to the truth about Lance.'

'The truth is' – she spaced out each word – 'that Lance didn't do it . . .'

'Oh, come on.'

'I did. It was my fault. But I keep telling you. It was an accident. She ran. I caught up with her by the lake.'

'Rita, this won't wash.'

'I only held her under for a moment. Just to teach her to keep away from him.'

'I see. First I carry the can. Now you. Anybody but your precious boy.'

'Davis was no accident, though. The blackmailer.'

195

'You're just making this up to protect him. You're obsessed with him. There's no hope for us . . .'

'Who do you think was the woman in the head scarf they're looking for? Who was the youth in the donkey jacket?'

'So I am right.' Triumphant. 'He was wearing my jacket, borrowed my car. It was him.'

'Sooner or later Davis was going to tell the papers I killed the girl in the park. I had to stop him.'

'Rita, please.' A hint of anxiety. 'These lies are making matters worse. Lance is going to have to face up to it. He needs treatment. No one's safe. Me. No one. I'll come back to you if you'll go to the police.'

She was no longer listening. 'He knew nothing about it till afterwards. It was my idea; all mine, not his. Davis was evil. Didn't deserve to live. I took his voice box out. He won't be doing any talking now.' A low laugh, mirthless, frightening.

'Rita.' Stunned.

'Lance went back to help him. He was prepared to tell the police it was him, if necessary. To save me. That's how much he cares. Not like you. You've never –'

'Rita. For God's sake, don't say any more.' An imploring tone.

'I had to kill him. There would have been no –'

'*Rita. Shut up.*' Panic now.

'I'm glad he's dead. Proud it was me.'

'*Quiet.*'

Two thuds on the carpet.

'Get off me.' Anger, alarm.

'I'm sorry.' Begging, pleading.

'Let me go. You wanted the truth. You –'

'*Shut up.*'

'*Off me.*'

The needle hit red and stayed there.

Caroline let go of Jacko's hand and turned the key. He pushed the door open and stepped out of the cupboard. He blinked in the light. Caroline slipped behind his back.

Rita had her knees clasped together beneath her chin so that Caroline could see up her blue pleated skirt. Harry was kneeling by her chair, hands clamped over her mouth. Her hands stopped clawing his when she saw Caroline. Her eyes went white and wide.

196

'Mrs Morris. You know I am Detective Sergeant Parker and you also know Inspector Jackson.'

Harry released his hands. 'Bastard.' A hiss directed at Jacko, whose eyes had adjusted now and gazed apologetically down on him.

'We are arresting you . . .'

'*Bastard*,' Rita screamed at Harry.

'*Bastard*,' Harry screamed at Jacko.

'. . . for murder. You are not obliged to say anything . . .'

'How could you?' Rita was wailing like Coronation Street's cornet.

'. . . but anything you do say will be taken down . . .'

'Shithouse.' Harry waddled on his knees towards Jacko. 'You knew. *You Shithouse.*'

'. . . and may be given in evidence.'

'Lance. Oh, Lance.' Rita pulled her knees right up under her chin, turned sideways, shaking, sobbing, her head on the arm of an easy chair.

Harry dived, catching Jacko in a weak hold round the backs of his knees. He flexed them so that he lost a foot in height. 'Easy, Harry.'

Heavy footsteps thundered on the stairs. Sirens sounded in the distance. The door burst open too fast to squeak. One squad man skipped towards Harry. He headlocked him from behind.

'Easy,' Jacko repeated, this time to the officer, who stood with legs splayed.

Two women detectives entered, breathless. They looked anxiously at Caroline, who gave them a terse nod.

In strolled the collator, always cool under pressure. 'All right, guv?' Jacko nodded.

The sirens grew deafening. Brakes squealed. A woman officer knelt by Rita and stroked her hair.

More footsteps on the stairs, heavier, faster, and four uniformed officers appeared. Two constables took Harry, an arm each. Jacko straightened. He stepped back to view Harry, arms outstretched, a contorted face, crucified on the cross of proof. And on the altar of my vanity, he thought, for in that split second of absolute honesty he knew that he, perhaps more than anyone, wanted, needed the plaudits that came with success.

197

He turned to the collator. 'One crew with her. One with him. Tell the Melton detail to bring Lance in.'

Harry was lifted to his feet and led to the door, like a Saturday night drunk. Two WPCs took longer to coax Rita out of her chair, one putting an arm round her waist. 'Come on, love.' She was half carried from the room.

Jacko lowered his head. A long silence was ticked off by the clock.

He threw back his shoulders, lifted his head. 'P-h-e-w.' He rummaged with his left hand to find his cigarettes.

Caroline walked slowly towards him, opened the packet, took one out, poked it in his mouth and lit it for him.

'Thanks.' Jacko spoke through the smoke. He waited, smiling at her. Then: 'How did you know?'

'Know what?'

'That I'm scared of the dark.'

Her bird-like smile, evasive. She nodded at the cigarette. 'I thought you needed that.'

My missus, Jacko thought, seeing through her lie. She got loaded at that party and blabbed my bedroom secret.

Caroline giggled at his discomfort. 'Turned off the tape?'

Shit, he thought. When that's played in court the whole squad will know that a lesbian held my hand because I was frightened in the dark. Does it matter? Does it really matter? No, it does not.

A smile, deeply affectionate. 'I don't half love you, you know.'

He turned quickly and only caught the beginnings of the glistening in her eyes at words which, he guessed, she had never heard before from a man outside her family and never would again.

He walked to the opened broom cupboard and bent over the machine. Tick, tick, went the clock.

This tape ends at nineteen fifty-four.

22

'On the first indictment, do you find Rita Morris guilty or not guilty of the murder of Katherine Burrows?'

'Not guilty.'

'On the alternative charge, do you find her guilty or not guilty of manslaughter?'

'Guilty.'

Mrs Burrows gave her husband a puzzled glance. A row behind, Harry Morris held his mother's hand.

The black-gowned clerk shuffled documents. 'On the second indictment, do you find Mrs Morris guilty or not guilty of the murder of Terence John Davis?'

'Not guilty.'

'On the alternative charge, do you find her guilty or not guilty of manslaughter?'

'Guilty on the grounds of diminished responsibility,' said the forewoman of the jury, positive, no doubts.

'Do you find Lance Frost guilty or not guilty of conspiracy to murder Terence John Davis?'

'Not guilty.'

'Do you find Lance Frost guilty or not guilty of acting as an accessory after the commission of a crime?'

'Guilty.'

Lance gripped his uncomprehending mother's hand. He towered over her in his pin-striped blue suit and black leather tie. She was wearing a plain fawn dress. She looked pale and frail, her strength and spirit sapped. They sat down together in the dock as the public stirred and sighed, the nearest they'd come to making a noise all week.

The prosecutor stood and let the jury into a secret. Both defendants had pleaded guilty in their absence to perjury at

Lance's original trial. 'I recall the arresting officer.'

Caroline slipped off a bench behind the barrister where she'd sat next to Jacko. He'd noted the verdicts with ticks and crosses in the way he checked his pools at his mother's on a Saturday before tea.

She had already taken the oath when she gave evidence, going through the taped conversation as a double act with the prosecution's QC, he playing Harry, she as Rita.

She did not pick up the bible again. No, she confirmed, neither mother nor son had previous convictions.

Rita's QC shook his head. No questions.

Lance's counsel rose. 'My client was held in custody for two months, was he not?'

Yes, said Caroline. On his arrest, she explained, he signed confessions in which he admitted causing the deaths of both Katie and Davis, absolving his mother from all responsibility. For nine weeks he would not retract, despite the fact that his mother was also accepting full blame in a written statement . . .

Three months without a clue, thought Jacko, his mind meandering, then two conflicting confessions to two separate killings.

Lance was claiming to have ducked Katie in the lake, like his mother ducked him in the sink bowl. He couldn't give much detail about Davis's death. 'My mind's a jumble.'

Finally, Jacko begged for the truth – for Katie's folks, the judge, the jury. 'And above all your mother. Her doctors haven't a clue how to treat her. You say one thing. She says another. If they don't know what ails her, they won't know how to help her.'

A tense silence, on the verge. He tried one last throw; to make him laugh. 'It's like you reporting sick to the prison MO, complaining of a broken arm while holding your balls. He wouldn't know whether to give you a sling or a jockstrap.'

Lance lifted his head from his hands, a smile on tear-wetted face. He looked for guidance at his solicitor, who nodded. The truth flooded out with the tears.

He knew Katie from school. They were snogging in the bushes. The sap rose within. 'Hold it for a minute,' he pleaded.

'Get away.' She pushed him, stepped out of the bushes and

200

came face to face with Rita, who screamed, 'Slag!' Katie ran, terrified, towards the lake, Rita chasing her. Lance fastened his flies with fumbling fingers. He saw them rolling on the grass at the water's edge. By the time he reached them Rita was ducking her face down in the shallow water. He pulled her off. Katie splashed up, turning to face them. He fled, his mother chasing him now. 'Katie was standing in the water when I left the lakeside. When the police arrested me, I couldn't shop my mum, could I?'

They'd misread Davis's involvement. 'She approached him and said she wanted his help or she'd tell on him over the bribe he'd taken.' Davis's idea was simple, really. All he had to do was blame Harry for everything he'd seen his mother doing. 'I wasn't keen. He's a good bloke. When he was around I felt safe from my mum's moods. But I was scared. I thought I'd be in prison till I was an old man.'

It came as a surprise when Davis called months later. 'How would you like to earn a grand or two?'

'Not likely,' said Lance when he heard how.

'I know what happened.'

'It was an accident.'

'Involving your mum, not Harry, though, wasn't it?'

'What could I do?' Lance asked Jacko. 'I had to go along with him or you'd have charged Mum.'

Davis wasn't interested in the whole truth. He allowed Lance to continue the pretence that Rita wasn't involved. He took the blame again in a 'My Terrible Truth' story, a tear-jerker, the guilt he felt over branding his innocent stepfather.

They met in the station forecourt. Lance was wearing the old jacket because it was handy and the night was cold. Jacko had totally misled Harry because implicating him had never entered Lance's mind. Rita told Davis she wanted a private word about money. 'Back in a jiffy,' she said to Lance.

He stood around, stamping his cold feet, then decided to find out what was happening. His mother ran from behind the car-park barrier. 'Come away.'

'Where's Terry?'

'Come away.'

He shook off her hand and went into the car-park, fearing the worst. 'He was in a pool of blood. I couldn't hear him breathing.'

201

Such was his panic he ran the wrong way out of the car-park and had no memory of a blind man standing outside or a black jogger running by. He circled the block and returned to the borrowed car.

'Why, Mum, why?'

'I had to. He knew. He would never have left us in peace.'

Next day Lance added to the fog with a back garden bonfire of her clothing, the donkey jacket, Davis's notebook and Harry's old protective gloves with screws drilled through the fingertips. ('She got that idea from a horror video.')

Since then he'd been caring for her. 'You're right, Mr Jackson. She is ill. But I couldn't tell on her. What would people think? My own mother.'

Lance was sobbing. Jacko put an arm round him so that his head dropped on his shoulder . . .

'As a result of that final statement,' Lance's QC was asking Caroline, 'you withdrew the charge of murder and your objection to bail?' She said yes.

'And it's also correct, isn't it, that he spent seven months in custody, awaiting trial, accused in connection with Katie Burrows' death, for which he was in no way responsible?' Another yes.

He beamed his thanks and Caroline backed out of the witness box and sat in a chair behind it.

Rita's QC, a man of few words, stood. He asked for a sentence in accordance with the medical evidence. His only witnesses had been doctors. Her paranoid schizophrenia was deep-seated and of long standing, one said. Added psychopathic disorders had surfaced with catastrophic results in the wake of her mother's death and her son's sexual misbehaviour, said another.

Lance's counsel, on his feet again, pleaded with pained politeness for his liberty. 'He has spent a total of nine months in custody when his real crime has been to love his mother too much.'

The judge, kindly and efficient throughout, put his elbows on his bench, shook his hands to straighten the ermine cuffs of his red robe, and formed a chin rest with them. 'Don't get up, Mrs Morris. Katie Burrows died at your hands through your act of recklessness and Terence Davis was killed to keep that fact a secret. The jury have agreed with the medical opinion –

and so do I – that you are in need of treatment. You will go to hospital to receive it. Your eventual release will be a matter for your doctors and the Home Secretary. All I will say is that you have a loyal son who, I feel certain, will give you the help and hope you need.'

He looked at two women guards sitting behind her. 'She may go.'

Rita appeared not to have heard a word. She sat, head down, knees tight together, hands on her lap, clasping a handkerchief she had not let go of for a week.

His son put his arm round her, kissed her cheek and held his nose to it. Gently he helped her to her feet while her guards hovered, uncertain. She threw her right hand across her chest up to his neck, craning her neck as high as it would go, her eyes tightly shut, weeping pitifully. He lowered his head so they walked nose to cheek, arms round each other to the door which led to the cells.

The court was hushed in a way that Jacko had never known before. People seemed to have stopped breathing.

Lance returned alone in a shambling defeated walk to the rail. He nipped tears from his eyes with finger and thumb. 'Sorry.' A cracked voice.

'Take your time.' The judge spoke at little above a whisper.

Lance let his arms drop to his side. The judge, chin still rested on his hands, raised his eyebrows. 'All right now?' A nod.

The judge began to speak clearly, thinking through each sentence. 'I am going to put you out of your agony straight away. I am not going to deprive you of your freedom.' A sigh went round the public gallery, led by Katie's mother. Harry closed his eyes.

'I owe a public duty to explain that decision. Perjury is a wicked crime which strikes at the very heart of justice.'

Every week some judge somewhere says that something strikes at the very heart/core/root of justice, and when they are talking of false testimony, they are right, Jacko had decided long ago.

'In normal circumstances this offence merits a long sentence. In your case you caused a kind, caring stepfather untold misery but I accept it was not your idea and you did so reluctantly.

'I accept, too, the jury's finding that there was no plot to dispose of Mr Davis but you did dispose of evidence which could have delayed, perhaps for ever, the facts coming out. This is another serious offence which usually merits a long sentence. I acknowledge you committed both crimes in misguided protection of your mother but, in doing so, you held back the treatment she so sorely needs.'

He folded his arms and looked to one side in a thought he decided to share. 'You know, parents are wonderful but there comes a time when they and their offspring have to let go of one another. It can be a painful experience on either or both sides. The timing varies but people know when that time is right. That moment is long overdue for you.'

He looked down at his papers. 'What makes it possible for me to take the wholly exceptional course I am proposing are three letters I have received.

'The first is from a doctor who tells me that the problems which you displayed and which added to your mother's anxieties are behind you.' Lance, Jacko knew, had been impotent since the night of Katie's death, such was the trauma he'd suffered, poor sod.

'The second comes from the family of Katie Burrows.' He picked up two sheets of blue paper. 'They accept their daughter's death for the tragedy it was and do not blame you. Moreover, they express their forgiveness to your mother and wish her a speedy return to health.' He shook his head in silent admiration.

'The third' – he retrieved three sheets of white paper from beneath the blue – 'comes from your stepfather.' He studied it. 'He expresses shame that he had not spotted what was all too apparent to you – namely, the depth of his wife and your mother's illness. He offers you a bolthole when the going becomes difficult; likewise, his mother. You'd be well advised to take up their invitations when you feel, as even grown men do now and then, battered and bruised by life. Two years' probation. You may go.'

The dock gate opened but Lance stood still, in a trance. A guard took his arm and led him to an approaching probation officer, who guided him down the aisle where Harry and his mother stood. All three hugged.

The public gallery coughed and shuffled. Some half stood to

put on their street coats. All settled back into their tip-up seats when they sensed the eyes of the judge upon them. They are all great whisperers in court, and the judge whispered now, looking down at the clerk, whose eyes searched out Caroline. He flicked his head at her. She stood. Another flick directed her back into the witness box.

She rested a hand on the edge alongside the bible and her anxious eyes sought Jacko, who smiled at her. The judge ignored her at first, turning to the jury to thank them for the close attention they had paid to a troublesome case.

Finally he turned to her. 'In my view, the charge at the original trial of Lance Frost was properly brought on the evidence then available and properly dismissed by that jury on the facts made known to them at that time. Your inquiry into the death of Mr Davis was the most complex imaginable. In getting to the truth of that, you uncovered the truth of what happened to Katie Burrows.

'It was you who detected that she may have been ducked face down, then, due to her strength as a swimmer and the purchase obtained from the tree roots, managed to surface. Sadly, because of shock and her congested lungs, she collapsed backwards into the water, as she was found – face up. Spotting that enabled you to theorize that a left-handed assailant may have been responsible for the predominant marks on her neck and you and your inspector proved it in a most ingenious fashion.' He gave her an admiring smile which he soon turned off.

'Mr Davis had been a serving police officer who used his legal knowledge to tarnish the fine reputation of his former force. During your inquiry a further cause for concern arose which you handled with efficiency and dispatch.'

This, as every reader of the *Mercury* knew, was a reference to his sentencing of Udden and Bullman to prison for fifteen months each. Too light, Jacko had grumbled. They'd ended up blaming each other, rats from a sinking ship.

The judge glanced along the row of barristers. 'Those of us who have regular business here know that on occasions, happily very rare, an officer of this court will fail our fallible system. They betray a trust, a solemn duty, a badge of office that should be worn with pride.'

He turned back to Caroline. 'You, your inspector and your colleagues bore that honourable burden with responsibility and dedication. Please accept our heartfelt thanks.'

Caroline bit her lip and nodded, embarrassed. Jacko felt a tingle running right through, proud and humble at the same time, a moving, emotional moment in his life. In one sentence, the judge had framed a testament to all that he had been brought up to believe in.

The judge rose. Everybody rose. The courtroom emptied. Jacko lit a cigarette and breathed in the end-of-term atmosphere in the foyer.

Reporters gathered round him. He filled in the gaps left by the evidence for them. Tony from Television was not among them. He'd already got an extended interview, embargoed till the end of the trial. Neither was Jason French. He had Chrissy Fixter at a hotel hideout, giving him 'My Secret Love for Slain Private Eye – by tragic ex-WPC'. Jacko had heard she was getting five grand for it.

Mrs Burrows took Caroline's hands in hers and squeezed them before turning with her husband to walk the gauntlet of cameramen outside. She stopped, posed and talked, willing and for free.

Jacko pulled on his new Bogart mac, a birthday present from Jackie, black this time, Caroline her white mac, and they stepped out on to the red-bricked walkway. No one took their photos.

'Some commendation,' said Caroline, preening a little.

Jacko pulled a pained face. 'The thanks of the management.' She looked at him, baffled.

'The three most useless things in the world are', he explained patiently, 'a man's nipples, Jack Frost's balls and the thanks of the management.' She laughed.

They strolled through an ugly concrete square. A fierce autumn wind chased cartwheeling leaves down the gutters.

'It would have been nice – poetic justice, really – if Mike Fixter had been in on the end,' said Caroline.

'There was no part in it for him. If they'd fought it all the way and he was in the box, imagine the questions about Davis and his wife.' Jacko believed in justice all right but there was no poetry in his soul.

'You then,' Caroline persisted. 'You should have taken the commendation, instead of leaving me standing there, feeling like a Brownie.'

'And if they'd fought it, I would have been questioned about my failure to nick Davis and nip all this mayhem in the bud.' That still rankled and so did his failure to catch Golden Jim or his new nark. In a sense he was back where he came in.

They were heading for the Barley Mow where the rest of the team waited. 'If I get pissed will you drive me home?'

'I thought you never celebrated court decisions – win or lose,' said Caroline as they turned downhill past a multi-storey car-park.

Jacko knew they hadn't lost or won. It was an honourable draw, the right decision. 'We're not celebrating that. We're celebrating my demotion. Now it's over, I'm no longer your chief but plain old inspector.'

She hooked her arm in his. 'You know, Jacko, it never suited you somehow.'

She's right, as usual, he thought as they picked up speed with the pub in sight. Who wants to be the chief of anything? They all wind up pushing paper around in the end, Tippexing out duty rosters.

This is where police work is. On the streets. Out and about with the boys and girls, doing the job as best you can and having a drink together afterwards.